# Fire and Cross

## Pride and Prejudice with a steamy mysterious twist

by

**ENID WILSON**

To

Sandy, Michelle, Hangnhu, Miaka, TEB and Gloria.
You urge me on!

**Enid Wilson** loves sexy romance. Her writing career began with a daily newspaper, writing educational advice for students. She then branched out into writing marketing materials and advertising copy.

Enid's novels, *In Quest of Theta Magic*, *Bargain with the Devil* and *Really Angelic*, received several top reviews. *Bargain with the Devil* has been ranked in the top 50 best-selling historical romances on Amazon USA, *Really Angelic* in the top 30 best-selling Regency romances on Amazon Canada and *My Darcy Mutates* in the top 21 romantic short stories on Amazon UK.

Enid loves to hear from her readers. You can contact her at enid.wilson28@yahoo.com.au or www.steamydarcy.com

Illustrations and cover design by Z. Diaz
First published 2010

# Chapter One

"Fire! Fire!"

The loud yelling woke George Darcy from his deep sleep. Blinking open his eyes, he saw smoke blackening the whole room. He jumped up from the bed and dashed to the door, but the thick cloud hindered his progress, especially as he was unfamiliar with the layout of the inn.

"Anne! Fitzwilliam!" he called out desperately as he stumbled around, trying to find the door to the corridor. His wife had not been feeling well and she had retired to a separate chamber. Their son had wanted to keep her company.

When he finally pushed open the door and came to the landing, a large piece of burning wood fell from the ceiling and hit him on the right shoulder, scorching his arm. Gasping in pain, he leaned heavily on the railing.

"Anne! Fitzwilliam!" Believing his wife and young son to be still trapped in their room, he continued calling out for them as he walked on. The smoke was less overpowering here. As he turned left at the corridor, a man of medium height emerged from George Darcy's right and pulled at his arms.

"Sir you cannot go that way!" The man had an educated voice, a gentleman perhaps. "The fire started on the left side of the building and it seems to be burning like Hades itself."

Mr. Darcy coughed heavily as he tried to pull away from the other man. Suddenly the sound of crying stopped his movement. The country gentleman was carrying a baby, half tucked inside his coat.

"Shh, my dear, all will be well!" The man rocked the baby quickly as he continued to pull Mr. Darcy away.

"No, I must go that way," Mr. Darcy said. "My wife and son are there."

"You are injured. They may have already escaped. We should look outside first." The gentleman was now using his shoulder to prevent George Darcy from passing through. He had clearly not been injured by the smoke or the fire.

"Let me go! I have to find Anne and Fitzwilliam!" Mr. Darcy cried out angrily.

"Even if you find them, you cannot carry them out. You are hurt." The gentleman became equally angry at George's stubbornness. With a shake of his head, he thrust the baby into Darcy's hands. "Take my daughter out to safety! I shall find your wife and son for you." Then he pushed Darcy towards the direction of the stairs.

"No!" George Darcy did not want the stranger hurt for his family's sake. But as the figure of the country gentleman dashed into the left side of the hallway, amidst heavy smoke, Darcy could do nothing but carry the baby girl down the stairs.

When he finally came out of the Bromley Inn and drew in a breath of fresh air, he was led by some servants to lie on the grass. He surveyed the crowd and could not see his wife or son anywhere. He wanted to raise himself to dash back into the inn again but his body was not under his control because the pain rendered him helpless. He could barely move.

As grim emotion gripped his heart, fearing for his wife and young son, the baby in his arms was strangely quiet. The bright moonlight permitted George Darcy to look at her more clearly. She was dressed in baby cloth of a modest quality, not expensive or fine but clean and neat. She had big expressive eyes and a few brown curls. Her silence seemed to bring him some calm.

His arm hurt like the devil and the smoke he had inhaled was making his head spin. Through the haze, his eyes turned to stare at the front of the inn. He prayed for the safe return of his family.

Suddenly the baby stretched her arms and touched his face. He turned to look at her again. She gave him a bright smile and George Darcy's heart seemed to constrict. He made a heartfelt wish upon seeing the babe's encouraging smile and hoped both Anne and Fitzwilliam would be safe.

"I am willing to part with the most important thing in my life for a miracle – that my family will be rescued!" he swore. He closed his eyes tightly and prayed. "A newborn signifies happiness. I pledge the future of the Darcy line to you, dear one. May you bring us forever joy."

He opened his eyes and looked at the baby girl. She had stretched out her hands from the blanket and seemed to be clapping her hands.

Darcy put his own hand into the pocket of his waistcoat and drew out a velvet box he had safely kept hidden. In it was a garnet cross with ruby red gemstones on an exquisite silver necklace. He had had it made by an exclusive jeweller for his wife Anne's twenty-eighth birthday and had had the words "Forever as One" inscribed on the back face. He put the necklace inside the pocket of the baby's dress. "You are too young to wear it yet but I pray it brings us all good fortune, precious baby girl. Bring back Anne and Fitzwilliam to me."

He shut his eyes and prayed again. He wished he could remember the baby's name. But everything was too painful for him at the moment.

"Agha! Agha!" The cheerful sound of the baby roused George Darcy from the fog of his pain. He turned back to look at the inn.

He heard someone calling loudly and through his smoke-strained eyes he saw the country gentleman emerging from the inn. In his arms was a woman. A young lad had his hand holding onto the man's coat tail as he ran along beside him.

The gentleman peered through the crowd and finally saw Darcy and the baby.

As the baby's father drew closer, George saw with a quickening heart that he was carrying Anne and the lad holding his waist was Fitzwilliam.

"They are safe!" George Darcy breathed out a sigh of relief and kissed the cheek of the baby girl. "Thank you! You are our saviour!" Then his words caught in his throat as the pain finally took hold of him and he fell into blackness.

It was two days before George Darcy regained consciousness. Mrs. Darcy was unconscious for several hours but their loyal servants were able to settle them in another inn and call their doctor from London.

When he inquired about the identity of the country gentleman and the baby girl, none of the servants was able to answer his questions. If Fitzwilliam had not said that the father and his baby daughter had left with a "God be with you" amidst the flurry of activity to bring the injured to another inn, the Master of Pemberley would have thought his family's saviours were mere apparitions.

***

Five years after the death of George Darcy, Mr. Fitzwilliam Darcy was astonished to meet the woman wearing the garnet cross.

In a letter left to him by his father, Fitzwilliam was told of the fire at Bromley Inn when he was eight years old, of which he had no memory. His father wished for him to find this gentleman and his daughter, whom George Darcy had been unable to locate, and offer to take her for a wife.

"A promise to the Lord cannot be rescinded, son! I had so many more years with your mother and with you, all thanks to this gentleman and his precious baby girl."

Fitzwilliam was resentful of this request. He did not remember his rescuer, let alone the baby girl.

*Where will I find this gentleman and his daughter? How long should I search for them before I give up? What if I meet another woman I love instead? Am I to give up my future for my father's moment of...insanity? Weakness?*

He had engaged the services of a man earlier who professed to have once plied his trade as a Bow Street runner to find the baby girl and her father. But after a year without success, he abandoned the search. "May the Lord help me plan my future as He sees fit."

It was an absolute shock to Mr. Darcy, at the age of eight and twenty, to find Miss Caroline Bingley wearing this garnet cross. He had known Charles Bingley since their days together at Cambridge. His elder sister was a lady who always treated people condescendingly and scornfully, especially servants and those from lower circles. She had set her cap at Darcy and was relentless in her pursuit of him whenever they were in company together.

Darcy would never have considered her as a partner for life, if not for finding out that she was in possession of the garnet cross.

One morning in the summer, without notice, she came with Bingley to visit Darcy at Ashford Hall, his townhouse in London. It was then that he noticed the ruby garnet cross seated comfortably on her over-powdered chest. She said that it had been her most treasured possession since she had been a baby.

"Why is it a treasure? I have never seen you wearing it before," Bingley said to his sister with a frown. Darcy was thankful that his friend was asking the question for him, because he could not shake the thought that he might be forever linked to her.

"Charles, you did not know because you were not yet born!" Caroline replied with a raised voice.

"The design looks quite unusual. So father gave it to you when you were a baby? It was a strange thing for a baby. I would have thought it suited a grown woman better," Bingley said.

"It was a mysterious gift from an acquaintance of father." Caroline looked at Darcy with a smile as she replied. "I have never worn it before because I only found it in father's treasure chest a few days ago with a letter of explanation."

"Was … was there an inscription on it?" Darcy finally managed to gather his wits to ask.

"It was so beautiful, why does it need an ins…" Caroline stopped in mid sentence. She fingered the pendant and then turned her eyes away from Darcy. "Oh, I had totally forgotten that I have another appointment with Miss Wolfring."

When the Bingleys had departed in haste, Darcy was left in total confusion. He feared for his future happiness if Miss Bingley was truly to be his betrothed. But a promise was a promise. He would not fail his dearly departed father's last wish.

But the way she had avoided answering his question about the inscription had made him suspicious. Perhaps Miss Bingley had somehow learned of the story behind the garnet cross and was trying to force his hand in marriage. His mind was in turmoil. He needed to go see his sister, Georgiana, to make sure that he would not act in haste and tie their future to this mean-spirited lady.

***

His luck was such that he arrived in Ramsgate in timely fashion to prevent his sister from falling into the hands of George Wickham, a childhood friend who had turned quite wild. Wickham was allowed to court Georgiana by the governess Mrs. Younge. Georgiana was persuaded that she was in love and had agreed to elope with the scoundrel. Fortunately, when Darcy talked to her about his own future in regards to the necklace, his sister then confessed to him the imminent elopement with Wickham.

After Darcy had sent away the rake and the irresponsible governess, and settled Georgiana back in Pemberley, he rethought his own future. He had to agree that perhaps Miss Bingley was truly that baby girl of long ago. She was the reason the Darcy family had been saved.

Therefore, he took up an invitation from Bingley, leaving Georgiana in Pemberley.

He went to stay at Bingley's newly-rented estate in Hertfordshire and nursed the heartache of failing to protect his sister Georgiana from the previous summer's embarrassment. He was seriously thinking of asking Miss Bingley for her hand. Perhaps she would know how to lift his sister out of her despondency.

But two days later, imagine his surprise when, on arriving at Meryton's Assembly, he came face to face with a second woman who was also wearing the unique garnet cross. A Miss Elizabeth Bennet. How could there be another garnet cross of the same individual design? And it appeared so similar to the other one Miss Bingley was wearing. How could that have happened?

He wanted to talk to the young lady about it but her mother, Mrs. Bennet, had no sense of propriety. She looked at Bingley and himself with calculating eyes, trying to push her daughters to dance with them.

He turned to see that Miss Bingley was also taken aback. She was not wearing the necklace this night. In fact, she had not worn it since Darcy had arrived in Netherfield two days ago.

*So who is to be my wife? Miss Bingley or Miss Elizabeth Bennet? Who is the woman my father swore my future to?* Darcy stalked off and leaned on the farthest wall of the Assembly room. He was suddenly very angry again.

*How can father connect me to either of them? Miss Bingley is mean, fawning and mercenary. And Miss Elizabeth – she is from such a family? The mother is loud and silly. The eldest daughter, Miss Jane Bennet, though very handsome, smiles too much. The other two or three daughters are running wild in the room, flirting with almost anyone. How can my connection with any of them help Georgiana through her trials? And this Elizabeth Bennet, she is hardly tolerable...with more than one failure of perfect symmetry in her form. Her manners are not those of the fashionable world. At least Miss Bingley is more elegantly dressed. That cannot be much better. My future cannot possibly be linked to either of them. Perhaps I am right. Miss Bingley somehow has faked that necklace and someone else must have given Miss Bennet the garnet cross necklace. I must find out the truth, somehow!*

# Chapter Two

Mr. Darcy strode decisively across the room to ask Miss Bingley for a dance. The young lady accepted with keen interest.

"Mr. Darcy." She spoke with a smirk. "Have you seen such savage society before?"

"Why do you think them savage?"

"Come, come, sir! Do you not see the dresses of the women? They are horrible, at least three seasons old. A definite imitation of the sophistication of the *ton* but with poor workmanship."

"I am no expert on women's fashion. But I am fascinated by Miss Elizabeth Bennet's."

"Miss Eliza's?" Did Miss Bingley's voice really appear to tremble? "How so?"

"She wore a garnet cross very similar to the one you said was left by your father."

She drew in a deep breath. "I see you are as astonished as I am."

"So you have no idea how such a coincidence could occur?" His voice turned cold.

"I could not possibly know why."

"If you do not mind my intrusion, could you share with me what your father said in his letter that accompanied this piece of jewellery?"

Miss Bingley hesitated for a few seconds before replying. "I do not understand your interest in the cross."

"What about its back? Does it have anything of interest written upon it?" he persisted.

"I see, you are asking about…the inscription." Miss Bingley's eyes darted to another lady in the room.

"So there is an inscription?" Darcy asked the question curiously, in order to throw Caroline off balance.

She turned her gaze back to him. "Well, I have not worn it since that day in London. I shall have to examine it more closely later on."

"You have brought it to Hertfordshire?"

"Indeed, I would not want to part with such a precious gift."

"And yet, you are unsure of the design on the back."

"I was more fascinated by the story behind it."

"But you prefer not to share it with me?" Darcy continued.

"It was rather private."

"Yes, I am sure," he nodded and murmured in a low, threatening voice. "So private that you may have known just the half of it."

Feeling the tremor in Miss Bingley's hands, he was sure that she possessed a fake garnet cross. Angry at her deception, he spent the rest of the dance in cold silence.

When the dance ended, he took Caroline to Bingley and said intently in front of her, "Charles, could you introduce me to Miss Elizabeth Bennet? She seems…intelligent enough for me to become acquainted with her."

Bingley laughed and shook his head. "Darcy, it is a dance, not a debate!" They left Miss Bingley alone, not before he saw her staring at Miss Eliza Bennet as if wishing her serious harm.

Miss Elizabeth was surprised by the introduction and the request for a dance. But she accepted gracefully.

Mr. Darcy observed the amazed looks on her mother's face, and on those of the other people in the room.

Never good at conversation with a stranger, he was considering with great intent how to interrogate this lady about the cross.

"We must have some conversation, sir," the lady said with a playful tone.

"Do you speak according to rule?"

"No, indeed. But would it not seem awkward to spend half an hour together without an exchange of a single word?" She arched her eyebrows. "I can talk about the dresses of the ladies. You can comment on the wine being served."

"Do you presume to know my interest?"

"If you ask a question every time you honour me with your voice, I shall have to presume a great deal."

*How very impertinent this young lady is!* Darcy thought. But he could not stop his lip from curling up to smile. *At least she is not agreeing with everything he said.* He wondered what she would say about the garnet cross. "I am interested in your necklace," he said.

She cast a glance at the jewellery on her bosom. "Indeed? May I ask why?"

"It is a unique design."

"Since I have not seen a great many pieces of jewellery, I cannot know if it is unique or not."

"But what attracted you to buy it in the first place?"

"I did not buy it."

"Your parents?"

She shook her head.

"I am intrigued now." He looked at her intensely.

"You would know soon enough anyway. Mama likes to talk about it."

He tilted his head to urge her on.

"It was left in my clothes when I was a baby."

Darcy missed a step and trod on Miss Bennet's toes. She cried out. He was so surprised by what she said that he was not aware of what had happened to his dance partner.

His mind was unprepared for this. He was hoping against hope that she had obtained the garnet cross through other means. He was praying that she would not be his betrothed. *What shall I do?* he thought. His mind was full of confused feelings and continued in an agitated silent manner until the dance ended.

When he brought Miss Elizabeth back to where her mother stood, he failed to give both ladies a polite bow. Mrs. Bennet blamed Elizabeth and for the rest of the evening lamented that her second daughter had upset the wealthy man.

***

Mr. Darcy spent the night in turmoil, arguing with himself about the morality of obeying his father's wish or not. The next day, he and Bingley went out to meet some officers stationed in the town.

Darcy was in no humour to meet more new acquaintances. But to have spent the day with the ladies would have been even worse. On their return, they learned that Miss Jane Bennet had been invited to Netherfield and had fallen ill while riding on horseback during torrential rain. Miss Bingley had sent for the apothecary and dispatched a letter to inform her family.

On the morning of the second day, Miss Bingley greeted the gentlemen angrily as they were taking breakfast.

"In addition to their lack of decorum, this Bennet family is entirely witless," she said.

"Caroline!"

"What? Did you not notice Miss Bennet's mother at the Assembly? She was saying Mr. Darcy must be attracted to Miss Eliza's form. How crude!"

*Indeed! But she does have a pair of fine eyes*, Darcy smiled. *Her bottom certainly appeared to be quite shapely, too. Stop it, man! A gentleman must not think such vulgar things about a lady. Did you not at first think that she was not handsome enough to tempt you at the Assembly? And do not forget she has a horrible mother.*

"Caroline, you appear even more crude for repeating such a remark." Bingley protested.

"Mrs. Bennet said Mr. Darcy's ten thousand a year would do very well for all her daughters when her husband dies, for their estate is entailed away. They have an uncle in trade, living in Cheapside, and another uncle, a Mr. Philips, in Meryton who is merely an attorney," Caroline continued on her course of exposing the unsuitability of the Bennets' lowly connections.

*Am I to be burdened with a whole circle of connections decidedly below my own?* Darcy frowned.

"You forget that our fortune comes from trade as well," Bingley argued.

Caroline gave her brother an irritated look, then said, "Mr. Darcy, you are very silent. What do you think of Miss Eliza?

Should we congratulate you on your good fortune soon, as you singled her out as a dance partner?"

"Thank you for your concern with my future happiness," Darcy gazed at her. "You seem very interested in Mrs. Bennet's conversation. Perhaps you find a friend in her."

Bingley grinned. Caroline was trembling, perhaps with anger. Mrs. Hurst, desiring to help her sister, provided more detail concerning their eavesdropping on Mrs. Bennet at the Assembly and their interrogation of Jane Bennet before she became ill.

"Mrs. Bennet also boasted of Miss Eliza's good fortune. She said her second daughter was given the exquisite garnet cross when she was a baby."

Darcy turned to see Miss Bingley winking at her sister. Perhaps she was trying to stop Mrs. Hurst from revealing the information as to how Miss Eliza had come in to possession of the garnet cross.

"The garnet cross!" Bingley said. "I did not notice it at first when Miss Elizabeth was introduced to me. But when I danced with her, I noticed that it looked very similar to the one you have worn, Caroline. I did not ask her about it for do you not agree it would seem rude for a gentleman to enquire about a lady's jewellery upon such short acquaintance?"

Mrs. Hurst looked at her sister with confusion. "You have a similar piece of jewellery? Why did I not know about it?"

"I do not tell you about all the jewels I have." Caroline tightened her lips.

*Ah, so she did not tell her sister of the treasure her father left her?* "Mrs. Hurst, do tell us more concerning Mrs. Bennet's story," Darcy said.

"If you would excuse me," Caroline said. "As I have a sick patient, I have a lot to do." She rose to take her leave. "Louisa, can you come? I have some private matter to discuss with you."

Mrs. Hurst was about to rise when her brother prevented her. "You go along first, Caroline. Louisa can join you in a few minutes, after she answers Darcy's question."

Caroline gave Bingley an annoyed look and seated herself once more. "I shall stay then."

"Mrs. Hurst," Darcy urged.

"Mrs. Bennet said they were staying in the Bromley Inn some twenty years ago. A fire broke out. Apparently her husband became separated from Miss Eliza for a few moments during the incident. When she returned home, she found this piece of expensive jewellery in Miss Eliza's baby cloth."

"I wager the Bennets have some unsavoury connection and they have embellished a stolen piece of jewel with a story," Miss Bingley added sharply.

"Caroline!" Bingley chastised her.

"Is there an inscription on it?" Darcy asked, though he knew there was no disputing his father's wish. The story was of a piece. But it seemed Mr. Bennet did not claim to be a hero. Darcy's respect for his saviour increased.

"Did you know about this jewel?" Bingley asked him. "You asked Caroline if her garnet cross had an inscription as well. In fact," he turned to his sister, "you failed to answer his question."

Caroline was breathing with difficulty now. "Yes, there is an inscription."

"On yours or the one that Miss Elizabeth possesses?" Darcy said.

Before Miss Bingley was able to furnish a reply, a caller was announced. "Miss Elizabeth Bennet."

Miss Bennet came into the room and smiled cautiously at the seated assembly.

She curtseyed. "I come to enquire after my sister."

The gentlemen rose. Darcy took in her appearance. *Did she really walk three miles alone to visit her sister? It is not proper. But her face is rosy pink and her eyes sparkle. She looks so lovely with the curls that escape her hairpins falling around her face.*

Caroline seized the opportunity and whisked her sister and the intruding caller away from the gentlemen. Darcy did not have a chance to continue the question about the inscription.

***

Darcy completed his dinner preparations far too early. He learned that Bingley had invited Miss Elizabeth to stay with her sister. Miss Bingley had sent a servant to deliver a note to Longbourn and to fetch the guest's trunk.

Earlier that day, the gentlemen had visited the patient. From the entrance to the sick room, Darcy could see that Miss Elizabeth was genuinely concerned for the wellbeing of her older sister. Before Bingley had made their presence known, she had been placing a cold compress on Miss Bennet's forehead. She was wiping the patient's neck and whispering tender words of encouragement to her sister.

Darcy's heart swelled on seeing the scene. He could imagine Miss Elizabeth caring for Georgiana, nursing her from sickness and heartache. For the first time since learning of the history of the garnet cross, he felt at peace with his father's pledge.

He decided to go to the billiard room for a game before dinner. On passing the corridor, he saw Miss Elizabeth outside the door of her guest room.

He was about to bow and greet her when a voice sounded from her room.

"Yes!"

It was Miss Bingley.

Miss Elizabeth's hand froze on the handle, seemingly unsure of what to do. A moment's hesitation gave Darcy an idea. He put his hand on hers. They both gasped on contact. She looked at him with wide eyes. He then helped her open the door.

Miss Bingley was crouching on the floor, in front of a trunk. Darcy was distracted by the sight of stockings, stays, corsets and dresses thrown haphazardly out of the trunk. Glancing at Miss Elizabeth, he noticed a shade of pink spread from her cheeks, down her neck and to her chest.

"Why are you searching through my clothes?" Elizabeth raised her voice.

Darcy turned his attention back to Caroline. "Is it because you want to exchange your garnet cross with Miss Bennet's?"

"What?" Elizabeth repeated in confusion. She did not see that Caroline was holding two garnet crosses in her hand.

Miss Bingley dropped one of them back into the disarray of clothes and closed the trunk immediately, with no regard to the garments thus caught by the lid. She stood up and dashed for the door.

"Not so hasty, Miss Bingley!" Darcy commanded loudly. He was not master of hundreds of servants and tenants for nothing.

Caroline stopped on the instant.

"What is the matter?" Bingley appeared at the entrance, looking at the three of them with confusion.

"I am sorry to upset you, Charles," Darcy said. "Your sister has been going through Miss Bennet's trunk for the garnet cross, in the hope of exchanging it."

"I did no such thing!" Caroline finally found her voice and protested.

Bingley drew in a deep breath. "Show me what you have in your hand."

"I take offence to your tone, Charles. Remember I am your elder sister."

"But as the master of this house, he has every right to see off a thief," Darcy added.

"I am no thief!" Caroline hid her hands behind her back. "This *is my* garnet cross."

Elizabeth opened the trunk and found the necklace easily. "Why would Mother pack the garnet cross? I do not wear it except during special occasions."

"Remember, Miss Bingley helped you send for the trunk." Darcy folded his arms. "She could have easily persuaded your Mother that *I* am the special occasion."

Miss Bennet's face turned even redder. She gave him a cold stare.

Before Caroline could open her mouth to protest, Bingley asked the guest, "Did your jewel have an inscription?"

"Yes, on—" Elizabeth began to reply. "But this is not my garnet cross! There is no inscription on it."

"Caroline, how could you go through Miss Bennet's belongings and exchange your necklace for hers? What is the importance of this garnet cross?" Bingley said in a raised voice.

"Whoever is in possession of the treasure is Mr. Darcy's intended!" Caroline said. "You cannot rescind your father's words. I have this garnet cross. We are to be married." She waved the jewel in front of Mr. Darcy.

Both Elizabeth and Bingley gasped. They looked at Miss Bingley's frenzied gesture.

Darcy was extremely calm. Finally the secret was out. "How did you come across my father's letter?"

"It is of no importance. I have the treasure. I shall be your wife and the next mistress of Pemberley." Miss Bingley tilted her head knowingly.

"Then you apparently did not read the letter in full," Darcy said. "Did you know why my father pledged my future to Miss Bennet?"

"I…I…" Caroline looked at Elizabeth. "My father and the late Mr. Darcy met in Bromley Inn and made the marriage contract there."

"In what year?" Darcy asked.

"I…I…was a baby. It must have been 1785."

"Miss Bingley, my father made the pledge in 1791, when Miss Bennet was a baby. You were six years old by then. His pledge did not only mention that whoever was in possession of the garnet cross would be my fiancée. There were circumstances you did not know. Please return the garnet cross to Miss Bennet," Darcy commanded.

Anger rose in Caroline's chest. She threw the necklace at Elizabeth, then lunged at her.

Darcy dashed to Elizabeth's side, embraced her and took the brunt of Miss Bingley's attack.

Bingley stood in a stupor for a second before restraining his sister. Amid her loud screams and abuses, the host hauled Caroline over his shoulder and carried her out of the room. "It is all your fault, trollop! Mr. Darcy was going to make an offer to me. I had the garnet cross made exactly like the drawing on the letter. I could have been the Mistress of Pemberley if not for you… you penniless country chit of a girl without suitable connection or fortune. I shall ...."

"Are you hurt?" Darcy tilted Elizabeth's head up to examine her.

"I am well," she replied and struggled from his embrace to retrieve the necklace on the floor.

"Is it damaged?" He frowned, not sure why she had shied away from his touch.

She smoothed her hands over the front and back of the garnet cross and shook her head.

"Good. My late Father would be happy that it is not broken." He walked closer to the window and looked out at the darkness. Thinking of his father gave him strength to tie his future with this unknown lady. He turned around to begin. He gave Miss Bennet a brief account of what had happened at the Bromley Inn. "Now that you have heard the story behind it, I am sure you are ecstatic to know that we are betrothed."

The lady was silent. But the high colour of her cheeks and her shortness of breath confirmed his estimation.

He felt the need to rein in her enthusiasm, setting the boundary of their marriage. "Frankly speaking, I was very resentful when I read my father's letter after he passed away. I did not appreciate the fact that my future would be tied to an unknown woman. She might have been ugly or witless. What was Father thinking? When I saw the fake cross on Miss Bingley, I regretted the fact that she would be my intended. You probably can guess that she treats servants and people from lower circles exceedingly badly. And then when I saw the necklace around your neck, I was even angrier. Your mother and younger sisters behaved in a highly improper manner at the Assembly. Your coming here alone on foot was not looked upon with favour either. Nevertheless I could see that you were genuinely worried about your sister's well-being. Your caring nature puts you in a good light. I am now at peace with my father's momentary insanity. I would like to make an offer for your hand. But your family would need a lot of guidance on proper behaviour."

After Darcy had completed his proposal he anticipated hearing Miss Bennet's acceptance. Instead, as he impatiently waited for her answer, he observed that the lady's countenance was surprisingly clouded with irritation.

"In normal circumstances such as this, even if the lady does not accept the offer, she should express her gratitude," she said. "However, I cannot. I never desired your offer and you decidedly bestowed it most unwillingly. Therefore, I release you from your father's pledge. Good day, sir!" She walked to the door and held it open for him to leave.

Darcy was astonished by her refusal. He drew in several deep breaths. Instead of walking to the door, he turned back to look out of the window. *How could this have happened, Father?*

A single cloud above the estate traversed the sky quickly. After a few moments of silence, he had himself under control and turned back to look at Elizabeth. Her eyes flashed with a burning flame. Why would she be so angry at such an eligible offer? Ire rose in his chest as well.

"Your father's estate is entailed away. Have my father and I not bestowed the greatest fortune on you! May I ask why you reply with such lack of civility?"

"Am I uncivil?" Her voice rose. "What about you? Were you civil when you criticised my family and me, directly to my face?"

"A less honest gentleman would hide his true concerns and offer you flattery. But masquerade of any sort is abhorrent to me. I am not in love with you and I would not express admiration where there was none." Darcy paced around the room.

"A true gentleman would do his duty with humility. You belittled your father's gratitude to the Lord. You reproached my family's behaviour without really knowing the circumstances behind it."

"How can you expect me to rejoice in a connection so decidedly undesirable and beneath my own?"

"Sir, your arrogance, your conceit and your selfish disdain of the feelings of others know no bounds. Although I have only known you for a few days, I already feel sure to say that you are the last man in the world whom I could ever be prevailed upon to marry."

"You have said quite enough, madam. I perfectly comprehend your feelings." With that he bowed and walked out of her room with fury in his chest. The loud slamming of the door by the lady was one last insult.

The dinner at Netherfield and the breakfast the following morning were quiet affairs, with Miss Bingley, Miss Elizabeth and Mr. Darcy absent. It seemed an epidemic of headaches had descended on the house, with all three individuals pleading their absence because of their suffering.

Darcy took his horse out for a ride very early. He was still outraged by Miss Elizabeth's uncivil and ungrateful refusal. *Perhaps this is for the best. I am relieved of this obligation and can marry whomever I wish now.*

Scanning the gentle slopes of Hertfordshire countryside, he realized the vast difference between it and Derbyshire's untamed beauty.

He suddenly felt a moment of regret for not knowing this contrasting county and its inhabitants more. Were the rocks and hills of Derbyshire truly superior to the flat horizon of Hertfordshire? Why did the Lord make such distinctive landscapes and people?

*Should I not congratulate myself on having my own wealth and connections, over her lack of it? What would be a more gentlemanly approach in the face of such disparity? And what of her foolhardy behaviour? To refuse an offer that could save her family should her father meet his destiny? What set her so decidedly against me?*

These conflicting ideas were assailing his thoughts until he came upon a gentleman walking in a field.

"Sir, are you lost?" The gentleman greeted Darcy with a tip of the hat.

Darcy was in no humour to meet any new acquaintances. But this man reminded him of someone. Darcy climbed down from his saddle and returned the greeting. "Darcy of Pemberley. I am a guest of Mr. Bingley at Netherfield."

"Fitzwilliam Darcy? You have grown."

"I beg your pardon. Have we met before?"

"You told me your name at the Bromley Inn some twenty years ago, though not where you hailed from. When I heard my wife talking about you a few days ago, I did wonder if you were the same lad." Extending his hand he made the introduction. "Bennet of Longbourn."

Darcy was in awe. Suddenly the frightening scenes during that fire so long ago flashed before his eyes. He remembered everything now. The sense of despair and helplessness when he had tried to move his mother to safety, she being overcome with smoke, sprang back into his memory. He had lacked the strength and had prayed to the Lord that she would be saved. He had prayed out loud, promising his life to the one who was their saviour. And this gentleman did come to their rescue. He remembered the encouraging words Mr. Bennet had murmured amidst the cracking sound of burning wood. The memory of dark choking smoke and intense heat which had stayed hidden at the back of his mind came rushing forth. He suddenly felt faint and as he started to sway towards the older gentleman, he grabbed the other's shoulders and hugged him.

"Mr. Bennet, I have wanted for such a long while to thank you…." His voice was trembling. "Thank you for saving my mother and myself."

"It was nothing, my boy. I did what any gentleman would have done."

The word "gentleman" sounded like thunder to Darcy's ears. He was utterly ashamed of his uncharitable feelings towards Mr. Bennet's family and his mode of declaration to his second daughter. If not for the older gentleman's bravery, Darcy would not have grown to be the master of Pemberley. His wealth and connections could not compare to the gift of life Mr. Bennet had given him.

"I must beg your forgiveness, sir." Darcy said with head lowered.

"Whatever for?"

"I behaved in an ungentlemanly manner towards Eliza…towards your second daughter."

"What? What did you do to my Lizzy?" Mr. Bennet pushed Darcy away from him and glared at him.

"I insulted her with my offer of marriage."

"What? Why would you offer her marriage? You have only known her for a few days."

Darcy squared up his shoulders and told the older gentleman of the pledge made by his father and then of his fiery exchange with Elizabeth.

"I did wonder where the garnet cross came from," Mr. Bennet said as he turned and walked slowly back in the direction whence he had come. Darcy followed him, not sure if his saviour would forgive his transgression.

"You are right, Mr. Darcy," the older man said. "I have neglected the silly behaviour of my wife and younger daughters for too long. It grieves me to know that Jane and Lizzy's future will be hurt by their impropriety."

"Sir, please do not dwell on my arrogant opinions. Miss Elizabeth was right to call me conceited. And please call me Fitzwilliam."

"Yes, Lizzy is correct. You are arrogant. But I do understand that those are your genuine apprehensions." Mr. Bennet stopped. He continued walking for some time, a variety of emotions passing over his face. He looked unhappy and angry. "I am abashed to admit that the fire at Bromley did change me for the worse."

"I do not understand, sir. You performed a brave act. How could it have changed you for the worse?"

"When I helped you and your mother outside, we stepped onto a man's body." The grey haired gentleman drew in a deep breath. "Do you remember that?"

Mr. Darcy shook his head. He had been too young or confused at that time.

Mr. Bennet continued. "I suddenly thought that I could have died like that man. How could I have left my wife, Jane and Lizzy to fend for themselves? I vowed to make up for them if I was fortunate enough to escape the fire safely. From then on, I started to indulge my wife, showering her with gifts and allowing her to spend beyond our means."

He stopped again, looking at a building not far away. It was a lovely house, about half the size of Netherfield. Mr. Bennet's countenance seemed tortured. Darcy was sorry to evoke such painful memories in him.

"Did you know that my estate is entailed away?"

Darcy nodded.

Mr. Bennet continued, "I always thought that Fanny and I would have a son. So when I died, my daughters and Fanny would be taken care of. By the time I realised that I would not have an heir, it was too late to start saving. Fanny started to fear for the future. She became sillier and sillier in her pursuit of rich husbands with which to match the girls."

He shook his head and picked up his pace. "It is all my fault. I should have been more prudent to save for my children's future. But instead of doing that, I laughed and joked about Fanny's silliness, allowing her to indulge the younger girls too. I am utterly ashamed of myself. It is too late now. What can I do at this late hour? Both Jane and Lizzy and all of them will have to suffer for my incompetence!"

Darcy was surprised and saddened by Mr. Bennet's revelations. He understood Elizabeth's earlier indignation. He had reproached Mrs. Bennet and her younger daughters without taking the time to know them personally or the circumstances that lay behind their present behaviour. Where was his humility or sensitivity to the feelings of others?

"Mr. Bennet, please do not blame yourself. But surely it is not too late to make amends. You are in good health. You can still start saving. You can still encourage your younger daughters to learn the proper ways of society. If you do not mind my intrusion, may I offer my assistance?"

"Do you really think I can?" Mr. Bennet stopped and looked at the younger man. Mr. Darcy's eyes conveyed a look of admiration. The esteem of a master who possessed a large fortune seemed to give the older gentleman courage.

"I suppose that if I were to live until my seventieth decade, I would still have many more years to do so. Good, my boy, we are almost at Longbourn, my estate. My wife and the younger girls are visiting Netherfield at the moment. She said she had to instruct Lizzy on how to use her arts and allurements to snare you," Mr. Bennet said with a sardonic smile. "Come, we will go to my study and start planning the grand scheme of saving the Bennet women!"

## Chapter Three

Darcy's face had turned a shade of pink when Mr. Bennet talked of Elizabeth's arts and allurements. The thought of her voluptuous figure, expressive eyes and passionate countenance made him very uncomfortable. He told the stable boy to take his horse. This activity gave him respite from Mr. Bennet's prying eyes.

And who would have the courage to take the master of Pemberley to task? Inwardly Darcy applauded Elizabeth's fierce defence of her family, her tender caring of her sister and her unmoving dismissal of his fortune, making him realize that indeed she was not covetous.

Would he be able to regain her good opinion? He considered the delights he would enjoy, engaging in fiery debates with her while appreciating her female attributes. Perhaps in return for her favour he could teach her something about the world, introducing her to a far superior circle than that with which she was presently familiar in the country.

He drew a breath and hastily asked the older gentleman, "Mr. Bennet, would you grant me permission to court Miss Elizabeth?"

The older man stared at Darcy. Then his mouth turned up in a smile. "You desire more witty torment in your life?"

Darcy laughed out loud. He felt genuinely happy, as though he were back at his father's side. But Mr. Bennet was more playful, reminding him of Elizabeth. After he had fought back his laughter, he told Mr. Bennet seriously, "I esteem your daughter greatly. I would like to fulfil my father's pledge one day, if I am lucky enough to earn Miss Elizabeth's forgiveness and love."

Mr. Bennet did not reply for several moments. This made Darcy anxious. Perhaps his saviour was not impressed with his character. The ten thousand a year would not save Darcy's estimation in the older gentleman's mind after all.

"Forgive me, my boy, but I cannot grant you permission."

Darcy was crestfallen, as though he had been slapped in the face again, twice in two days!

"Cheer up, my boy." Mr. Bennet clasped Darcy's shoulders and walked him into his study. He said in a whisper, "My Lizzy is a strange creature. If I force her to do something she does not desire, she will rebel. I think I know the way to help you advance your course, unless Mrs. Bennet has already learned of the story behind the garnet cross." He gave Darcy a wink as he closed the door.

Mr. Bennet and Mr. Darcy remained behind closed doors for several hours, until the mistress burst into the room.

"Mr. Bennet, Lizzy will be the death of me! She did not heed what I told her. She said she would not receive Mr. Darcy alone and encourage him with her charm. She would not cease her impertinent behaviour. How are we to survive after you die? And Mr. Darcy and Miss Bingley are not even present. They claim to have suffered headaches the night before. I suspect the lady is trying to use her charms to ensnare the gentleman. You did not see how Miss Bingley's face turned green with envy when Mr. Darcy asked Lizzy to dance at the Assembly. I was sure the gentleman could not keep his eyes from our daughter's bosom. But Lizzy is such an insolent girl! She will not be able to sustain his interest with her constant talk of books. Fortunately, Jane is still sick. I would not allow her to be moved back home yet. Perhaps a few more days in Netherfield will do the trick for Jane and Mr. Bingley. And I am so proud of Lydia! She asked Mr. Bingley to host a ball. Mr. Bingley said he would let her choose the date, after Jane is well again…"

"Mrs. Bennet, we have a guest here."

The lady's mouth formed an O when she saw Mr. Darcy by the wall with a book in his hand.

He gave her a bow. "Good day, Mrs. Bennet."

"Good morning, sir. I … I did not know that Mr. Bennet and you had met…"

"I was inspecting the field on the south side when I had some chest pain." Mr. Bennet rubbed his hand on his chest. "Mr. Darcy came upon me at that time."

Darcy turned his eyes to look at the older gentleman. He looked rather normal. Was that a plot of his in the grand scheme? They had been talking about how to improve the management of Longbourn and Mr. Bennet had not said a word about feeling unwell.

"Chest pain! You must have some hidden illness, like Mr. Thompson. He simply dropped dead during the church service two months ago. You must go and lie down. I shall send for the apothecary. We cannot have you dead before we have our girls married! Mr. Darcy, you do not know how I worry every day. I pray to the Lord all the time. I would do anything to see our girls well settled before the Lord takes Mr. Bennet away."

"Well, Mrs Bennet, perhaps the Lord would prefer to take you before me."

"Mr. Bennet! My nerves!"

"I know your nerves very well. But if you would do anything to see our girls get married, Mr. Darcy has the solution for us."

"Oh, Mr. Darcy, are you going to offer to take my Lizzy? Are you enchanted by her form? She was never as handsome and obedient as Jane but she has the best figure. Mind you, Lydia will surpass her in a few years. If Lizzy would only heed my advice and stop skipping around the lanes and fields all day, her complexion would improve…"

Darcy did not care to hear her belittling Elizabeth.

The elderly gentleman interrupted. "Mrs. Bennet, you have the wrong idea. Mr. Darcy suggested that I send you away."

"What?"

"To accompany Kitty to a school. Kitty will learn some artistic skills to enchant a rich young man while we arrange for you to learn how to present our girls to gentlemen of wealth."

"Present our girls? Why would I need to learn that? I host the best parties in the neighbourhood, much to the envy of

Lady Lucas. And what is the use of artistic skill? Men are not attracted to that!"

"Ah, so you do not want Lydia and Kitty to have a season in London? Well, Mr. Darcy, it seems we do not need to discuss how to increase the yield of the farms after all."

"A season in London for Lydia? Really?" Mrs. Bennet turned to look at Mr. Darcy for confirmation.

"Yes, I have looked at Longbourn's accounts and suggested that Mr. Bennet let some fields lay fallow to allow the soil to rest and encourage some of the tenants to use the French notion of *orangeries* to grow flowers or fruit all year round…"

"You do not need to go into such detail for my wife. Mrs. Bennet, let me just say that we will have the money to launch our younger girls in society, and also Mary, if she is so inclined. You would not want to commit any mistakes during the season in town and possibly ruin Lydia and Kitty's chance to make a good match, I daresay?"

"Of course not! I would do anything. But is there a school for a matron as old as I?"

"Who said you are old? You are still the young Fanny I met in the meadows some twenty years ago. The school is for Kitty but Mr. Darcy knows the headmistress there. Mrs. Watson used to be a companion of a Duchess. He is sure she will be willing to give you private lessons and teach you all the skills required to launch our girls into London society."

"Oh, Mr. Bennet!" She jumped up and went to give her husband a kiss on the cheek. "You are the best husband and father in the world. I shall go and pack…When are we going? Why is Lydia not coming too?"

"Perhaps in three days time. This school does not accept girls of Lydia's age. And I thought you would prefer to go with Kitty rather than Mary."

"Of course. I would not understand a word of the sermons Mary says. But that means Kitty and I shall miss the ball at Netherfield. I cannot do that. What if Jane and Mr. Bingley were to become engaged then?"

"Mr. Darcy has another grand idea to help Lydia and Mary find rich husbands. He will ask Mr. Bingley to postpone the ball until later," the Master of Longbourn said.

Mr. Darcy looked at him with a frown. They had indeed talked about how to improve the management of Longbourn and "educate" Mrs. Bennet, under the pretext of sending Kitty to school. It was a type of "divide and conquer" strategy to separate the two major silly forces of Mrs. Bennet and Miss Lydia. But they had not discussed how to manage the behaviour of the latter yet.

"Oh, Mr. Darcy, I do thank the Lord the day Mr. Bingley decided to let Netherfield and that he invited you to stay with him," Mrs. Bennet said with joy. She ran to Mr. Darcy's side to give the younger man a kiss on the cheek too.

Mr. Darcy was surprised by such a familiar gesture from a near stranger. He almost held her at arm's length, but Mr. Bennet nodded at him and he allowed her to approach.

"Yes, Mr. Darcy is the best of men to come to Hertfordshire in many a year," the older gentleman said with a humorous expression.

"So tell me your idea about Lydia and Mary, sir?" Mrs. Bennet went to seat herself and looked at Mr. Darcy eagerly.

The younger gentleman looked at his fellow conspirator for help.

"Let me do the honour, my dear," Mr. Bennet said. "Lydia and Mary may not go to London yet. They have not observed how people in higher society live and behave. Before we give them a season, it will be advantageous to let them become accustomed to such a way of life first. Mr. Darcy will ask Mrs Hurst to invite Lydia and Mary to stay at Netherfield for the winter, to learn how best to conduct themselves in society. If our younger girls become good friends to Mr. Bingley's eldest sister, she may even invite an accomplished friend to come teach Lydia and Mary how to dance the latest dances and dress in the most fashionable ways."

"Oh, my girls!" Mrs. Bennet fanned her flustered face. "What a great opportunity! I shall go tell Lydia about it now." She jumped up and left the room like a whirlwind.

Mr. Darcy looked at Mr. Bennet with trepidation. *How could I demand that Bingley ask his eldest sister do all that? And how can I find such a friend for Mrs. Hurst?* he thought.

"Now, Fitzwilliam, you must be careful and ask Mr. Bingley nicely to fulfil these duties for us."

"I am afraid Bingley does not have a great influence on his elder sister." Mr. Darcy paced around the room. "And I doubt Mrs. Hurst would have such a friend who would be willing to take on the task of educating Miss Lydia."

"Ah, but I am sure you know such a lady. And are not all your friends welcomed by the Bingley sisters too? I am certain that Mrs. Hurst and Mr. Bingley would not want me to send the magistrate for Miss Bingley, for stealing Lizzy's garnet cross. After all, you were witness to the theft." Mr. Bennet folded his arms and rested his back comfortably on the chair.

A jovial smile spread across Mr. Darcy's face. Although he hated to use blackmail on his friend, it was an excellent idea to engage a governess to teach Miss Mary and Miss Lydia correct manners. However, he did not understand why Mr. Bennet desired them to be installed at Netherfield instead. He did not relish the idea of living under the same roof with them for an extended period just yet. Perhaps after Elizabeth and he were married, and the young Bennet sisters had learned proper manners, he would not be averse to inviting them to stay in Pemberley for a holiday.

"While the younger girls are learning their way in Netherfield, I shall invite you to stay at Longbourn to help me implement the farm improvement tasks," Mr. Bennet said. "Lizzy has been helping me to deal with the tenants for a few years now. I am sure you two will work wonders to increase our income. And I cannot have you riding over here every day. What if you catch a cold from the rain like my poor Jane?"

Mr. Darcy's smile became even wider. He took his leave of the older gentleman quietly, avoiding the loud cries and laughter of the ladies in the parlour.

***

When Mr. Darcy returned to Netherfield, he discussed Mr. Bennet's requests with Bingley first. He confirmed the story behind the garnet cross but did not reveal to his friend

Elizabeth's rejection of his proposal. Later they talked to Mrs. Hurst. After first declaring that she could not possibly assent to such an arrangement, she at last agreed to the scheme with resignation.

Darcy also learned from Mrs. Hurst that Miss Bingley had interviewed all the servants extensively, despite her proclamation of having suffered a headache the evening before, and ensured that no one would spread gossip about the incident in Elizabeth's room.

*So she did not want her shameful exchange of the jewellery and that my father had pledged my future to Elizabeth, to become known abroad,* Mr Darcy thought.

This suited him. He now understood that it would not provide for his future happiness if Elizabeth was forced to marry him. He wanted her to come to him willingly.

What he needed to do now was to persuade and even seduce her with his wit, his conduct and his admiration.

That evening, he dressed with special care. He hoped she would not dine in her sister's room or claim to have a headache again.

Much to his delight, she came down for dinner. The elder Miss Bennet remained in her room, still endeavouring to recover her full health. Elizabeth had dressed in a shimmering green gown that accentuated her form, with the garnet cross adorning the slope of her neck and her cleavage.

Close behind her came Miss Bingley with a face of thunder. She passed quickly by Elizabeth and hurried to seat herself next to Mr Darcy.

"Miss Bennet, Miss Bingley, I hope you have recovered from your headache," he said.

"Thank you, I am well," Elizabeth said, her eyes sparkling with challenge.

"Oh, Mr. Darcy..." Miss Bingley was about to say something when he spoke at the same instant.

"And you look exceptionally lovely, Miss Bennet."

Miss Bingley sent her rival a look that would kill while Elizabeth seemed taken aback by his compliment.

"I agree," Bingley said. "And how is your sister?"

"She is feeling much better. We have decided to take our leave and return home tomorrow morning."

"Surely it is too soon to move Miss Bennet," Bingley said with alarm. He must have wanted more time with Miss Jane. "Your mother said so this morning, too."

The mention of Mrs. Bennet brought a shade of red to Elizabeth's face. Darcy could imagine the embarrassment and frustration she had felt when her mother had demanded that she tempt him.

"We do not want to intrude for too long."

"Charles, let her be. I am sure Miss Elizabeth misses her father," Miss Bingley said with false kindness. "I heard from Miss Bennet that they are very close."

"I met your father today," Mr. Darcy said.

The words sent both ladies into panic.

"I hope…the meeting was pleasant." Elizabeth said, fidgeting on her chair. "Did you…discuss anything interesting?"

"He recognised me and I had a very interesting discussion with him and later your mother," he said cryptically.

She bit her lips, seemingly desirous of asking more questions.

Miss Bingley instead jumped into the conversation. "Ah, Mrs. Bennet is such a lovely mother. Although I did not meet her this morning owing to the severity of my headache, I passed the small sitting room on my way out and heard her teaching Miss Eliza how to…obtain the company of a certain gentleman by pulling down the neckline of her gown and thrusting her…bosom out to tempt him."

"Caroline!" Bingley and Mrs. Hurst chastised their sister. It was a vulgar piece of conversation to repeat.

Elizabeth's face turned bright red but she drew in a deep breath and retorted, "Were you eavesdropping on our conversation, Miss Bingley? What a pity the door was too thick and you did not hear it all. We were actually talking about a theatre performance." She stopped and shook her head, "There are so many scandalous deeds that some women are willing to perform in order to ensnare a gentleman. Next, I am sure an author will write on the subject of a woman resorting to theft in order to marry a rich gentleman."

The Bingley siblings gasped for air. Darcy wanted to applaud Elizabeth's wit. Seeing that she had shut up Miss Bingley, Elizabeth turned her gaze directly to him. He could see that she was livid. Her eyes seemed to convey the message: "Do not cross swords with me or you shall be cut up like Caroline." But she asked sweetly, "Mr. Darcy, I am eagerly awaiting to hear of your discussion with my parents." Too sweetly, in fact; she sounded uncannily like Miss Bingley.

Darcy pondered carefully. He did not wish to be slapped on the face, figuratively speaking, yet again by the lovely lady. "Your father invited me to Longbourn and discussed how to improve the farm yield there. When your mother returned from her visit, he told her of his chest pain earlier in the day."

"Father is not feeling well?" Anger left Elizabeth's eyes. She had asked with such concern that Darcy suddenly felt guilty about taking advantage of her caring nature.

"But he dismissed Mrs. Bennet's request to send for the apothecary," he added casually. "Perhaps he had just walked too much today."

Elizabeth nodded. She remained silent for a few minutes before asking again, "What conclusion did father and you arrive at concerning improvements to the estate?"

"I did not know that Miss Eliza acted as a steward at Longbourn," Miss Bingley said with a grim smile.

Her siblings glared at her. Darcy shook his head. *Perhaps Miss Bingley needs to learn her manners from head mistress Mrs. Watson too*, he thought.

"Miss Bingley, as you know my father's estate is not very large. Father does not hire a steward. He consults Uncle Philips, who is a lawyer and lives in Meryton, if there is any legal matter requiring attention. As I do not have any brothers, I have been assisting Father with the management of the estate for some time." She said to Mr. Darcy, "I am therefore interested in hearing of your discussion."

Darcy admired her forbearance of Miss Bingley's rude behaviour and her true concern for the estate. She would make an excellent Mistress of Pemberley.

He told her the practical details of his discussion with Mr. Bennet. The remainder of the dinner passed without incident afterwards. He thought it best to leave her father to inform her of the departure of her mother and younger sister. As for his own stay in Longbourn, he would not touch the subject at all until he arrived at her doorstep.

He could also see that Bingley wanted to tell his sister that Miss Mary and Miss Lydia would be lodging shortly in Netherfield. But his friend seemed to decide not to do so at dinner, with guests present.

The next morning, Bingley watched attentively as the Bennet sisters departed. Darcy's farewell was short and formal. The Bingley sisters did not rise in time to see them off.

"It is so good to have the house to ourselves again!" Miss Bingley exclaimed when she sat down in the parlour nearly an hour later. She smiled and fluttered her eyelashes at Darcy.

"Not for long," her brother said.

This statement startled her. "What do you mean? Whom have you invited this time? I hope you have invited some of your London friends instead of the savages of Hertfordshire."

Bingley drew in a swift breath. "Louisa invited them to spend winter here. Perhaps she will tell you when she comes down."

He was attempting to avoid answering her question, and fortunately, at that moment, Mrs. Hurst came in.

"Whom have you invited? I hope not the annoying Barrymore sisters," Miss Bingley glared at her elder sister.

"It was really more Charles's decision." Mrs. Hurst was prevaricating too.

"Indeed it was not…" Bingley argued.

"I would much prefer it if you two ceased placing the blame on each other," Caroline declared, as though she were the matron of the family. "I insist on knowing whom you have invited."

"Miss Mary and Miss Lydia Bennet," Mrs. Hurst said at last.

"What? Have you been deprived of your senses? Why would you want those foolish Bennet girls here again?" she rose and demanded of her eldest sister.

"Miss Bingley, I would suggest you refer to the Bennet sisters with respect in future," Darcy said furiously.

"Yes, Caroline," Mr. Bingley added. "Mr. Bennet desired his two daughters to improve in music, fashion and proper manners, and he has honoured Louisa by requesting her guidance."

"I forbid it." Miss Bingley slammed her hand on a side table. "I am acting as your mistress here and I shall not allow those two trollops to pollute the atmosphere of Netherfield. If the old goat wants to educate his daughters, tell him to engage a governess or send them to a seminary! Yes, it will do well for Miss Eliza to stay in a nunnery."

"Mr. Bennet is not requesting us!" Mrs. Hurst raised her voice as well. "He is *demanding* this be done or he will send the magistrate to arrest you for stealing Miss Eliza's garnet cross. You stupid—!"

"Who would dare to gossip about my household? I shall fire all the servants this instant!" Miss Bingley readied herself to pull the bell for the housekeeper.

"It was I who told Mr. Bennet of the incident," Darcy said, holding back his temper. On the surface, Miss Bingley was always polite, elegant and refined when she visited Georgiana in London or at Pemberley. Although he had previously glimpsed some of her ghastly treatment of people, especially servants and those from lower orders, he did not know that she had so much contempt, vulgarity, and vindictiveness in her character. Mrs. Bennet's behaviour was ten-fold more acceptable than hers. He shuddered at his fortuitous escape by failing to ask for her hand on his return from Ramsgate.

"Mr. Darcy!" She tried to lower her voice but her anger was so beyond limits that Mr. Darcy was afraid she would draw close to cuff him. "How could you?"

He was not afraid of her.

"I think it is best you leave for London, Caroline, and stay with Aunt Pamela," Bingley said with a sigh. "Darcy was invited by Mr. Bennet to stay in Longbourn for a while so that he could help with the improvement of the estate. He and I shall be busy with estate business and Louisa with her two protégés."

Stamping her foot with annoyance, Miss Bingley left the parlour and heaved the door closed behind her with an ear-splitting slam.

## Chapter Four

Three days later, Mr. Darcy sent his grand carriage to Longbourn to pick up Mrs. Bennet and the younger Miss Bennets. The Mistress of Longbourn saw to the settling of Miss Mary and Miss Lydia in Netherfield before going on her way with Miss Catherine to the school in Kent.

Darcy divined from Mrs. Bennet's parting enthusiasm that she was certain that Bingley and he would make proposals for her two eldest daughters upon her return.

She hinted that the use of his grand carriage and the interest of Mr. Bingley's sister in improving her young daughters were both endearing means for courting Elizabeth and Jane. It was unfortunate that she was not able to meet Miss Bingley as the latter was once again abed with a headache.

On arriving at Longbourn later in the day, Mr. Bingley and Mr. Darcy were received by a quietly happy Mr. Bennet, a blushing Miss Jane and a subdued Miss Elizabeth. Dinner was a comfortable success with all five present taking part in intelligent conversation. Mr. Bingley stayed until very late.

Darcy did not sleep well that night. He was not used to less than perfect accommodation. But more importantly, the proximity of Miss Elizabeth was creating havoc with his thoughts. He could hear hushed voices and the sound of footsteps on the floor boards across the corridor. Images of the lovely lady in her night gown, sleeping sweetly with her hair down to her shoulders, occupied his mind. The sight of her stockings, stays and corsets in Netherfield came back clearly in his memory.

The next morning, he rose to greet a strangely quiet Miss Elizabeth.

While at breakfast, Mr. Bennet said to his eldest daughter, "I hope, my dear, that you have ordered a good dinner today, because I have reason to expect an addition to our family party."

Miss Bennet's face turned bright red. Was Bingley expected for dinner again, Darcy thought?

"I have not, Papa. But I shall do so immediately. Whom are we expecting?" Miss Bennet asked.

"It is a person whom I never saw in the whole course of my life."

Such a revelation raised general curiosity. Miss Elizabeth urged her father to continue.

"I have received a letter from my cousin, Mr. Collins, who, when I am dead, may turn you all out of this house as soon as he pleases."

Both ladies gasped but determined to be calm. They asked for more information concerning this stranger. Mr. Bennet read his cousin's letter aloud. Darcy was astonished to learn that Mr. Collins was his Aunt Lady Catherine de Bourgh's clergyman. From the tone of his over-flowery letter, Darcy could see why his aunt had appointed such a person. Mr. Collins would defer to the ladyship for every decision.

Equally alarming was the clergyman's indication of offering an olive branch to heal the disagreement between his family and Mr. Bennet's.

"At four o'clock, therefore, we may expect this peace-making gentleman," said Mr. Bennet, as he folded up the letter. "He seems to be a most conscientious and polite young man who might make an offer of marriage to one of you and relieve my constant worrying about the entail. Mr. Darcy, who do you think would suit Mr. Collins better?"

Both ladies turned, flustered with alarm. They were both intelligent enough to judge from the content of the letter that Mr. Collins was an oddity.

"I hope we can devise some method of improving Longbourn's income, sir," Darcy said. "Then you would not need to worry about your daughters' future too much."

Mr. Bennet rubbed his chest with his right hand and replied, "It may take some years to save enough to give each of them a decent dowry. But if Mr. Collins is willing, I do not object to his making an offer to my girls. Lizzy, I think you are the bravest of all of your sisters. What say you to taking him on?"

Elizabeth seemed to be holding back her irritation. Darcy sensed that the older gentleman was trying to push her daughter to see him as a more sensible alternative. But he did not welcome the fact that she was being embarrassed in the meanwhile.

"Should you not leave the decision until after you meet the gentleman, sir?" Darcy said. "And I must impart an intelligence as well. Lady Catherine de Bourgh is my aunt."

The Bennets expressed astonishment at such a coincidence. "Capital, Darcy! I hope you do not object to lowering your connection and staying in the same house as your aunt's pastor."

It was now Darcy's turn to get flustered. He did not look kindly on Mr. Bennet's mocking words, especially in front of Miss Elizabeth. The lady looked at him with an apologetic eye that lifted his spirits. It was the first time she had looked at him with an expression of concern. He could not prevent himself giving her a smile. When he turned to reply to the older gentleman, he saw Mr Bennet wink. Perhaps he had done it on purpose!

"Your home is very comfortable, sir. Perhaps we should ride out to talk to your tenants about the fallow land and the orangeries." Darcy said.

"Yes, well I want to discuss tonight's dinner with Jane and the arrangements for my cousin's stay. Lizzy, you take Mr. Darcy out. You know all the tenants anyway. He will tell you how his grand scheme works. You can use our curricle, Mr. Darcy. Yours will be too big for the narrow lanes here. And Lizzy is no horsewoman. Jane, come with me!" With those parting words, Mr. Bennet left quickly for his study.

Miss Elizabeth was now deep in thought. Darcy coughed to request her attention. She nodded and went to get her pelisse and bonnet.

He dismissed the servant and held out the garment for her. When he pulled it up to her shoulders, he remembered his thoughts of the previous night, of her sleeping with her hair down. Feeling the blood rise in his veins, he let out a quiet sigh of relief when she was finally dressed for the outdoors. He saw the white skin of her neck faintly trembling. There would be no more gentlemanly acts such as clutching her bonnet in future. He turned to quickly take his great coat from his valet, buttoned it up and walked ahead.

By the time he had settled himself on the other side of Mr. Bennet's curricle, he had cooled down enough to speak to the lady when she finally caught up with him.

"Miss Bennet, where should we begin?" he asked.

She was breathless and a rosy pinkness adorned her face. He thought he should leave her to run after him more often.

"The tenants have recently completed the harvest at Michaelmas. They should be preparing to rest for the winter. Do you need to talk to all of them?"

"I think only a few of the more progressive ones would be best. And they should have more than merely one man in the household because if they accept this new venture, they will need to work on the greenhouse this winter and grow flowers throughout the year."

"We should begin with the Jones family on the west of the estate then," she said, and was about to climb up into the curricle when he put out his hand to help her.

She took it with grace. When he had first stepped into the curricle, he had understood why Mr. Bennet wanted him to use his. It was the smallest curricle he had ever ridden in. He could feel the lady's shoulder, arm and thigh touching and stirring every inch of his body.

When he took hold of the reins and urged the horses to a slow pace, he could feel her bosom, hip and leg chafing him down one side. Luckily they both had their thicker outer cloaks on for otherwise he would surely have disgraced himself.

He did not understand how this country girl could cause such a reaction in him. She was not as handsome as her elder sister nor as pretty as many ladies in the town.

He stayed quiet throughout the journey, taking her direction and pondering her wit and character.

Fortunately the lady took the hint.

"Mr. Darcy, it seems you have brought about many changes in my family," she said.

"That has only been possible because your father was willing."

"That is what I find astounding. Not only is my father, who tends to be, shall we say, enlightened as far as his management of the lands is concerned, taking a keen interest in improving the estate, my mother is also excited about introducing my younger sisters in London. I do indeed wonder what you said to my parents in the course of that day when you first met my father."

"Did your father not explain it to you?"

"He seemed to be very busy suddenly. Or he is avoiding me. Did you tell my mother about the garnet cross?"

"No."

"But you told my Father?"

Mr. Darcy nodded.

"Even about your father's pledge?"

"That was the truth. I did not want to hide anything from him. As you know, he saved my life."

"And you told him I rejected you?"

"The truth again. Though I confessed that it was more my fault."

"Can you ever be less than candid?" she said in a level voice.

"That is not my nature."

"My father has been behaving very strangely these few days. I fear he is trying to force me to accept you!"

"I do not think so. You are not of age. If he were attempting to force your hand, he could easily demand that you simply did as he said. He told me he regrets indulging Mrs. Bennet after his close proximity to death in that horrifying fire at Bromley Inn. Improving the estate and educating your siblings are his way of making amends. He wants to act in the best interests of his family. My appearance in Hertfordshire merely happened to prompt him into action."

"You will not try to change my mind about our future?" She raised her brows sceptically.

"You have expressed your opinion very decidedly a few days ago. I would not make an offer for your hand unless…" – he turned to gaze at her – "... unless you were to ask me."

She opened her mouth, possibly ready to confirm that she would never beg him to court her. But at that moment several lads ran up to the curricle. They greeted her warmly. They were the sons of Mr. And Mrs. Jones.

The Jones family was a happy lot. The father and his three oldest sons welcomed Miss Elizabeth. After she had introduced Mr. Darcy to the tenants, he asked them about their crops, their farming routine and their harvest.

"I have been talking to Mr. Bennet about some of the new farm methods I have tried in Derbyshire. I think as Longbourn is relatively near to London, you can do better by growing flowers and fruit. A greenhouse will ensure that you can grow them even in the winter."

"We have often discussed planting more crops to harvest," Mr. Jones said. "But new seeds are costly and we don't know any market or tradesmen to sell our crops. And we certainly know nothing of greenhouses."

"It is a building with glass and where the temperature is kept warm throughout the year. It can be hard work to stay vigilant in regards to the heat throughout the day. But the rewards are immense. Mr. Bennet said he would provide the seedlings and glass materials to build as a loan. As for the market, I have sent an express about this to my steward. He will be able to find some people who would want to buy your crop."

As he continued to discuss the merits and problems of building a greenhouse with the Jones men folk, he noticed the surprised expression on Elizabeth's face.

He was happy to show her his knowledgeable and persuasive side. He felt more at ease talking about farming than the trivial, polite but dull conversations required by those of the town or upper circles of London society.

After almost an hour of discussion, the Jones men were eager to participate in the new venture. Miss Elizabeth would inform her father and uncle to draft the loan agreement. Her face again showed a degree of bewilderment when Mr. Darcy said he would instruct two of his men who were familiar with constructing greenhouses to come help the Jones family.

Before the pair took their leave, Mrs Jones invited them to take some tea in their house. When Grandmother Jones learned of the new development, she could not help commenting. "Sir, I am so happy that you're helping Miss Lizzy. She is a strong girl but it's not proper that she should worry about us constantly."

"I am happy to be of help to the Bennets," Mr. Darcy said.

"Mrs. Jones, I do not worry about you at all," Elizabeth said. "You rule your house like a queen."

"Nonsense, I am just an old girl with more white hair than most. Sir, I have known Miss Lizzy all my life. She is the cleverest one of her sisters. Don't be alarmed by her sharp tongue."

He smiled and said, "Miss Bennet's words maybe sharp but she is often correct in her opinion."

"Ah, so you've already received Miss Lizzy's pointed view! That's good. For a girl won't set you right if she's not interested in your welfare." The elderly lady's comment put a shade of red on Elizabeth's face.

*Could that be true?* Mr. Darcy thought.

Mrs. Jones continued, "And you will do well with our Lizzy. She has the widest hips of all her sisters. She would be able give you many healthy babes."

"I ... I think we should be on our way," he stammered, his face now as pink as Miss Elizabeth's.

When Elizabeth and Mr. Darcy had crammed themselves into the curricle again, he could not avoid feeling her hip. He vowed to think of Grandmother Jones's words no more.

The lady directed him to take a different route along the river back to Longbourn. Half an hour into the journey, the curricle became stuck in mud on a slightly downward slope.

Mr. Darcy jumped down to push the curricle from behind.

"You must urge the horses forward gently, Miss Bennet," he said.

She nodded and used the whip with a light hand. Her first attempt did not produce any result.

He took off his greatcoat and pushed again with full force while she whipped the horses slightly harder. Suddenly the horses startled and dashed forward.

Mr. Darcy was caught off-guard, falling forward and then landing face-down in the mud.

"Mr. Darcy, are you hurt?" Elizabeth cried. She reined in the horses, descended from the curricle and ran back to his side immediately. She knelt down to help him stand.

Except for the mud on his front and on part of his jaw, he was not injured. "I am unhurt, thank you. But your dress is covered in mud," he added, seeing that the hem and the knee portion of her dress had been smeared by mud as she had helped him to rise.

"It is of no consequence. Let us..." She turned and was about to ask him to get back to the curricle when she saw that the horses had taken off without their passengers. "Oh, we have lost our curricle!"

"We are not far from Longbourn, are we?" he asked, feeling the indignity of his muddy appearance in front of his companion.

"No, perhaps a mile or two. But the river is not far. Would you like to wash off some of the mud first?"

Mr. Darcy agreed with this plan at once, not wishing to enter her home in such disarray. They walked down to the river. He held out his hand to assist her when required. Every time their gloved hands touched and their eyes met, he felt his heart racing. He was also encouraged by the shade of pink on Elizabeth's face. He told himself it was his attentive presence, rather than the exercise, that made her blush.

When they arrived at the river, he begged for her forgiveness as he took off his gloves, cravat, coat and waistcoat. Using his cravat, dampened with water, he removed the mud as best he could. He also took the occasion to glance at Elizabeth from time to time. She had used a handkerchief to wash the area of the dress around her knees but did not bother to address the mud that had dried around the hem.

Once that was done, he rolled up his damp clothing and helped her to ascend the river bank. Now and then he felt the heat of her gaze on the skin of his neck because the cravat was not fit to wear once more. She had also taken off her gloves when she had washed her dress, so this time their hands touched skin to skin. He could not help but gently rub her soft palm. He could see that she shivered at his ministration. The blossom on her face had now spread down her neck and chest.

Sensing that she was too busy fighting her feelings to protest, he did not let go of her hand when they reached level ground and continued to hold it as they walked back to Longbourn.

Breathing in the sweet lavender scent from her body, he was happy with the progress he had made today. He hoped Elizabeth would soon forget his inconsiderate proposal of the other day and give him another chance to win her heart.

At last she broke the silence. "How did you learn of this greenhouse method?"

"Using a greenhouse to grow crops was used as far back as Roman times. It became common in France and Italy a few years ago. My father wanted to use them in Pemberley but he died before he could do so. I learned more about it from books and by talking to other landlords who were successful with the scheme."

"Was it very difficult for you…when your father died?"

He nodded. In the previous five years he had not talked to anyone about the anger, resentment and sadness connected to his father's passing. He had always pretended to be strong. It seemed fitting that Elizabeth was the one now to ask him about it.

"I could contend with the responsibility but I still miss him greatly." A feeling of loss welled in his chest. "And I fear I have failed my sister."

She looked at him with questioning eyes but he could not go on to recount his failure as a brother. He turned his head away from her intense gaze, hoping to conceal the depth of his feelings. To his surprise, she stopped and gave him a quick comforting hug.

His heart warmed by her action, he embraced her tightly for a moment, lowered his mouth to kiss her hair but released her immediately afterwards, not wishing to take advantage of her considerate gesture.

They walked on in silence again, this time side by side, without holding hands. When they entered Longbourn, they moved towards the back garden as they did not wish to enter the front door with mud on their shoes.

They were taken aback to discover Mr. Bennet conversing with another gentleman.

"Ah, what has happened to you two? Did you decide to frolic in water and mud together?"

The young couple attempted to conceal their embarrassment. But before they could reply, the stranger said, "If my distinguished patron the Right Honourable Lady Catherine de Bourgh was here, she would perform the respectful duty of instructing people not to disregard propriety. The wild behaviour of young people today is alarming, she would say. She would not allow her daughter to ramble in the countryside with a young man without chaperone. Such enterprise would only encourage young people to take the liberty of committing licentious acts." The man shook his head as Elizabeth tried to pull the lapels of her pelisse together to conceal her dress, which had been made damp by Mr. Darcy during their embrace. "Frolicking in water, improperly attired, is not to be condoned."

Mr. Darcy stood to his full height and bowed to Mr. Bennet. "Sir, I am sorry for the state of my attire. The curricle became stuck in mud. I fell to the ground while trying to dislodge it. Miss Elizabeth was made wet when she tried to help me. We went to the river to cleanse ourselves as far as we were able."

"I knew that some misfortune must have befallen you two when Nelly and Mimi returned without their occupants. But you must pardon me and let me introduce you to my cousin, Mr. William Collins. He arrived early. Cousin, this is my second daughter, Elizabeth, and Mr. Darcy of Pemberley."

"Mr....Darcy, you say?" The clergyman's tongue seemed to have been caught between his teeth. He continued to bow deeply and stuttered. "I...I did not know that the....esteemed nephew of Lady Catherine de Bourgh was in the neighbourhood."

Darcy gave Mr. Collins a short nod. He saw Elizabeth's lips curl up in a teasing smile. "Sir," he turned to Mr. Bennet.

"Please excuse us. We had best enter through the back door in order to launder ourselves more effectively."

"Yes, we do not want our *dirt* to distress my cousin," Elizabeth added sweetly. She put her hand on Mr. Darcy's arm and walked with him around her cousin, who was still bent double, bowing to Darcy.

# Chapter Five

When Mr. Darcy and Elizabeth entered the kitchen area, they were greeted with gentle disapproval. The servants were in the middle of preparing dinner and did not relish the idea of arranging baths for the wayward pair.

But there was no avoiding the task. Miss Lizzy and her beau were not fit to be seen. Speculation also spread among the servants and knowing glances and secretive smiles were exchanged.

Being the less muddy of the two, Elizabeth was to go upstairs after she had taken off her boots. A pitcher of water would be brought up for her to wash in her room.

A maid helped take off her shoes and Darcy caught a glimpse of Elizabeth's feet in stockings. He was enchanted by how tiny her feet were. His hands seemed to him larger.

His errant thoughts were interrupted by his valet, Winston, who came down to help him bathe. As Winston discussed with Longbourn's servants the matter of setting up the bath, Darcy saw Elizabeth glancing at him from time to time.

She was surprisingly slow in her preparations and seemed to be lingering in the kitchen, Darcy thought.

Only when the water was ready in the laundry room and he was asked to leave the kitchen did the lady ascend to her room in haste.

Behind the laundry sheets, Mr. Darcy took off all his clothes, save for a pair of trousers.

He was relieved that the servants were busy in the kitchen and none of them dared to venture into the room. With the help of his valet, he washed away the mud and thought about the events of the day. The curricle ride was intimate. Grandmother

Jones's comment made them felt awkward. Falling into the mud was embarrassing, but Elizabeth's compassionate embrace gave him hope. The most annoying occurrence was the appearance of Lady Catherine's clergyman. Mr. Collins was a silly and exasperating man.

With that last unpleasant thought, he rose from the bath tub and wrapped himself in a robe made ready by his valet. As he emerged from behind the sheets, he bumped into a soft form near the door of the laundry room.

"Ouch!"

"I beg your pardon!"

It was Elizabeth. Her tumbling mane of hair was let down to her shoulders and the shawl that covered it had dropped to the floor.

They both bent to retrieve it. His eyes caught the low neckline of her gown while he felt her gaze on his bare chest, which was not covered by the robe. He remained unmoving while heat rushed through his body.

Luckily the movement of his valet startled him. He grabbed the shawl and wrapped it around her shoulders.

"I…I came down…to find my cor—" Elizabeth stammered.

"I…I had just finished my bath," he interrupted. His eyes remained fixed on her bewitching eyes, framed by thick dark-brown curls. "I shall…I shall go upstairs to dress."

She curtsied and stepped aside for him to pass. But her eyes still seemed to burn a hole in his chest.

Risking a glance at his valet, who pretended to be busy with his chores, Darcy lowered his head and whispered into her ears, "Did you come down to steal a look at me? I hope you take some pleasure in it." He was happy to hear her gasp for air and exclaim "Insufferable men!" under her breath.

"Men?" He frowned. "Who else has irked you?"

She glanced at his valet. Darcy signalled for Winston to leave, which the latter did quietly.

"Did Mr. Collins do something inappropriate?" He held her arms and his tone was grave.

She struggled from his hold and blurted out. "What is Miss Anne de Bourgh to you?"

"Ah I see. Mr. Collins has been spreading lies." He paced around.

"So you are not engaged to her?"

"No, though my aunt Lady Catherine always wished it." He stopped in front of her, agitated. "Did you not trust my integrity and honour? Have I not told you my father's wish? Did I not ask you to marry me?"

"But Mr. Collins…"

"Yes, what exactly did he say?"

"He said that you have been engaged to Miss de Bourgh since your birth and you visit her every year, waiting for her health to recover. And that whatever…feeling you had for me, you are probably acting like any young man bewitched by the…arts and allurements of young maidens."

"He accused me of trifling with young women and you of loose morals!"

"I did rebuke him most fervently about my character."

"But you believed what he said of mine?"

"I did not." She stamped her foot in annoyance. "But I did not know your relationship with Miss de Bourgh."

He stepped forward and held her arms again. Gazing into her eyes, he said slowly, "Anne is only a cousin. You, however, mean a lot more to me…if you would allow it." Then he lowered his head and kissed her.

It was not a brotherly kiss. It was fast and fierce. He tasted her soft yet fiery lips. Savouring the moisture of the caress, he withdrew from the kiss as abruptly as he had begun.

Not trusting himself, he dashed from the laundry room, leaving her with her mouth partly open, followed swiftly by another murmur of "Insufferable man!"

As he dressed with care for dinner once again, Darcy was both furious and anxious. He was angry with his aunt's meddling parson and anxious about Elizabeth's response to his transgression.

When he entered the dining room he was unhappy with the seating arrangement. Mr. Collins was seated beside Elizabeth while he was to be seated facing Miss Bennet and to one side of the clergyman.

Mr. Bennet was smiling slyly. Darcy shook his head. He had difficulty understanding the elderly gentleman's actions.

They passed most of dinner listening to a monologue from Mr. Collins. He praised the size of the chimneys in Rosings, the large number of windows and how considerate Lady Catherine was to all her tenants. Miss Bennet was the only person who occasionally responded to his speech, while the other three ate in silence.

When they had almost reached the end of the meal, Mr. Collins repeated to Mr. Darcy how well Lady Catherine and Anne were when he left Rosings, Darcy decided to put the clergyman in his place.

"Thank you for relating the news, Mr. Collins. I have heard that you appear to be privileged to some other news about myself as well," Darcy said.

"Your most esteemed Mr. Darcy, what type of news are you referring to?"

"About my cousin Anne and myself."

"Oh..." Mr. Collins's hand stopped in the middle of the table, and did not continue to reach for the wine glass.

"Yes, Mr. Collins told Lizzy and I that you were engaged to Miss de Bourgh," Mr. Bennet added at once. "How thoughtless of me not to congratulate you, Fitzwilliam."

Jane gasped and threw a concerned look at her sister while Mr. Collins retracted his hand and pulled out a handkerchief to wipe his brow. "Yes, your most honourable Mr. Darcy..."

"I am afraid, Mr. Bennet, that Mr. Collins is mistaken. Anne and I are not engaged."

"But my most respectable Fitzwilliam," Mr. Bennet imitated his cousin, "Mr. Collins has mentioned to us that your most admirable Lady Catherine de Bourgh informed him of the engagement. The agreement was reached with your gracious mother Lady Anne' and had been in place from the time you were in the cradle. Mr. Collins even told me that I should not take any of your...intentions in respect of my daughters seriously."

Darcy put down the cutlery heavily and announced, "Mr. Bennet, it is unfortunate that my integrity has been questioned. I shall examine the source of this slander carefully. Perhaps I should ask the Archbishop, who is a personal friend, for guidance in this matter."

Mr. Collins dropped the fork with a loud clatter. He then rose and bowed deeply. "I am not…feeling well, my dear cousins. Pray excuse me…I must retire now." He then fled the room in haste.

Miss Bennet looked at the retreating form with concern, then Elizabeth and her father burst out laughing.

"So Mr. Collins was in error?" Miss Jane turned to look at Mr. Darcy.

"Yes, I am not engaged to Miss de Bourgh and I am always honourable in my… intentions." His eyes stared at Elizabeth as he replied. The lady stopped laughing and became flustered.

"Mr. Bingley invited us to dine with them tomorrow," Mr. Bennet said. "Perhaps Mary would enjoy discussing Fordyce's Sermons with Mr. Collins. Fitzwilliam, you may stay to entertain my girls. I think I ate too much. I shall retire now."

The occupants in the room rose and Elizabeth said with concern, "Papa, you have complained about not feeling well these past days. Should you not send for the apothecary?"

"It is only a minor irritation." Mr. Bennet waved his hand in dismissal.

Elizabeth turned to look at Mr. Darcy and bade him to help.

"Mr. Bennet, it is better to be on the safe side. I can ride out and fetch the doctor now," he said.

"You will lose yourself in our unfamiliar countryside. Tomorrow morning will be fine. Take Lizzy with you. She can show you where Doctor Smith lives." The elderly gentleman then left the room.

When the occupants had moved to the sitting room, Miss Jane expressed her concerns. "Papa has not been well lately?"

"I first heard of it from Mr. Darcy on the last day of our stay in Netherfield," Elizabeth said.

"He told your mother he had chest pain," Darcy explained.

"And tonight the food did not seem to agree with him," Jane murmured. "I hope he is not worried about the changes that have happened in the household and the estate lately."

"Mr. Darcy, I meant to ask you earlier, can we really afford the glass house for the Jones family?" Elizabeth said.

"I have promised to loan Longbourn some capital for the new venture."

Elizabeth's face turned crimson. She opened her mouth to speak but closed it firmly all of a sudden.

"We are indebted to you," Jane said, and looked at her sister with concern.

"Please do not be uneasy, Miss Bennet. Mr. Bennet saved my life during the fire at Bromley. I would be most happy to assist him in any way that would ease his mind about the estate," he replied and turned his gaze to Elizabeth, "Regardless of the outcome of other matters."

Miss Bennet seemed to be mollified by this reply. She rose, took up the sewing basket and sat herself in a chair further away from the other two.

Elizabeth fidgeted on the chaise. Darcy moved closer to her and whispered, "I want to apologise for my behaviour in the laundry room."

"You promised you would not change my mind," she replied huskily, her eyes glancing at his profile before turning away.

"Did my kiss change your mind?"

"No…yes…no…You behaved in a less than gentlemanly fashion in order to steal a kiss from me."

"But you stole a look at me while I bathed."

"I did not! I came down to the laundry room to collect my corset." During this declaration of innocence, however, a scarlet flush spread from her face to her chest.

"Your maid was busy?" His eyes lowered to assess that piece of clothing. "I shall thank her for sending you my way."

"Impossible man!"

He moved closer to her on the chaise, as they had been in the tiny curricle. "I hope you will change your mind, on your own." He breathed the words into her ear. "Soon."

Suppressing the urge to bite her adorable earlobe, he rose, bowed to the ladies and bade them good night.

***

The next morning, Mr. Darcy awoke in an embarrassing condition. He had just experienced the most erotic dream in his life. Not even in his younger years had he undergone such a vivid and detailed event.

In his dream, he had wandered around Pemberley in search of someone from dawn till dark. After passing through each room with frustration, he had finally arrived at the pond and found the most striking woman standing there.

When she had turned around, he could see with the assistance of the setting sun that it was Elizabeth.

Her dark-brown hair had been released to her shoulders. Her sensual body was sheathed in a corset that was almost translucent. Through the white fabric he could see the dark cherry colour of the tips of her breasts and the dark secret at the apex of her thighs.

She arched her eyebrow and gave him a teasing smile before trying to untie the garment.

Darcy swallowed hard and stood there in anticipation. He was intensely aroused.

He waited one minute. Two minutes, then three.

Her hands were most ineffective. She continued to smile and gaze at him.

Impatient, Darcy stepped towards her and offered to help her untie the corset. But then she suddenly began to flee from him, running along the border of the pond.

She was laughing, stopping to splash water at him.

With a loud howl that did not in fact produce any sound in the dream, Darcy gave chase. But she was like a butterfly, escaping his grasp the moment he could smell the scent of her skin. By now, she was thoroughly wet. The white fabric moulded itself to her figure, outlining every valley and delicious mound.

His aroused senses were heightened to an unbearable degree and hindered his pursuit.

On and on he ran after her awkwardly, from the pond to the formal garden and into the house.

After the ballroom and the library, Darcy finally found Elizabeth in the dark laundry room. Behind sheets of laundry, in the dim wavering light from a host of candles, she started untying the corset and taking off the wet garment with deliberate slowness.

He caught his breath and parted the sheets. His eyes bored into her skin as he savoured her measured undressing.

When the top of her corset dropped down, she pulled her long hair to the front and covered one tempting nipple. But its twin was left standing proud and hard.

Then Elizabeth bent forward and pushed the garment down her wide hips. Darcy's breathing became fast and shallow. His eyes followed the path of the white fabric.

Slowly, her adorable navel was revealed. Then, the covering of her most private secret came into view.

His gaze moved downward, following the drop of her garment, along her round buttocks.

He focussed on her petite toes for a moment but she turned around, hands on the edge of the bath tub and tried to climb into it.

With lightning speed, he stood behind her, preventing her movement. Then he wrapped one hand around her tiny waist and used the other hand to cup her creamy mound.

She squirmed and murmured some silent words. Bending her forward with his body, he started squeezing and pinching her nipple while undoing his breeches.

Shaking and trembling, she began to press her buttocks against his body. Once his thick shaft was freed, he seized her inner thighs, parted her legs and stood between them.

He thought it was impossible to feel any sensation in a dream. But he could feel the actual grip caused by the sheathing of his hard rod into her warmth. She was tight and burning. With a forceful thrust, he pounded into her up to the hilt.

The heat, perspiration and friction assailed his muscles. His manhood was clamped so hard that he thought he would soon stop breathing.

He felt that he had pushed her so high that he had taken her feet off the ground. She was leaning with her weight supported by her hands on the edge of the bath tub, with his hands grasping her hips.

Elizabeth turned her head and mouthed the words "Ride on." Darcy obliged with eagerness. With legs firmly on the ground, he pounded, thrust and impaled her welcoming core, on and on, again and again.

Minute by minute, she shook and rode with him. It seemed like hours passed before he awoke from his frantic thrusting and experienced the most extraordinary climax. When he opened his eyes, he found himself alone inside the guest chamber of Longbourn, a drenched pillow clasped between his legs.

Shocked by such a vivid dream and by the task of restoring the ruined pillow, Darcy entered the morning parlour later than usual.

Mr. Bennet was reading his paper, looking well and perfectly normal. Miss Bennet was mending a ribbon. Mr. Collins was still abed, not feeling well.

Darcy enquired after everyone's health and Elizabeth told him that she had already asked a servant to fetch the doctor.

Mr. Bennet pitied him for losing an opportunity to drive out this morning.

Darcy bore it with good grace. He sat down at the far end of the room but could not seem to drag his eyes from the arc of Elizabeth's neck as she paced about the room, impatient for Dr. Smith to arrive.

His gaze followed her movement. He had developed a sudden fascination with her buttocks, fresh from the memory of pummelling them so many times in his dream. *Do not think about the dream!* he warned himself. *You have a long way to go yet before you may win her affections.*

# Chapter Six

Dr. Smith arrived soon afterwards and took the Master of Longbourn to his room. Much to the relief of his daughters, Mr. Bennet was found to be well. The doctor was asked to examine Mr. Collins. But the latter came down at that instant and dismissed the services of the doctor.

He excused himself without catching the eye of any one in the room, and said that he had a letter to post instead.

"You can leave it for Hill to do that for you," Mr. Bennet offered.

"The morning air in Hertfordshire appears to be quite good, though not as fresh as that of Rosings. I think I shall walk to your little village … Meryton, that is, and post this important letter myself." He bowed to Mr. Bennet.

"Ah, but you do not know our roads. I would not want you lost. Lizzy, pray take Mr. Collins to Meryton," Mr. Bennet said.

The clergyman's face lit up at this offer and agreed. Elizabeth rose from her seat reluctantly. Mr. Collins for once did not proclaim the likely problems associated with rambling in the countryside alone with a young lady, Mr. Darcy thought. He debated how to ask Mr. Bennet for permission to join them.

A few minutes after the pair had left the parlour, Mr. Bennet relieved his suffering. "Fitzwilliam, you should go too. Have a look at the roads around Meryton and see if they are good for the winter transport of fruit and flowers."

Mr. Darcy rose at once and gave the elderly gentleman a smile of gratitude.

It did not take long for Darcy to catch up with Mr. Collins and Elizabeth. Mr. Collins had stopped under a tree, saying he had some stones in his shoes, and bade the other two to continue.

"Oh, you have business in Meryton too?" Elizabeth asked Mr. Darcy. He told her what her father had said.

"I think you have scared my cousin off." She turned her head and signalled Mr. Darcy to look back.

Mr. Collins was following them, but at a safe distance, with no intention of catching up.

"That is good!" he said, raising his chin. "I prefer not to listen to his flowery speeches concerning my aunt and my cousin."

"You are being condescending and arrogant again!" she grimaced.

Darcy's face turned ashen. How could he forget her censure? "I am sorry for my boorish behaviour. My dearest Elizabeth, I shall look to you for guidance. How should I behave in front of such an oddity?"

He was happy to have raised a scarlet flush on her face with his endearment. She tilted her head with an expression of exasperation and replied, "Flattery! Simply listening to the first and last portions of Mr. Collins' speech will suffice."

"It seems I have to learn from you about pretence."

"It is called gentlemanly behaviour."

"And what do you do in the middle of his speeches?" he asked.

"Often I contemplate the beautiful weather, the fresh air or one of Shakespeare's sonnets."

"I shall think about a certain young lady, then, when Mr. Collins embarks on his monologue."

Elizabeth blushed again. "Flattery!"

"I am only talking about my sister," Mr. Darcy smiled.

She stamped her foot with irritation, then picked up her pace. He caught up with her easily, as his legs were rather long. But the pastor had fallen quite far behind.

They had almost reached Meryton when Elizabeth stumbled on a rock by a tall oak tree.

With good fortune, Darcy was right beside her and prevented her fall. He had his hands around her waist and pressed her against him to steady her. The closeness of her shoulders and hips sent a tremor down his body. Her sweet scent evoked memories of his dream. He gazed at her lips and drew in a deep breath.

Panting hard, she seized his hand, then passed her tongue over her lips. He groaned out loud at her gesture and lowered his head. Before he could kiss her ardently, she turned her head away.

Releasing her, he held his hand behind his back and twisted the ring on his finger.

"A carriage is coming," she murmured.

He sighed with relief. She turned away not because she did not welcome his eagerness. But he blamed himself for lacking control, for almost kissing her on a public road.

Once the carriage had passed, they continued at a slower pace. Mr. Collins had caught up but was still walking a few yards behind.

When they reached Meryton, Darcy looked around with interest. It was slightly larger than Lambton, a small town near Pemberley. There were shops for ribbons, food, books and other supplies. Many people were out and about and Elizabeth seemed to know many of them. They greeted her from afar with curious eyes but did not approach to ask for an introduction.

She returned their greetings with good cheer and politeness. Once she had arrived at the shop where Mr. Collins could post his letter, she waited with Mr. Darcy while her cousin went inside. The clergyman entered the shop quickly but stole a glance over his shoulder.

Darcy had the suspicion that Mr. Collins did not wish Elizabeth and he to enter the shop. That suited Darcy perfectly. He would rather talk to his beloved.

Not a few moments later, two horses drew up near them.

"Darcy! It is good to see you. Bingley is taking me to visit you at Longbourn."

Darcy turned around and saw his cousin, Colonel Fitzwilliam, and Mr. Bingley dismounting.

"I did not know that you were coming too." He shook hands with his cousin.

"Susan was talking about this secret mission of yours, and I have some leave. Of course I could not stay away," Colonel Fitzwilliam laughed.

"Yes, he simply arrived with Lady Susan yesterday evening and demanded the best port and a room," Bingley joined in. "But we should not forget our manners. Miss Bennet, how are you today?"

"I am well," Elizabeth said. "And you?"

"Very well! Excellent!" Bingley smiled.

"This is my cousin, Colonel Fitzwilliam." Mr. Darcy made the introduction. "Mrs. Hurst has invited his eldest sister Lady Susan to stay in Netherfield for the winter."

"And I tagged along," the Colonel said. "I am delighted to make your acquaintance, Miss Bennet. Bingley has not exaggerated. Your beauty rivals that of an angel!"

"Richard!" Bingley chastised his guest with a red face while Darcy looked on without expression.

Elizabeth smiled. "I see you possess the same skills in flattery as your cousin, Colonel Fitzwilliam. But the angel in Longbourn is my eldest sister."

"Darcy flirting with young ladies? That is unheard of," Colonel Fitzwilliam said. "Have you served him a special 'Charming' wine in Longbourn?"

The easy banter was cut short by Mr. Collins who came out of the shop with another gentleman.

"Cousin Elizabeth..." Mr. Collins's greetings were interrupted by a sudden uproar.

Darcy had noticed the gentleman standing by Mr. Collins and anger seized him.

"Wickham!" he exclaimed.

"You bloody scoundrel!" Colonel Fitzwilliam yelled and lunged at Wickham. Darcy wrapped his arms around Elizabeth and pulled her away from the mayhem.

Wickham ducked away from the Colonel and aimed a punch at his stomach, causing him to double over. Bingley stepped forward in an attempt to help the Colonel regain himself when Wickham turned on him.

Bingley twisted his body to avoid Wickham's fist and responded with a right-handed blow of his own. Wickham avoided the strike by pulling Collins in front of him.

Unable to stop his momentum, Bingley hit Collins's nose with a powerful blow and knocked the clergyman to the ground.

Colonel Fitzwilliam regained his balance and slapped the distracted Wickham, his ring scoring a deep cut on Wickham's face. When the Colonel tried to strike again, Darcy pulled him back. Wickham took this opportunity to steal away from the scene.

While Darcy was trying to calm his cousin, Elizabeth and Bingley crouched down by Mr. Collins.

"How is Mr. Collins?" Darcy asked Elizabeth when the Colonel had calmed down.

"He is unconscious," she said. "We need a carriage to take him back to Longbourn and to a doctor."

"I am sorry, Miss Bennet. I wounded him accidentally," Bingley begged for forgiveness.

"It is not your fault. It was Wickham who used the clergyman as a shield."

"Let me get the carriage and take him to Netherfield instead," Bingley said. "It was I who injured him and I would not permit Miss Bennet and yourself to be burdened with the task of taking care of the patient."

Elizabeth turned to look at Darcy. He agreed with Bingley and asked the lady to consent. Netherfield had more servants and could take better care of Mr. Collins but Darcy did not explain these details to Elizabeth.

Bingley went to fetch a carriage and the doctor. Colonel Fitzwilliam apologised to Elizabeth profusely for starting the brawl but did not explain his past history with Wickham.

The party left for Netherfield in a carriage amid the hushed voices of Meryton locals and left Mr. Darcy and Elizabeth with the two horses. Darcy and Elizabeth would take them back to Longbourn and return them that night during dinner. Clothes for Mr. Collins would be sent as soon as possible.

***

As Darcy walked alongside Elizabeth to return to Longbourn, his mind was in turmoil. He had not seen Wickham since that fateful day in Ramsgate. Why had he appeared here in Meryton?

"Mr. Darcy, who is this Mr. Wickham?" Elizabeth's question broke his thoughts.

"He is nobody." He dismissed the question quickly, as would any man who did not want to worry his loved one.

"A nobody who made you mutter disapprovingly? And it would appear he is a scoundrel who caused your cousin to assail him without any outward provocation on his behalf?" Her eyes flared with fire and anger.

He looked away, unable to comprehend either her anger or her compassion.

"I do not want a marriage like my parents, where life is not shared but is merely a matter of coexisting," she said. "I would like to engage in a marriage of equal partnership, sharing not only happy circumstances but even painful ones with my husband."

Darcy hesitated for a moment, but then realized he must heed her words. Hence he began, "George Wickham was my father's godson,"— the words tumbled out with intense vehemence— "who squandered every opportunity my family gave him to succeed by repaying us with disrespect and deceit."

"Your father looked after him?"

"He was the son of my father's steward. My father sent him to Cambridge after his own father died."

"He enrolled in the school of debauchery instead of respectability?"

"His indulgence in wickedness occurred well before he attended Cambridge. We played together as boys and I noticed his transformation. I regretted not exposing his dissolute manner to my father earlier."

"And why did you not?" Elizabeth asked softly.

"Mother died not long before and I could see the sadness and dejection in my father's eyes. I did not know how to comfort him and Wickham had an easy manner which brought some lightness to Father's life. I did not want to kill that little happiness in him."

She patted his arm and said, "You were correct in your intentions. It is time to look forward rather than to live in regret."

Their eyes met and he felt his shoulders unburdened.

"What kind of deceit did Mr. Wickham practise on your cousin?"

He stopped near a tree and raised his hand, wanting to smite it. But he feared that Elizabeth had seen too much violence that day. Clenching his fist tight, he lowered his arm and barely uttered the words. "It is too painful to tell."

Elizabeth stepped in front of him, placed her hands around his waist and laid her head on his chest. "Tell me of the day it happened."

As he took in her lovely scent, the weight of her head seemed to slow his heavy breathing. He described how he discovered Miss Bingley with the garnet cross and how he went to Ramsgate to visit his sister in order to discuss their future. Much to his astonishment, Georgiana confessed to him her impending elopement with the scoundrel Wickham. He continued the story of how he had acted in regards to Wickham and his accomplice, Mrs. Younge.

"Georgiana was then but fifteen!" He tightened his hold on Elizabeth. Tears threatened to fall from his eyes. He looked up at the sky. "I failed my father, my cousin and my sister."

She gripped him once, tightly, before stepping back from his embrace. Her eyes held his as she took his arms in her own. "We live our own lives, Fitzwilliam. You gave your sister a comfortable home, a sensible education and an abundance of love. She was imprudent to allow her companion and Mr. Wickham to prey on her but she will learn from her ill-advised actions. You must allow your loved ones to experience life's trials and tribulations for themselves."

A single tear fell from his eye. He seized her hand and raised it to his mouth. Then he wiped away the tear and whispered, "Thank you, Elizabeth."

He did not know whether he had exonerated himself from the dereliction of his duty to his father, cousin and sister. But now he did not feel so overwhelmed by the guilt and regret that had been plaguing him since the Ramsgate affair. He was relieved that Elizabeth did not pity, censor or mollify him. He did not need absolution. He simply needed understanding.

He held her hand for the remainder of the journey back to Longbourn, not speaking a word, while pondering life's lessons. Her hand warmed him. Her silence fostered a sense of connection. He could walk to the end of the world now, embracing the future, as long as she was with him.

When they arrived at Longbourn, she told him to rest while she explained the absence of Mr. Collins to her father and sister. Later Darcy was able to appear for the dinner at Netherfield in a refreshed and peaceful frame of mind.

***

"It is most unfortunate your cousin is removed to Netherfield," Mr. Bennet said to his daughters. The four occupants were assembled in the parlour at Longbourn, taking tea before heading over to Netherfield.

"Miss Bingley must be frantic, what with the care of our sisters and guests and now our sick cousin," Jane said.

"Yes, you must tell Mr. Darcy what Mary has written just now about the events in Netherfield," he smiled.

Miss Bennet was flustered. "I do not want to bore Mr. Darcy with mundane chatter."

"Nonsense! Fitzwilliam has a young sister. He must be used to such illuminating discussions."

Darcy did not know how to reply. He looked at Elizabeth for assistance.

"How did Mary find her stay at Netherfield?" Elizabeth asked.

"She said Mr. Bingley was very kind and went out of his way to make their stay very comfortable. Her room was spacious and delightful."

"It seems your relative, Lady Susan, has made a great impression on my girls, despite arriving only last evening," Mr. Bennet added.

"Has she?" Darcy was puzzled by this line of conversation.

"Mary found Lady Susan fashionable, witty and...with a great sense of right and wrong," Jane said.

"That is an interesting observation." Darcy said. He would classify his eldest cousin as quietly overbearing with both a sweet and sour tongue.

"Yes, Lady Susan discovered Mary's weakness immediately and compelled her to behave by providing the most interesting sheets of music from Vienna," Mr. Bennet smiled knowingly. "And her Ladyship has clashed with Lydia in wonderful style already."

Elizabeth eyed Darcy, who turned a shade of red. He had begun to feel some anxiety.

"Oh, I hope Lydia did not do anything...hasty," Elizabeth said.

"It seems Lady Susan has drafted a...a plan to help Mary and Lydia learn how to become accomplished ladies. But Lydia finds it...trying," Jane commented.

"A plan?" Mr. Bennet snorted. "Jane, you always find the best word to describe things. I would call it a military regime. Wake up at seven in the morning for breakfast. Exercise in the garden for one hour. Then another hour and a half of English history, French, Italian and Latin languages. By ten, how to oversee household accounts. Eleven, the manners and fashions of London society. Twelve, European poems and novels... I have lost count of the other activities."

Darcy's face turned even more scarlet. He had provided the music sheets, lesson ideas and other conceits. But he had not known that Lady Susan would combine all of them into one day for the two Miss Bennets!

"That would be very trying for Lydia." Elizabeth's eyes fixed on Darcy's flustered face. "Since she usually does not wake up until almost noon, if possible. But the disagreement...?"

Jane did not continue so Mr. Bennet took up the pleasure of the story. "Half way through the English lesson, Lydia threw a fit and would not continue. So Lady Susan asked her what she wished to do with her life."

"That was a good question," Elizabeth noted.

"Your sister's answer was that she wanted to dance and flirt her life away with a camp full of soldiers!" Mr. Bennet said. "And she did not need to know about all these household accounts, society and languages."

The two sisters were blushing now, ashamed of the thoughtlessness of their youngest sister. But Elizabeth, like Darcy, seemed to want to know what had happened next. They were relieved that Mr. Bennet continued without further prompting.

"So Lady Susan showed her how her life would be if she wished to follow that path. She told Lydia that a young lady who liked only to flirt and did not learn would never be taken seriously by a good soldier and would only be used and discarded by the rakish ones. If she wished for a life of debauchery, Lady Susan would let her start now."

Elizabeth gasped. "What did Lady Susan do?"

"She called for tea immediately, with her own servants bringing in the most exotic food such as hot chocolate, bananas, grapes and other wonderful creations. While Mary and she were partaking of the heavenly food, she asked her nanny to make sure Lydia stood aside, exactly as a servant must do."

"Oh, but Lydia loves her food," Elizabeth exclaimed.

"Yes. Then Lady Susan brought out two most beautiful gowns. She said they were her gifts. One was for Mary and the other was originally intended for Lydia. Since Lydia did not need it any more, as a discarded-gentlewoman-turned-servant, Lady Susan asked her maid to alter the gown for Mary directly in front of Lydia."

"Oh dear!" was all Elizabeth could find it in herself to utter.

"Lydia was distraught. She cried and begged to be brought back home," Jane said. "Papa, perhaps we should bring her back and teach her at a slower pace."

Mr. Bennet shook his head. "Lydia is quite set in her ways. I am ashamed to say that I was slack in the education of all of you in the past. Lydia needs a strong hand. I have a feeling Lady Susan will be good for her."

Elizabeth now wore a deep frown. She cast a look at Darcy. He did not know how to respond. His sister Georgiana had never been rebellious and had enjoyed her lessons. He hoped Elizabeth would not blame him for her sister's unhappiness.

"What happened next?" Elizabeth asked.

"Lydia remained locked in the room while Mary began a music lesson instead," Jane said. "By the time Mary had finished, Lydia seemed to have calmed down and agreed to continue with the lesson plan. Mary said Lydia was in fact very good at learning about household accounts. Of course, she excelled in society manners and fashion."

"I do hope Lydia will soon acquire a passion for learning," Elizabeth said, breathing out a sigh of relief.

"I hope she will be able to keep this up and not have another fit again," Mr. Bennet said. "At least she was rewarded with another new gown, less magnificent than the one she lost to Mary, though."

"Mary said Lydia still loves it," Jane added.

"Papa, is it right for Lady Susan to give them so many gifts?" Elizabeth asked.

"It is perfectly acceptable. When Fitzwilliam said Mrs. Hurst would invite Lady Susan to help educate Mary and Lydia, I had asked your Aunt and Uncle Gardiner to visit her in London. The first two gowns may have been from Lady Susan but the remainder of the gifts are mostly from your uncle and me." Mr. Bennet smiled. "It will be Christmas soon. Now let us go to Netherfield. I must say, I surprise myself, for I am eager to see how Mary and Lydia have changed in a day. I think I miss them!"

## Chapter Seven

Darcy was sure that he would not enjoy the dinner for with Miss Bingley as the hostess, he would surely find himself placed beside her.

When the Longbourn party arrived, he could see that Miss Bingley wanted his family near her and had positioned her brother with the locals from Meryton.

He could well understand the hostess's ploy of placing Jane Bennet as far away from her brother as possible, and Elizabeth from him. He looked longingly down his side of the table for his beloved.

Placing Miss Lydia across from, and next to, a Redcoat perhaps demonstrated Miss Bingley's intention to cause havoc during dinner.

And by sitting Elizabeth's youngest sister next to him, Miss Bingley probably expected him to frown upon Miss Lydia's total lack of propriety.

"I had to make my feelings well known to certain influential people in order to have you seated next to me," Lady Susan said.

"Truly?" Darcy looked at his eldest cousin. He could see that her eyes were full of mockery. "Where was I supposed to sit first?"

"In my seat," Colonel Fitzwilliam said. "Susan had to emphasise to Miss Bingley that as a son of a Lord, even the younger one, I have higher standing in society than a rich, lazy landlord."

Darcy smiled at his cousin's words, observing that the hostess had turned crimson. Susan lowered her voice and whispered in his ear, "I would have liked to place Miss

Elizabeth next to you. But I am afraid someone might put poison in my soup if I interfered too much."

"I do not think you are intimidated by anyone," Darcy replied. "I think you just take pleasure in seeing me suffer."

"A dinner away from your lady-love causes suffering already?" Lady Susan snorted. "Has the elusive Mr. Darcy finally fallen in love? It is a pity I am not able to educate your beloved too, for I would love to teach her a few things to prick your arrogance."

"Do I appear haughty to you too?" Darcy frowned. "I do not think Elizabeth requires your help. She has already ensured that I do not rise above myself."

"You have permission to call her Elizabeth already?" Lady Susan burst out laughing.

"Mr. Darcy, what words of wisdom did you say to put Lady Susan in such a jolly mood?" Miss Bingley leaned over to ask him.

Lady Susan replied with a superior smile, "My dear cousin confesses that he is pleased to be tortured."

"Men generally are," Colonel Fitzwilliam added. "If their tormentors are women."

"Brother, you are a lady's man. That is of course true for you. But our cousin has been a saint for so many years, I thought he was immune to the meanness of our sex."

"Men are the breadwinners of a family. Why would we want to upset them?" Mrs. Hurst asked with wide eyes.

Lady Susan shook her head and replied to Mrs. Hurst directly, "Did I not hear Miss Bingley telling young Charles not to invite more guests to Netherfield? Your sister did not hesitate to tease the breadwinner."

Miss Bingley's mouth appeared to grow even narrower as she defended herself. "Taking care of an injured patient who is wholly unconnected to us is foolhardy. Mr. Collins should stay in Longbourn."

"Oh, did your brother forget to tell you that he struck Mr. Collins so hard that his shoes needed new soles?" Colonel Fitzwilliam said.

Miss Bingley and Mrs. Hurst gasped loudly.

"Now what have I missed during your visit to Darcy at Longbourn?" Lady Susan raised her eyebrows. "Did Mr. Collins do anything rash with Charles's *inamorata*?"

"The Bennets are wild people," Caroline raised her voice. "I am sure they provoked my brother."

"Actually it was my fault," Colonel Fitzwilliam said. "Wickham was in town and I could not contain myself."

Lady Susan drew in a loud breath. "What was that rake doing here?"

"I do not know and I hope he has run away with his tail between his legs," the Colonel continued.

"Who is this Mr. Wickham?" Miss Bingley demanded to know. "And why was Charles involved?"

"You do better not knowing about this Wickham," Colonel Fitzwilliam said. "Your brother was trying to protect me when he hit Mr. Collins accidentally. Since it was his doing, your brother wanted to take care of the injured man here."

"And how is Mr. Collins?" Darcy asked.

"He has recovered consciousness," Colonel Fitzwilliam replied. "But the doctor ordered him to stay in bed for at least a week as he had lost some blood. That reminds me, I should talk to Colonel Forster and apologise. Captain Denny told me Wickham had originally joined the militia that was stationed here."

"There is no loss to Meryton's neighbourhood with him having taken flight," Lady Susan said.

Seeing that she could not obtain more information about this rakish figure, Miss Bingley steered the conversation to another topic. She opined, "Miss Lydia had a trying morning."

Lydia, who was busy talking to the Redcoats, turned her head when she heard her name. "Yes, Miss Bingley?"

"I was just telling Mr. Darcy what a trying morning you had, shattering a beautiful dish in our guest suite and setting off a rumour that you had been imprisoned."

Miss Lydia's face turned bright red. She opened her mouth to retort but Lady Susan spoke first. "Miss Lydia is an exuberant young woman and I would love to have her under my wing. I have been thinking of inviting her to stay at Nevan House when I leave Hertfordshire."

"Would you do that, Lady Susan?" Lydia's eyes sparkled. To be invited to stay at a Lady's townhouse in London was beyond her imagination. "I shall try my very best to swallow all this dry history of England and learn these ridiculously difficult languages!" She turned to Captain Denny and laughed out loud. "I could only remember '*je vous aime*' because it means I love you. Oh, did I say it correctly?"

Miss Bingley attempted to whisper to Mr. Darcy, as much as distance allowed. "Some country savages can never be taught the proper manners of society. Imagine how shocked my family and friends would be if I were to be related to some country maids without an iota of sense."

"I always tell Darcy to be careful of any woman who resorts to meanness to advance her cause of securing his attention," Lady Susan interrupted. "A jolly young girl who has seen little of the world could learn to be more sensible than a trying old woman who puts wealth and connection above character. A burnt orange can never revert to its original sweetness but an immature one has the potential to gain great depth."

Darcy choked on Susan's mention of a burnt orange. Colonel Fitzwilliam smiled broadly while Lady Susan continued to dine with great style.

***

After dinner, Darcy and the gentlemen left the ladies for their port. He was worried about leaving the women to their own entertainment, for he could see that Miss Bingley was on the verge of an outburst should Lady Susan continue to provoke her.

He also did not want Elizabeth and her sisters to bear the brunt of Miss Bingley's malicious remarks.

He was therefore very inattentive to the discussion of the other men during the short duration they remained in the study. In a rather impatient manner, he charged the others that they should join the ladies soon.

It was not soon enough, for mayhem had broken out in the room. Miss Lydia's new chestnut-coloured evening gown was covered with splashes of red stain. Mrs. Foster and Miss

Bingley were tearing at each other's hair, while Mrs. Hurst and Lady Lucas were trying without success to separate the two of them.

Mrs. Philips was about to help or join in the fight, but Elizabeth and Miss Bennet tried to restrain her. Miss Mary sat on the chaise with her mouth hanging open while Lady Susan was fanning herself frantically.

"Desist!" Mr. Bennet yelled out loud.

The ladies halted momentarily, except for Mrs. Foster who could not stop in time and her hand slapped Miss Bingley on the face.

"Harriet, stop!" This time Colonel Foster joined in.

Miss Bingley kicked her assailant on the shin, smashed a tea cup on the ground and walked out of the room. Mrs. Hurst dashed out to follow her sister.

Mrs. Forster groaned in pain and burst out crying. Her husband and Miss Lydia rushed to assist her immediately.

"Charles, perhaps you should prepare a room for Mrs. Foster too. She is injured," Lady Susan said.

"I would not stay in this horrible woman's house for an instant longer!" Mrs. Foster demanded her husband to take her home.

"Papa, I don't want to stay here either!" Miss Lydia joined in.

Jane Bennet had tears in her eyes and Elizabeth was holding her hand. Darcy stood by their sides, helpless to console them.

Colonel Fitzwilliam pulled his sister aside and talked to her in a hushed voice.

Mr. Bennet said, "Mary, take your sister to change her attire and come down again. I want to hear what happened."

After Bingley apologised to the guests, the Fosters, the officers, the Philips and the Lucases took their leave.

Darcy saw Elizabeth approach her father.

"Papa, can I have a word in private with Mr. Darcy?" she asked. He saw that she was wringing a handkerchief as if to starve it of life.

Her father looked at her for a moment before asking Mr. Bingley to allow them use of the library.

"I shall leave you two here," Mr. Bennet said and walked from the library, leaving the door open. "Do not take long, as I want to return to Longbourn soon."

Elizabeth agreed and Darcy acknowledged to himself that he was baffled by her request for a private talk.

"Would you sit down?" she said, looking up at him.

He sat down with an air of bafflement. She then began pacing around the room before stopping in front of him.

"Do you still wish to comply with your father's pledge?" Her voice was hoarse and shaky.

"To marry you?" He thought she had been decidedly against him and therefore had to confirm that he understood her present disposition.

"Yes." She looked at him intently, drew in a deep breath and said slowly, "I have changed my mind and I would be honoured to accept your father's heartfelt promise."

His eyes widened. He had expected to spend months changing her mind. He did not understand from whence had arrived her sudden transformation.

He rose from the chair and held her hands. "May I ask why, and so suddenly?"

She glanced away, withdrew her hands and sat down. "You give me your answer first."

He sat down once again, very close to her, and pulled her hands into his again. "Miss Bennet, it is my greatest honour and pleasure to have you as my wife."

She opened her mouth to say something but he was so happy that he could express himself as only a young man violently in love could. He lowered his head and kissed her.

Her lips were soft and tender. She tasted of tea and lavender. The delectable scent stirred him. Turning his head slightly, he touched her lips with his own. He felt her gasp slightly and heard her release a low moan.

His hands let go of hers and wandered to her waist. Pulling her closer to him, he could feel her lush bosom pressed onto his hard chest. He groaned in ecstasy as her soft form cleaved to his masculine shape. He put his mouth to her delicious earlobe and nibbled at her neck.

As he lowered his head to breathe in the aroma of her bosom, he would have pushed down the sleeves of her elegant evening gown had she not seized his hair.

The pull on his head startled him. He raised his eyes to her face and breathed deeply to calm himself. She had her eyes closed and her head rested on the chaise. How he wanted to teach her the pleasure of union! But he remembered her father's words: Mr. Bennet was waiting for them to return to Longbourn.

He traced his fingers from her neck down the neckline. His knuckles touched the smooth texture of her skin and the silky porcelain flesh. The trembling moved from her body to his own, and then down his spine.

"Elizabeth, thank you for agreeing to be my wife. I shall talk to your father when we get back to Longbourn."

His words woke her. She blinked open her eyes and stood quickly up. Her face was a deep shade of scarlet. Her lips were swollen and her hair dishevelled. She said, "I would prefer a long engagement and could we remain in London for the time being?"

He watched with a frown as she now paced the room. He was still caught in the memory of the heat of her body. He could not think clearly yet.

"I mean, could we spend the time of our engagement in London, or Derbyshire later?" she explained.

"How long do you want our engagement to last?" he asked.

"Until I am convinced."

"Of what?"

"That, Mr. Darcy, you love me and that I love you."

His whole being told him that he was already in love with her. He remembered how she had encouraged him to talk about the events concerning Georgiana. He wanted to spend the rest of his life with her, only her. But would she be convinced of his ardent feelings so soon after their first acquaintance? He was not sure and decided to be cautious; he asked her to explain instead: "Why do you wish to be away from Longbourn?"

"I simply do not wish to be near Miss Bingley."

"What did she do?" he asked with concern.

Elizabeth's eyes flashed suddenly, the mistiness of romance had turned to anger. "She has been ghastly to Lydia and Mary. She even said some cruel words about Jane."

"Then she ruined Miss Lydia's new dress?"

"Her aim was at me," she said.

"What?"

"She was so loathsome about my family, and how she was as superior as you were, that I retorted."

"What did you say?"

"I told her she would never have an opportunity with you, for not only did your father promise you to me, you had asked me for my hand too." She smiled and blushed. "She threw a tantrum then."

"And Miss Lydia tried to protect you?"

"I ducked to one side and Lydia was hit instead."

"But why was she sparring with Mrs. Forster then?"

"Are you certain that you wish to know?"

Darcy nodded.

Elizabeth raised her hands and continued as if she could not prevent what he was about to hear. "Lydia said Miss Bingley was like a savage, uttering barbaric words and having fits. The hostess responded and said that all Hertfordshire women were wild and stupid. Mrs. Foster, being herself a local, protested. She said she was indeed clever enough to catch a colonel, more so than Miss Bingley, who was old and desperate. Miss Bingley scoffed at Mrs. Forster's husband, saying that he was ancient and fat. And Mrs. Foster refuted this, saying she was a dry orange. Then things became intolerable."

He could not suppress the laugh and she joined in. When they stopped, his head was clearer. "So you have agreed to marry me simply to quieten Miss Bingley?" he asked, unsure of himself.

She stood in front of a shelf of books, tracing her fingers along the volumes. "Well, you have taken several liberties."

He could barely hear her. "You did not seem to object."

She turned around swiftly and glared at him. "You took me by surprise!" she protested loudly. Colour swept into her face.

He stood, walked towards her in a few quick steps and trapped her against the books. "But you enjoy it."

She breathed swiftly and looked up at him. He swore to himself that she was gazing at his lips in anticipation. But then she said, "Not as much as you!" She went on, "Excuse me, Mr. Darcy. I think it is time we return to my father. We have been here for too long. It is not proper."

He stood aside. She stepped away from him and added, "Even though we are engaged." Then she turned and walked from the library, swaying her figure in an exaggerated motion.

Did she just display her figure outrageously for his enjoyment? He shook his head and remained in the library for a few more minutes to suppress his passion before returning to the sitting room.

# Chapter Eight

When Darcy returned, Mr. Bennet seemed to have persuaded Miss Lydia to stay, for Lady Susan, Miss Mary and she were nowhere to be seen. As the Longbourn party prepared to leave, his cousin pulled him aside.

"Susan told me you are engaged to Miss Elizabeth?" Colonel Fitzwilliam asked.

Darcy nodded. He glanced at his intended and could not suppress a satisfied smile.

"Oh, please conceal your admiration for her from the rest of us," his cousin said. "It's too annoying. Are you certain of this? She did not trap you or something? Susan said Miss Elizabeth had spoken about your father promising you to her. Why have we not heard about it before?"

Darcy was irritated with the Colonel. Elizabeth was not the person he had described. He glanced at her as a servant assisted with putting on her cloak. He felt the deprivation of not providing that service to his betrothed on the first available occasion after their engagement. "I am sure," he said. "Elizabeth has not done anything untoward that would force me to ask for her hand. In fact I had to persuade her. I did not know how Susan reached her conclusions about Elizabeth and me. But I shall tell you the story concerning my father in the next few days. I must leave now."

"Shocking!" Colonel Fitzwilliam swore under his breath. "You cannot take your eyes from the lady. You are totally besotted. Tomorrow I shall visit you and you must give me the full story. Now, I am riding out to the camp too."

"Is it not too late to be visiting?"

"I want to talk to Chamberlayne and Denny about Wickham. Just to make sure the scoundrel will not come back to bother your intended."

Darcy was alarmed. But he thanked his cousin.

"And I want to apologise to Colonel Foster, for causing a scene with his potential recruit. Of course, some beer in a warm tavern is preferable to the chilly atmosphere here, with Susan goading Miss Bingley to madness at every possible opportunity she finds."

"Susan had some connection with the fight between Mrs. Foster and Miss Bingley?" Darcy was puzzled.

"Did Miss Elizabeth not tell you about it?" Colonel Fitzwilliam raised his brow. "You two were shut in the library for a very long time. What did you do?"

"The door was open and we were not that long!"

"That is your opinion," Colonel Fitzwilliam said, then continued. "Apparently Susan has been describing your virtues during tea and how you have never found any woman to match your highest standard. But then you wrote to ask her to come and help you win the heart of a local beauty. You praised this woman to the sky, saying she is so much more superior than the women you have known so far, in particular twenty times better than a certain sister of a friend who has been chasing you for years."

Darcy groaned out loud. "I did not write such a letter!"

"Miss Elizabeth is not twenty times superior than Miss Bingley?" Colonel Fitzwilliam asked playfully.

"Elizabeth is the best lady I have known but I did not tell Susan about it. I did not even tell her Elizabeth's name when I wrote to her. I have no idea how she concluded that I wanted to sit with Elizabeth tonight."

"Susan has an uncanny way of setting pieces of information side by side so that they eventually make a natural order," his cousin smiled. "Especially since Miss Lydia and Bingley are both rather talkative."

Darcy shook his head and bade his cousin good night.

He spent the carriage ride in silence, taking in the beauty of his intended. He was sure that Elizabeth darted her fine eyes to look at him much more often, as she chatted with her eldest sister. The blushing shade did not leave Elizabeth's face and she wore a half-teasing and half-smiling expression that made her all too enticing.

He hoped that they could walk out tomorrow to discuss the date of their wedding. Earlier would be better, for he could not wait to share his days with her, and his bed.

When they arrived in Longbourn, he asked to talk to Mr. Bennet, if he was not too tired.

"Well?" Mr. Bennet asked, as they entered the elderly gentleman's study.

"Elizabeth… ah—Miss Elizabeth has done me the greatest honour and agreed to be my wife. I ask for your permission and blessing." Darcy bowed and asked formally.

Mr. Bennet gave him a clap on the shoulders and embraced him.

"Fitzwilliam, I am very happy for you two. I am sure you will take prodigious good care of my favourite girl. You are a conscientious young man."

"I promise, Mr. Bennet. I shall respect and honour Elizabeth, provide for her and make her the happiest woman in the world for the rest of my life," Darcy replied solemnly, promising to his future father as much as to Elizabeth and himself.

"Welcome to the family!" Mr. Bennet said and fetched the whisky. "Take a drop and tell me what is troubling you."

Darcy was surprised that Mr. Bennet had noticed his careworn demeanour. "You knew the reasons for tonight's skirmish?"

Mr. Bennet nodded. "Lydia and Lady Susan explained it to me."

"I am worried that Miss Elizabeth entered into the engagement without due consideration."

"You need not be worried about that," Mr. Bennet said. "Lizzy is not the kind of girl who rushes into things, even under provocation."

Darcy thought for a moment and had to agree with Mr. Bennet's assessment. Could he hope that she had begun to have feelings for him? "She wanted a long engagement, saying that she wishes to make sure she is in love with me before we marry."

Mr. Bennet raised his eyebrow and asked, "And you do not?"

Darcy felt flustered by such a direct question. He replied honestly, "Sir, your daughter has enchanted me. I do not want to part with her from now onwards."

"Ah, the romance of youthful devotion. Perhaps it is good that Lizzy asks for a long engagement. It can test your fortitude and constancy. Now, should we have your wedding in three years' time?" the older gentleman jested.

Darcy swallowed and then shook his head in disagreement. "I hope to persuade her to marry me before Christmas. I am not a young man of one and twenty, Sir. And I have resisted the temptation of sirens and maidens for many years. I know my heart."

"But Lizzy is not yet one and twenty. Perhaps when you present her to your society, she will run off with a more charming man," Mr. Bennet said with a sly smile.

Darcy stood up and paced around the room. He had not thought about this before. His Elizabeth had not seen much of the world. She might not put another suitor's wealth before his character, but could she resist the charms of a gentleman who was ten times more amiable than he?

"Now stop worrying, young man! You simply need to learn how to charm her. For someone as unsuccessful as I in marital bliss, I do have advice for you." Mr. Bennet raised his cup for a toast. "Learn and observe from other happily married couples. I dearly wish Lizzy and you will be forever happy!"

Darcy stopped pacing and raised his cup. Yes, his late parents would be a good example. He needed to treat Elizabeth with respect and tender loving care as his father had done with his mother. He was looking forward to charming Elizabeth, commencing as soon as possible the next morning.

***

But his plan to have a heart-to-heart talk with Elizabeth the next day was foiled by the early arrival of an agitated Bingley.

Mr. Bingley had declined breakfast with the family. Not even sparing a glance at his angelic Miss Bennet, he asked for a private word with Mr. Darcy.

The two of them walked out to the fields at the back of Longbourn.

"What is the matter?" Darcy asked with concern. He had not seen his best friend in such a state as this before. "Are you well, Charles?"

"It is Caroline." Bingley sat down heavily on a fallen log and cradled his head in his hands.

"She is not well?"

"Earlier this morning a loud scream woke me and she was found …" Bingley choked with emotion.

"Found …?" Darcy prompted. He feared for the worst.

"Caroline was found…inside Mr. Collins's room."

Darcy hid his shock. "How did it happen?"

"She was ... asleep on top of ... Mr. Collins."

"What?"

"She was fully clothed, but Mr. Collins ..." Bingley found it difficult to continue again.

"He is well?"

"Mr. Collins was tied to the bed, face down. His trousers were stripped off. His buttocks had signs of heavy lashing." The words tumbled from Bingley's mouth. "Caroline held a leather whip in her hand."

Darcy swore, then asked again, "How did it happen?"

"That deranged sister of mine was so drunk that I could not interrogate her. Fossett and I untied Mr. Collins. Our guest said he was suddenly woken up, stripped, tied up, gagged and whipped for almost an hour. It seemed Caroline was …" Bingley's choked explanation was stopped in mid-sentence.

"Your sister was what?"

"She was…she thought Mr. Collins was you …"

"What?" That was the only response Darcy could utter.

"Mr. Collins said she cursed you vehemently while she thrashed him, and said you should not have allowed yourself to be engaged to Miss Elizabeth," Bingley murmured. "She said you needed to learn a lesson, to be appreciative of her masterful quality. You could not escape her, now that you were in her clutches for the whole night. I know in times past Caroline has used some cutting horse spurs on the horses. Louisa and I have talked to her about that. She has given up riding in the countryside, except she still appears fashionable with her horse in Hyde Park. I did not know that she could be so violent, so horribly enraged."

"My goodness!" Darcy exclaimed.

"What am I supposed to do?" Bingley looked at his friend helplessly. "Mr. Collins said he would not marry such a mad woman. But two or maybe more of the servants saw them in that state this morning. It was the scream of one of the maids that woke us. Lady Susan and the other Miss Bennets were in the other side of the guest wings and did not hear about it, but they were bursting with questions after the busy goings-on this morning."

Darcy paced to and fro in search of the best way forward. "Nothing can be done. You must bribe Mr. Collins to marry Miss Bingley. After the ceremony, you can set up a separate household for her."

"I did suggest that already. I offered to purchase a small estate in an area far from London for Mr. Collins. But he said he could not leave his honourable patron Lady Catherine de Bourgh. If he married, his wife must reside with him in Hunsford, until Longbourn is available." Bingley said. "He said Lady Catherine would not approve of my sister. He is demanding to leave this morning, even if he must kneel on the floor of the carriage the whole way back to Kent. I asked Fossett to give him some sleeping draught, to calm him for a short time while I came here to ask for your advice. Can you go with Collins and me to Kent to persuade your aunt to approve this marriage? I have to take Caroline with me too. I dare not leave her here. She may harm the other Miss Bennets."

Darcy paced again.

"Mr. Collins said Miss Elizabeth and I were engaged?"

Bingley nodded. "At least that was what Caroline told him. Is it true?"

"Yes, I have been granted Mr. Bennet's permission just last night. I do not think my aunt will listen to me, now that she knows I am not to marry her daughter," Darcy said. "What about my cousin? We can ask him to go with you. He advises Lady Catherine on estate issues from time to time too, when I am not available."

"Colonel Fitzwilliam did not return last night. But we found his room in complete disorder," Bingley said with a sigh.

"What?"

"I suspect Caroline went there first, before she found Mr. Collins. We found one of her slippers inside Colonel Fitzwilliam's room. She must have been on the hunt to find you …"

Darcy's lips tightened. "It is fortunate my cousin went to the camp last evening, though I doubt Miss Bingley could tie him up in her drunken state. I shall go with you back to Netherfield. If Richard is not yet returned, I shall ride to the camp to find him. You will need two carriages, to transport your drunken sister and the drugged Mr. Collins."

The two of them returned to the house and bade the curious ladies a hasty goodbye.

When Mr. Bingley arrived at Netherfield, he immediately arranged for the carriages and asked Mrs. Hurst and Fossett to prepare Miss Bingley and Mr. Collins for the journey.

Colonel Fitzwilliam had returned from the camp, and was taking coffee in the library. That spared Darcy a trip.

"Visiting so early? Did you know what the Devil happened to my things and my room?" the Colonel asked.

"Hurst did not enlighten you?" Darcy replied.

"He is still deep in sleep. Mrs. Hurst is busy and Fossett's lips are sealed. My best morning coat has been torn to pieces. Bingley will have to replace them, immediately!"

"Bingley needs your help to go to Rosings and persuade Lady Catherine to sanction Miss Bingley's marriage to Mr. Collins."

"Good God, something outrageous must have happened here last night, if the snobbish orange lady will give you up and lower her sights on the good pastor!" Richard laughed out loud, rubbing his hands eagerly. "Do not spare any detail. I will be more than happy to help young Charles to secure the lovely Miss Bingley's future."

Darcy told him about the events of the previous evening.

Colonel Fitzwilliam could not keep his composure. He was laughing so hard that he had tears in his eyes. "What a lucky escape for me!"

"You do not think that Miss Bingley is capable of tying you up?"

"After a glass or two of cheap port, I could be putty in the charming Miss Bingley's hands."

"Do you think Mr. Collins could be persuaded?" Darcy asked.

"I shall work on him as soon as the carriage leaves here. He is too idealistic to wish that his wife should be at his side all the time. With Miss Bingley's twenty thousand pounds dowry he could put his feet up and cease listening to Lady Catherine's well-meaning instruction."

"You sound like you envy Mr. Collins's forthcoming nuptials."

"I would not touch the exquisite Miss Bingley if you gave me double the money. Braving the guns of Boney is much easier than facing her whip."

"Bingley would be grateful for your help. But try not to appear too happy about it. He is really troubled by the whole affair."

"Ah, gentlemanly concern! The pair of you are too good. This old soldier has seen the world's ugliness. Miss Bingley has dug her own grave and she has to lie in it!"

"I hope you can keep Lady Catherine in Kent for a few days too."

Colonel Fitzwilliam shook his head. "What are you afraid of?"

"There are many demands being made of Elizabeth at the moment. I do not want our aunt coming here to cause her further grief."

"Your betrothed is a lot sturdier than you, I suspect. But if you want to act like the protective hero, who am I to dissuade you? That is an additional favour. You will have to pay dearly."

"A good bottle of French champagne?"

"Promise your first born to me."

"You want to be godfather to my first daughter? I have to discuss it with Elizabeth first."

"Ah, thinking of a herd of children already?" Colonel Fitzwilliam shook his head again. "Who said I wanted to be a godfather? I just want to manage young Miss Darcy's finances. What old soldier would not want to skim off a rich relative?" He laughed as he merrily left the library to prepare for the journey.

When Darcy returned to the study, Bingley was not there but Lady Susan was waiting for him.

"My dear cousin, what a lovely surprise! What brings you back to Netherfield so early?" Lady Susan said.

"Bingley needs some assistance with a family matter."

"You are not going to tell your good cousin about it? I thought I was your ally. Tsk! Tsk! Did I not help you get Miss Elizabeth to admit to your secret engagement?"

"Elizabeth and I were not secretly engaged."

"Then what is this juicy revelation that Uncle Darcy promised you to her?"

Darcy sighed and told Lady Susan the story behind the garnet cross. "But we were not yet engaged last night."

"Of course, you must have been boorish, as you always are with strangers, and offended her. Now you must thank me for making her see you in a better light."

"I cannot understand how you were able to deduce so much from a mere letter I sent you, asking you to come here and help Miss Mary and Miss Lydia."

"Typical men, they do not tell us anything. It did not take me even a full morning of conversation with Mrs. Hurst and the two Miss Bennets to determine that you were besotted with Miss Elizabeth. Well, you can keep the secret about this mission to Rosings. I know more than you think."

Darcy grimaced. "Then why did you ask me just now?"

"To give you an opportunity to be open with your amicable cousin."

Darcy shook his head. He hoped Elizabeth was less difficult to understand than his cousin.

"Well, since most of the Netherfield hosts will not be in residence, do you want me to continue with Mary and Lydia's transformation here or in London?"

"Are you really at leisure to invite them to Nevan House?"

"Darcy, you have to learn to socialise with your future sisters. If you present such a grim face every time you see them, Elizabeth will not warm to you."

"I know. But Miss Mary talks only of religious matters and Miss Lydia of men and Redcoats. I feel uncomfortable discussing such topics with them."

"They are just young girls who did not have the benefit of good guidance in the past. They may sound silly now but they are never malicious or mean. I think you need some education in conversing with 'ordinary' young ladies. I shall make time to talk to Miss Elizabeth next."

"I hope Elizabeth does not learn too much from you."

"You are afraid she will gain control over you soon?" Lady Susan laughed. "Darcy, your fate is sealed! Miss Elizabeth does not need to do that, she delivers her instructions with such sweetness."

Darcy shook his head. "We were talking about London. I shall consult Mr. Bennet about his daughters when I return to Longbourn later today. Now, I must see Bingley off."

When Darcy walked out to the carriage yard, he could see that Mr. Collins and Colonel Fitzwilliam were settled in one of the carriages. The former lay on his stomach on a seat. He had his eyes closed and his face was contorted in pain.

Mr. Bingley was helping a tipsy Miss Bingley into the other carriage. When the latter saw Darcy, she struggled free of her sibling and threw herself at him. "Sweetness ...urh... Did...you...enjoy what I did...last night?"

Darcy tried to pull her hands from his neck. "It is late! You must get into the carriage."

She dropped her hands and pinched his bottom. "So ... firm! Do you love the pain?"

Darcy yelled and jumped back. Bingley grabbed his sister by the waist and pulled her away.

"You were ... magnificent last night! I am sure I ... I brought you to heaven. I loved licking your ... buttocks. You tasted like … wood." Miss Bingley shouted over her shoulders. Bingley's face was as red as a ripe tomato. He threw his sister into the carriage roughly, locked the door and dashed back to Darcy.

Bingley bowed, with tears threatening to fall from his eyes. "Darcy, I am utterly ashamed of my sister. Please accept my apology for her vulgar gestures and crass outburst. I gave her another cup of wine to make her come with me willingly. If you decide to sever your ties with my family I shall understand and not blame you. Oh, yes. Be so kind as to apologise for us to Miss Bennet. Say that urgent business calls us away immediately. Please conceal the unhappy truth as long as possible, I know it cannot be long."

When he turned to go, Darcy grabbed his shoulders and gave him a hug. "Charles, you are a good man and my best friend. I shall not end our friendship for something over which you have no control. Elizabeth told me once that we must allow our loved ones to experience life's trials and tribulations. I am sure you will rise above this difficult circumstance. Do not give up on your own happiness. Miss Jane Bennet is stronger than you think."

Bingley wrapped his arms tightly around Darcy's back and released a sob. Then he pulled himself away and brushed away the tears. "Darcy, you are right. I should concentrate on helping Caroline and getting her married to Mr. Collins. I shall come back soon."

Darcy nodded and added, "I have only told Richard. I shall apologise to Miss Bennet for you but leave you to explain the situation when you return."

Bingley shook Darcy's hands heartily and then stepped into the carriage.

## Chapter Nine

After bidding goodbye to Mrs. Hurst, Lady Susan and the Miss Bennets, Darcy mounted his horse and galloped away from Netherfield and Longbourn. The wild wind cooled his tense body and the sight of the passing green fields lightened his heavy heart.

When he reached a small hill, he reined Osias in and surveyed the houses beyond in the valley. As his eyes gazed upon the homely countenance of the buildings, he felt a sensation of dissatisfaction rise in his thoughts. He felt compassion for Bingley, who was such an amiable person. His younger friend probably met the description of a gentleman more than he himself in Elizabeth's eyes - young, handsome, polite and a love of company.

And yet, just when Bingley had reached the age when he should become a vital member of society, his reputation could be tarnished by a moment of drunkenness on the part of his sister.

Georgiana, his own sister, had caused him some worries and concerns last summer. But she was only fifteen years old and, under the persuasive charms of Wickham, had acted foolishly. Miss Bingley was older than Charles and yet she had resorted to lies, theft and assault in order to coerce Darcy into asking for her hand. What had directed Miss Bingley in the first place to this road of self-destruction and degradation? Charles had said in times past she had used cutting spurs to discipline her horse harshly. Could she have been born with such a violent temper? Or had she acquired a taste for ruthlessness in her youth? He shook his head and relinquished the idea of finding an answer to those disconcerting questions.

When he was ready to ride down the hill, a flash of silver charging toward his horse disturbed his composure. Osias was startled and raised his hooves high. Without having had the time to prepare himself, Darcy was thrown from the horse's back. He landed on the ground heavily but was able to roll to safety.

As he turned to examine his horse, a sword was pointed at his chest.

"Wickham!" Darcy swore. In his haste to persuade Colonel Fitzwilliam to go with Bingley to Kent, he had forgotten to ask his cousin about Wickham.

"What wonderful luck I have, Darcy boy!" Wickham exclaimed with a charmless smile. "Now you can repay me for what that damned fellow Richard did."

He used his free hand to stroke the deep cut disfiguring his cheek that had been made by Colonel Fitzwilliam in Meryton, then raised his sword to Darcy's face menacingly.

"I would enjoy turning you into a scar-face," Wickham swore. "No woman would be interested in you, even with your grand estate at Pemberley."

"How can you sleep at night, being so intent on bringing harm to Georgiana and me? Do you not have a modicum of decency or gratitude for what my father provided for you?" Darcy retorted.

"Decency indeed! I prefer to have a nice warm bed and a willing woman than the satisfaction of behaving correctly. Well, to save your pretty face is easy. Merely hand over your wallet, your ring and your watch."

Darcy sat up, feeling some pain in his right ankle. He pulled out his possessions and threw them to Wickham.

With eyes fixed on his victim, Wickham picked them up and looked through them quickly.

He whistled and laughed. "Wonderful. With these and your horse, I should be well set for several weeks. Now stand up and turn around."

"What do you want?" Darcy stood up slowly as instructed. He was facing a downhill slope, with a sword to his back. He felt a chill course down his spine and thought he might never see Georgiana or Elizabeth again.

"No need to fear for your life," Wickham laughed. "I am not a murderer."

Darcy turned his head and gauged whether he could seize the reprobate's sword. At that moment, Wickham leaned forward and pushed him in the back. "Now enjoy the valley while I ride your horse to find the next pretty wench!"

Darcy's leg buckled and he braced his hands over his head as his body rolled down the hill. The branches and spiky bushes scratched and grazed his hands and body. Finally the downward motion stopped and he landed forcefully on his back.

He panted heavily. When the dizziness and pain seemed to subside, he tried to raise himself from the ground. Both his hands were bleeding, though not profusely. His right ankle was injured and he felt the pain as he attempted a few steps.

He stood with great effort and painfully limped through the overgrown branches at a slow pace. After almost an hour, he had only covered a short distance. He wondered whether he might reach either Longbourn or Netherfield by nightfall.

With great fortune, after another hour he found his way out of the valley and onto a lane. Not two hundred steps further on, he was met by a small horse-drawn wagon.

"Fitzwilliam, what happened?" Elizabeth exclaimed and jumped out to his side.

He had never been so happy to greet someone. With no regard to his painful and dirty body, he embraced her tightly and breathed in her calming scent.

"It was Wickham!"

"You are injured." Elizabeth's voice trembled with fear. "Let me help you onto the carriage."

Once again, after several painful manoeuvres, Darcy was sitting snugly by his beloved's side.

"Your hands are bleeding. Let me take care of them first." She took out a saddle bag containing a small flask of water and gently washed his hands. "May I use your cravat to cover them?"

He nodded.

Her head drew near his and she started untying the neckcloth. After the traumatic events of the morning, Darcy felt relieved now, safely in her hands. The manner in which she tenderly took care of him made him feel like a child once more, back in the embrace of his mother. He felt the urge to lay his head on her bosom and let her sing him to sleep. His head dropped onto her shoulder. He whispered, "I love you, Lizzy," before closing his eyes.

Shortly after, he was woken again.

"Please, Fitzwilliam, you cannot fall asleep. Wake up please, my love." He heard the begging voice of Elizabeth. "You will fall out of the wagon if you do not stay awake for I cannot hold onto you at the same time as hold onto the reins."

With great difficult, he forced open his eyes. He could feel the shaking motion of the wagon and Elizabeth had one hand on the reins and another around his waist.

"Yes," he answered drowsily.

"Hold on to me tight."

He obliged and put both his arms around her. "Is that…better?"

"Yes. No. Can you not sit up straight?" she stammered.

"Why? It is easier to…balance by embracing you."

"You do not sound like you are quite that injured."

Darcy felt less sleepy now, with her chatter keeping him alert. "What would a more seriously injured man sound like?"

"Talking nonsense, perhaps," she commented.

"You smell wonderful."

"It is lavender water. Are you pretending to talk like a fool?"

"Why would I? Do you bathe in it?" He drew in another deep breath, happy to forget the quarrel with Wickham and the pain in his body.

"Yes."

"Can I bathe in lavender water with you?"

"Fitzwilliam!"

"What?"

"We are yet to marry. It is scandalous to think about bathing together now. Did you also hurt your head to be talking such nonsense?"

"I do not think so. But my body hurts. I would rather contemplate us in the bath. It gives me pleasure." He touched his lips to her neck.

The wagon jerked slightly and she exclaimed, "Fitzwilliam! You will send us into the mud again if you keep doing that."

"I cannot…sleep." He yawned. "And I cannot kiss. What can I do?"

"Tell me why Mr. Bingley needed you this morning."

"I cannot do that. Charles wanted to explain to Miss Bennet himself, when he returns."

"Do you not realize the worries my sister and I suffered this morning? We have never seen Mr. Bingley this serious and grim. And then you were gone for hours. I have been looking for you for nearly an hour. If I had not met you here, I intended to go straight to knock on Netherfield's door." She raised her voice. "I beg your pardon…what did you say? Returns? Where did he go?"

"Miss Bingley and he have urgent business to attend to."

"And you cannot tell me about the business?"

"It is Bingley's private matter."

"Perhaps I shall visit my other sisters after I deliver you back to Longbourn."

"I did not tell Susan or your sisters."

"They must have heard something."

"You want to speculate on gossip?"

"Obstinate man! Why am I betrothed to you?"

"You asked me to ask for your hand, remember?" he responded defensively.

"It is all that vexing Miss Bingley's doing."

"I should thank her profusely when I next meet with her."

"I am sure she will be ecstatic. But then how did you meet up with Mr. Wickham?"

"I rode up a small hill for a breath of fresh air after I left Netherfield and he startled me there."

"What did he do?"

"He robbed me of my possessions and took Osias."

She gasped out loud. "With a gun?"

"With a sword."

"Blackguard! He injured your hands and leg. How could he harm an unarmed man? Does he not have any sense of honour?"

"No! He only pushed me down into the valley."

Elizabeth stopped the wagon and turned to wrap her hands around his neck and bury her face there. "He could have killed you!"

"He said he was not a murderer."

"But you could have knocked your head and been left bleeding to death."

"It is fortunate for him and for me as well."

"Fitzwilliam, I ..." She started sobbing. "I could have...lost you forever."

He tried to run his hands over her back but came to the realisation that they were wrapped and could not move easily. He rocked her gently as she cried. It was bliss to feel her body so close to him again, to know that he had not come to any harm and that they would indeed have their future lives together.

"Do not cry, my dearest and loveliest Elizabeth. All is well now."

She slowly regained her composure. Raising her head, he brushed away the tears with his bandaged hands. When their lips touched, it was a moment of confirmation. It began tender and slow.

And then their passion grew as he opened his mouth and bit her sensuous lips gently. She followed his actions timidly. He pushed his tongue slowly into her warm mouth, moving in and out, grazing her soft muscle and hot tongue. She panted, squirmed and moaned heatedly for a few moments and then shook her body against his violently, before becoming limp.

Darcy drew back slowly. Did he just bring Elizabeth to her climax on a country lane with only his kisses? He held back his ardour and reluctantly left her alluring mouth. Turning away from her, he tried his best to suppress his own arousal.

"What just happened?" she whispered.

"Did you find it pleasant?"

She drew in a deep breath and nodded. "I felt like I was on fire and as if I had flown to the sky. And you?"

He gazed at her and answered solemnly. "I love you, Elizabeth, with all my heart and body."

"I love you too, Fitzwilliam."

Darcy had never felt such happiness before. There was a sense of completeness in him on hearing Elizabeth's declaration. He could not help but lower his head to her again. This time their lips met just briefly, sealing the memory for all eternity. Then she drove the wagon on. He sat upright, shoulder to shoulder, thigh to thigh, by her side as they journeyed home.

***

When the couple arrived at Longbourn, Dr. Smith was sent for despite Darcy's protests. Elizabeth took on the disposition of Mrs. Bennet and fussed over the injured profusely, until her father forbade her to dash up and down the stairs.

Darcy was bemused by the reaction of his beloved. She was behaving like an old wife who worried about a tiny sniffle from her husband. He shook his head. He was touched by such an endearing gesture but a little concerned that the future Mrs. Darcy might be developing a nervous condition much like her mother.

After washing, changing his attire and being attended to by the doctor, all supervised by Elizabeth down from the parlour, Darcy settled in his guest chamber. Winston brought in some light refreshment, according to Miss Elizabeth Bennet's instruction. Unfortunately Mr. Darcy had no use of his hands. He did not want to ask Winston to feed him, so he sent his valet back down again with the tray.

That caused thunderous footsteps to be heard on the stairs moments later. Elizabeth pushed opened the door of his room, dropped the tray of refreshments on the side table and then stood next to his bed with her hands on her hips.

"Why did you not take any refreshment?" she demanded. "You need to eat to get well quickly."

He gazed at her angry countenance and smiled at her response to his difficulty. With a look of contrition, he held up his hands. Both were bandaged, this time more neatly and tidily by Dr. Smith. "I have no use of my hands, for at least a week."

"Winston cannot feed you?"

"He is not as pretty as a certain lady." He suppressed a smile and pretended to be sick. "I am afraid of indigestion if he feeds me."

"Am I to be reduced to your maid?" She folded her arms across her bosom.

"Far from it. You are my guardian angel."

She stepped forward and put her hand on his forehead. "Fever must have overcome you. You talk like the amiable Mr. Bingley."

"You prefer the brooding Mr. Darcy?" He frowned, wrapped his bandaged hand around her waist and pulled her down to sit on his lap.

"Fitzwilliam!" she scolded him in a low voice. "The door is open. Jane or Papa may see us."

"That will be good. You will be compromised and we can get married much sooner – perhaps some time this week!" He darted a glance to the empty corridor, making sure no one was to be seen, before lowering his mouth to nuzzle her neck.

She gave an embarrassed laugh and moved from his lap. Then she scowled and said sternly. "Behave! I shall cut the meat for you." She turned to take the dish and placed it on her lap before cutting tiny morsels of food and beginning to feed him.

He was delighted that she did not move too distant from him. His hands were around her waist as he partook of the most wonderful meal he had ever tasted at Longbourn. With the close proximity of his beloved, each morsel tasted exceptionally delicious and every sip of wine was a sensory delight.

He took a small piece of bread and then nibbled her adorable earlobe, mere inches from him. She squirmed and moved away, nearly falling off the edge of the bed. He tightened his hold of her waist and pulled her back. She was once again sitting on his lap.

As she tried to twist to settle herself on the bed once more, she felt him becoming aroused.

Her eyes widened and she opened her mouth to ask, "What have you got… ?"

His face turned bright red and she closed her mouth. With hands over her blushing face, she sat rigidly still.

"Um, perhaps it would be better if you moved from me now," he stammered.

She put the dish down on the side table heavily and hurriedly scrambled from his lap.

But it was not speedy enough for Darcy, for when she moved her behind, she accidentally caressed his manhood. At that moment he almost reached climax.

As she muttered about taking the tray back to the kitchen, a loud commotion was heard downstairs.

"Lady Catherine de Bourgh!" Hill's loud announcement was heard even upstairs.

A sense of consternation rose in Darcy's mind. How did his aunt find her way here? It was still early afternoon. She must have left Rosings early that morning. Damn! Bingley would have missed meeting her. "Elizabeth, please get Winston here for me. I need to get dressed and see to my aunt."

"But your leg is hurt."

"He can help me down. My aunt is probably here to see me."

She agreed reluctantly and went downstairs. As Darcy waited upstairs, he could hear raised voices: "trifle", "scandalous falsehood", "contradicted". But Winston was nowhere to be found.

Darcy stood up from the bed and grabbed a nearby robe. He would not be able to properly attire himself without the help of his valet. This would have to do. As he pulled himself along the corridor and down the stairs by leaning on the walls, he could hear the argument more clearly. It was between his aunt and his betrothed.

"Because honour, decorum, prudence, nay, interest, forbid it. Yes, Miss Bennet, interest; for do not expect to be noticed by his family or friends, if you wilfully act against the inclinations of all. You will be censured, slighted, and despised by everyone connected with him. Your alliance will be a disgrace; your name will never even be mentioned by any of us," Lady Catherine exclaimed.

Her aunt had trapped Elizabeth at the bottom of the stairs. Miss Jane was looking on from inside the parlour, trying to interrupt Lady Catherine's speech, but she could not come to Elizabeth's side. No wonder Winston had not been called.

"You have said quite enough, Madam!" Darcy addressed his aunt. He could see that Elizabeth had high colour on her cheeks and her eyes were flashing with anger.

"What has happened to you, nephew?" Lady Catherine asked. "Did the Bennets injure you in order to keep you here?"

The Bennet sisters gasped loudly. Darcy held back his anger and explained. "I was struck by a thief and Miss Elizabeth found me. I am indebted to them."

"That sounds all too convenient. My parson sent me an express detailing the lack of propriety of the lady. She is tempting you away from your duty. I demand that you announce your engagement to Anne now!"

"I was never engaged to Anne and I never shall be."

"How can you abandon the keen wishes of your mother and me? The engagement was agreed when you were both in the cradle," Lady Catherine exclaimed.

"Mother did not mention this agreement to me. In fact I have been promised to Miss Elizabeth these past twenty years."

"What nonsense are you talking?"

"Mr. Bennet saved Mother's and my life during a fire some twenty years ago and Father had promised my future to Miss Elizabeth since then. Not only that, I had the good fortune of winning her affection and her own father's blessing. Miss Elizabeth and I will be married soon."

Elizabeth stood on the last step to help Darcy down. She held onto his arms. "Yes, as soon as Fitzwilliam recovers!" she tilted her head and added.

Darcy was surprised by her change of mind, but he was not unhappy. He gave her a smile.

Lady Catherine banged her walking stick on the floor to draw his attention. "George Darcy never told me this. I am sure Lady Anne did not know about this either. I have never heard her talking about this. I demand to see the proof and I shall ask Lord Matlock to decide the matter."

"There is nothing to decide. Father left me a letter in his Will detailing the pledge. I have been engaged to Miss Elizabeth Bennet since she was a baby. Our betrothal will be published soon. I shall not allow you to interfere with my personal affairs."

"Obstinate, headstrong man! I am ashamed of you! Is this your gratitude for my attentions to you these past years? You refuse, then, to oblige me. You are determined to throw away your duty, honour, and gratitude for this girl with no connection and wealth. I shall know how to act. Do not imagine, Fitzwilliam, that I shall allow our family's name to be tarnished. I take no leave of you. I am most seriously displeased." With that parting line, Lady Catherine walked out of Longbourn and ascended her grand carriage, muttering further imprecations about the shades of Pemberley being presently tainted.

# Chapter Ten

Darcy breathed out a sigh of relief and frustration. He patted Elizabeth's hand one more time before bowing solemnly to Miss Bennet. "I am sorry for the untutored behaviour of my aunt. And for her abusive language against Miss Elizabeth and your family."

Mr. Bennet, having heard the commotion from his library, had just stepped forward to see the retreating Lady Catherine as he slapped Darcy on the shoulder. "Come, Fitzwilliam, you are not going to be faint-hearted about this, I hope. For what do we live, but to make sport for our neighbours and family, and laugh at them in our turn? Now what is this talk about getting married when you recover? Have you two taken some liberties?"

Darcy was caught off guard. His mind was still reeling from Lady Catherine's loud voice. And then there were the worries about the Bingley party. He murmured, "Um…" And then his eyes were drawn to Elizabeth's lips.

"Papa!" Elizabeth protested. Her face gained yet another shade of red. "Fitzwilliam!" she whispered her chastisement. Then she left Darcy's side and pulled her sister into the parlour. "Mr. Darcy, I shall send for Winston to assist you upstairs. You are not fit to be seen!"

"Um, are we to be married next week or not?" Darcy asked in a confused manner, at the retreating figure of his betrothed.

"Well, well, ladies like to change their mind," Mr. Bennet said. "You had better take some rest now. I shall send her to bring you a tray of dinner tonight. You can practise your persuasive skills on her then."

Darcy felt hot and flustered suddenly, remembering the light refreshment in bed just now. Did Mr. Bennet know about their transgression or was he acting like Mrs. Bennet, to ensure a wedding would occur soon?

"But do I not need to wait for Colonel Foster and the magistrate?"

"I shall send them upstairs when they arrive. As Lizzy said, you are not fit to hobble around downstairs."

"Perhaps I should apologise to Miss Bennet first before I go up."

"Jane? Why?"

"Mr. Bingley asked me to apologise to her. Miss Bingley and he have some urgent business. He said he was sorry he did not stay long this morning and he would not be able to visit her, I mean, the family in the next few days."

"Ah, the issue relating to the removal of Mr. Collins…" Mr. Bennet said.

Darcy's eyes widened. "You knew? Um, did…Elizabeth…the two eldest Miss Bennets know too?"

Mr. Bennet shook his head. "Hill heard from a maid and told me about it. I asked her to rein in the wagging tongues downstairs."

"Charles is very upset about the whole situation. I fear he does not feel that his family is worthy of Miss Bennet."

"Young man with a sensitive soul." Mr. Bennet shook his head again. "I shall tell Jane about his apology. But it is up to him to come back and talk to my daughter. I am not boasting about my daughter. Jane has the kindest heart. I think she will be a good person to help Mr. Bingley through this trial."

"I have said similar words to Charles. I hope he does not give up on his own happiness."

***

Colonel Foster and Magistrate Robinson arrived not long afterwards. They took a statement from Darcy about the incident with Wickham.

"Why is the man loitering around near Oakham Mount?" asked Mr. Bennet, who was also present. "Has he deserted the militia already?"

"That weasel! I gave him a chance because he said he was only acting in defence of his honour during the brawl with your cousin in Meryton," Foster said. "At dinner, your cousin told me more about Wickham's past sins. I was going to confront the blackguard the next day. But that scoundrel…!"

"What did he do?" Mr. Bennet asked.

"Colonel Fitzwilliam came to the camp rather late. I went out with him and some of the men to the tavern. When we returned in the early hours, we found Wickham trying to ... persuade one of the wives to leave town with him. I expect he was slavering over the tiny portion of money the woman has!"

Mr. Bennet and Darcy looked at each other and speculated who the lady could be. They had their suspicions but they did not want to offend the Colonel.

"We almost caught him stealing the money," Colonel Foster continued. "But he ran away. It was most unfortunate that you ran into him, Mr. Darcy, when he was most desperate. Luckily you were not gravely injured."

Mr. Bennet said seriously, "I hope you will make sure Wickham does not loiter around the village. I do not want any of my daughters hurt."

"I will assign some men to patrol the area during the next few days," Colonel Foster promised.

"And I shall send a detailed report to the neighbouring towns and London," magistrate Robinson added. "Hopefully that will get this scoundrel arrested when he tries to sell your possessions."

Darcy nodded. He wished only that the Bennet ladies were safe from Wickham.

After the visitors had left, Darcy took a short rest. At dinner time Winston walked into his room with one tray, and Elizabeth hard on his heels with another. She instructed Winston to pull a table next to Darcy's bed, where the food was laid down. A chair was also positioned close by. Once Winston took his leave, she sat down on the chair and folded her hands on her lap. Darcy understood completely: there would be no liberties to be taken with the lady this time.

"I hope you are well, Mr. Darcy." No Fitzwilliam any more? Formality was the key.

"I am very well, Miss Bennet."

"Father asked me to assist you with your dinner."

"I am most grateful."

She raised a spoonful of soup. Darcy leaned near, but it was too far away for him to reach. He moved closer to the edge of the bed and tried again. He managed to drink the soup, just barely. As he swayed a little on the edge, making her hand shake, some of the soup splashed onto the linen.

"Dear me!" she murmured and looked for something to wipe away the spatter.

"I have some handkerchiefs in my trunk," he said, but then suddenly remembered something. His face turned red and he added quickly, "No, do not open my trunk! I better ring Winston to bring in a cleaning cloth."

She regarded his sudden change of mind with suspicion. "There is no need to bother Winston," she said. Then she walked purposefully towards his trunk.

Once she had opened it, she started searching for a handkerchief. He saw that her face turned crimson as her hand touched one of his undergarments. She was about to withdraw from the search when she pulled out something.

"Why is my pillow in your trunk?" she asked. After examining it closer, she added, "And it is stained."

Darcy's face turned bright red, like a clay brick left in the sun. That was indeed her pillow because he had noticed that there were the initials EB embroidered on it when he had first slept on it. He had ruined it during his erotic dream, even though he had tried to repair it. It was still not clean. "Was that your pillow?"

"It has my initials on it."

"Why did you let me use it?"

She blushed and did not answer. "Why did you hide it in your trunk?"

"I am … sorry to have smudged it. As it is your prized possession, I … I think I shall bring it to London to clean it before returning it to you," he stuttered.

She looked at him suspiciously. "You cannot give it to the servants to clean it?"

He tried to divert the question. "The food will get cold. May I continue with dinner?"

She seized one of his neck ties and the pillow. After she had placed the pillow on the chair, she rinsed the cravat with water and cleaned the stain on the bed linen. Oh-oh, he thought, she was going to take the pillow back to her room!

"Should you not sit on the bed to feed me?" he suggested. "We do not want more damage to the bed linen."

She scrutinized him quietly for a minute before sitting besides him once again and starting to feed him the soup.

After the meal was almost over, she asked suddenly, "How did you dirty my pillow?"

He was caught off guard by her question and a piece of fruit went down the wrong passage. His coughing fit brought her closer to him. She laid down the cutlery and rubbed his back to help him breathe.

"I am sorry, Fitzwilliam. Are you well?" she asked with concern. Her caring hands moved over his chest.

Her close proximity, the caressing hands and the reminder of the sensual dream sent Darcy's thoughts racing. Without care of the open door and possible discovery by her father, he stopped her rubbing motion, tilted his head and kissed her lips, hard.

Her eyes widened, surprised by his sudden amorous gesture. He could see that her pupils dilated as he took her tongue between his lips. After savouring her mouth for a long time, he finally released her to breathe. Her eyes were half-closed, her gorgeous bosom heaving deeply. His eyes were drawn to her nipples which had turned hard and pointed beneath the thin muslin.

How he wanted to pull down the sleeves of her dress and suckle her soft breasts! In fact, he wished to do much more. He wanted to bury himself deep inside her and to bring her into a heavenly bliss. When he was about to lower his head to kiss her breasts, voices were heard from downstairs.

He knew he could not dishonour Mr. Bennet's trust. *He must not compromise his betrothed.* But he would need to persuade her to hold the wedding soon.

Taking a deep breath, he whispered in her ear, "I was dreaming about you, I mean, how to teach you the ecstasy of our union, when I ruined your pillow. Do you want to hear more in detail?"

Her half-closed eyes sprang open. Her mouth opened in a lovely O. She began to nod before she stopped herself. He was extremely tempted to thrust his tongue into that sweet opening. But he had to maintain his gentlemanly behaviour. "If you do not want me to ruin more pillows, I think we should marry soon, very soon."

Her mouth closed and the blush on her face turned full red. She jumped from the bed, seized the ruined pillow and dashed from his room without further word.

***

The next morning, Elizabeth came alone with a tray of food to help Darcy with his breakfast.

"Good morning, Mr. Darcy," she said. Her fine eyes sparkled and her scent was fresh. "Papa has allowed me to help you again."

"Good morning, Miss Bennet. That is very good of your father."

As she fed him with bread and meat, she chatted casually. "Did you sleep well, sir?"

"Indeed I did, madam."

"I sincerely hope that no shocking dreams intruded upon your peace."

Darcy had anticipated her approach. Her eyes had darted away before she spoke. He swallowed the meat and stroked the tip of the fork she held out with his tongue. He waited for a few seconds before answering, "I did have a dream. It was not bad at all. Quite the contrary."

She arched her eyebrows, silently urging him to continue. He denied her the pleasure. Instead he asked, "May I have a sip of the hot chocolate?"

She raised the cup to his lips and asked, "You do not want to go into more detail about your dream?"

His eyes were held fast on hers as he drank. After a mouthful, he stopped and licked his lips. "Well, if you tell me why you allowed me to use your pillow, I shall be happy to enlighten you about my dreams."

"Why, Sir! You are so eager to know about my thoughts that you are willing to offer an exchange for them. Let me tell you, I am not interested to know about your dream or dreams. Now what can you say?"

Darcy shrugged his shoulders and said, "It is immaterial to me. For you cannot take away my pleasure of reliving the dreams anyway. They were deliciously…" he stopped and gazed at her, "satisfying."

"Satisfying?" She laughed. "How can a dream be satisfying? I fear you must have dreamed of some strange food."

"Not strange at all, mostly wonderful fruit that could fill my stomach and quench my thirst."

"Such as?"

"Red and firm cherries." He lowered his eyes as he spoke.

"I would think cherries would be too small and delicate for your taste." She dismissed the idea quickly.

"I may be tall and cumbersome, but I appreciate forms that are light and pleasing. In fact I was having a sumptuous dinner in my dream."

Darcy thought back to the delicious dream. Elizabeth and he were having dinner at the grand dining room in Pemberley. But there was no food on the table and he had complained about his hunger.

She had graciously undressed in front of him and laid down on the long table in all her glory. "Come and feed on me," she had said huskily.

He sprang from the chair and climbed up on the table, starting to feed his hunger on her sultry lips, delectable neck, sweet nipples and searing womanhood. He was licking, laving and nibbling every inch of her skin for what seemed like endless hours.

But she was no blushing maiden either. While he was worshiping her hot sex, she palmed his manhood and admired it with her mouth. Her adorable tiny tongue brushed down the length of his hot velvety rod, from base to tip, several times. As he was rubbing the folds of her sex, she swallowed his huge shaft into her mouth, slowly, inch by inch. Her tongue played a dancing tune on its tip.

He was nearly undone when she withdrew from him and cried out loud, "I am hungry for you, fill me!"

He did not need more urging. Moving to lie on top of her, with eager fingers, he parted her thighs and positioned his thick shaft at her entrance. With one mighty thrust, he filled her tightly, completely to the hilt. She shivered and pressed against his manhood, devouring him.

He grabbed hold of her hips. As his mouth suckled her sweet cherry nipples, his rod moved into her with constant rhythmic thrusts. The grand table shook beneath them. He filled her up, again and again, until they both reached their peak. She convulsed with him, squeezing his essence into her burning core.

That was quite a feast and he had ruined his night gown and bed linen too.

Darcy woke from his musings and gazed at Elizabeth with an intensity of longing. He was hot and hungry for a real feast. When he darted a glance at the corridor, he could see Mrs. Hill approaching.

"An express for you, Sir!" She handed him the letter and left the room.

He drew his thoughts back from the dream and glanced at the writing. It was from Bingley. But why did he write from London?

He looked up and saw Elizabeth watching him with curious eyes.

"May I read the express in private?" he asked.

Her lips curled in a disappointed pout. She rose from the chair and left the room with flashing eyes.

He tore open the letter roughly with his bandaged hands. Bingley's untidy writing filled the sheet.

*Darcy,*

*We arrived at Hunsford around two o'clock yesterday. After we settled the injured parson at his home, I took Caroline to stay at an inn while Colonel Fitzwilliam went to Rosings to request a meeting on my behalf.*

*But his mission was unsuccessful. Lady Catherine de Bourgh had already left her estate early that morning after receiving an express the day before. Your cousin was unable to gain information as to where she had gone or how long she would be away.*

*We decided to stay in Kent for a day or two to wait for the ladyship.*

Darcy read the first part of the letter, knowing that Bingley's party would not be met with success. The beginning of Bingley's writing was legible but then the second part became unreadable, with many blots and broken sentences.

*Since writing the above, Darcy, something has occurred of a most unexpected nature. It relates to poor Caroline. My sister has disappeared. She took her maid, the carriage and my bag of money and ran away. Gone! Lord knows where!*

*Shortly after we started the journey from Hertfordshire, I gave her some coffee to cure her hangover. She slowly came back to her senses and returned to her normal self. I asked her if she knew what she had done the night before. She did not remember.*

*When I started recounting the sordid details, she remembered more and more. At first she insisted that she had tied and beaten you. She protested vehemently that she had not mistaken Mr. Collins for you. But when we stopped at Bromley and she saw the injured pastor walking out of the other carriage in limping steps, she remembered her misdeed.*

*She was still acting illogically and dissembling about the whole affair. She begged me to turn the carriage round. She said she would send the servants to America or New South Wales, to make sure they would not talk about her lapse of judgement. When I told her that sufficient time had passed since then that the whole of Meryton would probably know all by now, she turned silent and pensive.*

*I should have been more observant. I should have known she would not accept her fate so easily. She would never be so compliant as to marry a mere clergyman who possesses little wealth.*

*When I had decided to travel with Colonel Fitzwilliam to Hunsford to discuss the delay as a result of Lady Catherine's absence, Caroline took my belongings and left Kent. Colonel Fitzwilliam and I chased after her on horseback but she had over an hour's head start on us. We followed her as far as Clapham but no further.*

*I was praying that she would return to Hurst's residence at Grosvenor Square but that was not the case. I have visited all her friends and our relatives who are in town this morning but none of them have seen her.*

*I write to beg for your assistance. I am at my wit's end. I have written a separate express to the Hursts and asked them to return. I need them to help with the search. Lady Susan and the two younger Miss Bennets are welcome to remain at Netherfield but I desperately hope you can come at once.*

*Please try once again to conceal the nature of my request. I am full of shame in regard to my sister's behaviour and do not wish Miss Bennet to learn of it at the moment.*

*Your humble friend,*

*Charles Bingley.*

Darcy rushed through the second part of the express. With his injury, he wondered how he could assist Bingley in his search for his sister. But he did not want to let down his friend. Even if he could not physically help in the search, he could support Bingley with his mere presence.

But that meant leaving Elizabeth. He did not want to part with her, not for long. Perhaps her father would be agreeable to her going to London.

When he was about to ring Winston to request a meeting with Mr. Bennet, Mrs. Hill once again came to his room and announced Lady Susan's arrival.

"Darcy, I heard you were injured. Are you well?" Lady Susan asked briskly.

"I am well, Susan. Thank you."

"Who did this to you? Have the authorities been informed?"

"I had an altercation with Wickham at Oakham Mount. Yes, both the militia and the magistrate were informed."

"That scoundrel! That is how he repays Uncle Darcy's kindness?"

"He will have his punishment one day. But Susan, Bingley urgently needs the Hursts and I to go to London. Do you still want to invite Miss Mary and Miss Lydia to your townhouse or do you prefer to stay here? He said you are welcome to have the use of Netherfield."

"What happened? Why such an urgency?"

"It is Bingley's private matter."

"It must be his despicable sister! Hmm, I think it is best I return to London. It would be my pleasure to invite all four Miss Bennets to my town house. What say you if I hold an engagement ball for Miss Elizabeth and you?"

"You know I do not like to dance! And I may be quite busy with Bingley."

"You cannot neglect your betrothed for long. She may find a richer gentleman who loves to dance!"

"You jest! My Lizzy is not like that." Darcy looked at his cousin's smug expression. She was going to cause trouble. "Very well, organise whatever party you want. I shall ask Mr. Bennet and Elizabeth about going to London. But I have to leave today."

When the matter was raised with the Master of Longbourn, Mr. Bennet was happy to have the house all to himself and to have his girls stay in London for some time. But Elizabeth declined Lady Susan's invitation and would stay with her eldest sister in their uncle's house in Cheapside. Mr. and Mrs.

Hurst would leave with Darcy today and the rest of the party would leave the next day.

When Elizabeth saw him off in the carriage, she looked unhappy.

"I am sorry, my love." Darcy touched her hands.

"I understand you promised Mr. Bingley not to reveal the nature of the affair."

"As I told Miss Bennet, Bingley has some urgent family business and he needs my help. He particularly wants to explain the details to her personally."

"But he does not know that you are injured. How can you help him with your leg and hands bandaged?"

"Even though I cannot help in the search physically …" He stopped mid sentence.

"Search? Someone is missing … Miss Bingley is missing?"

"Elizabeth, please do not ask me any more. As I said, even though I cannot help him physically, I want to offer him my support. It is good that your father permits you to go to London to shop for your wedding clothes. I can introduce Georgiana to you and we can still see each other often. It is just unfortunate that you cannot stay at my town house."

"Perhaps that is a blessing," she said archly. "One will not be tempted to act rashly."

"Me? Or you?" He raised her hands for a kiss.

"Me? I shall only be tempted by the best silk and feather. It is good that Lady Susan has offered to host a ball for us."

"I will be happier if we omit the ball and move straight to the wedding."

"Father told me you wanted to get married before Christmas."

"Yes, but he suggested later, so your younger sisters and mother would have more time to dedicate to their learning."

"Yes, he told me too. What about St. Valentine's Day? I hope the crisis with Mr. Bingley will be resolved by then and Jane will be in better spirits."

"It is not as early as I hoped but I shall accept that." He lowered his head and touched her lips softly. "I must go now."

"Take care, Fitzwilliam."

"You too, my Lizzy."

## Chapter Eleven

After washing off the dust of the journey, Darcy went to Grosvenor Square immediately. Colonel Fitzwilliam and Bingley were closeted in the study. When they saw the condition Darcy was in, they could not prevent themselves asking at one and the same time, "What on earth has happened?"

"Wickham inflicted these minor injuries on me," Darcy explained.

"I should have dealt with him last summer!" Colonel Fitzwilliam swore.

"Let us forget him for the moment and concentrate on Miss Bingley. So she took everything and went off with the carriage and maid?"

Bingley sighed and nodded.

"What did you find in Clapham?"

"They were seen at the carriage stop but there are conflicting reports of where the carriage has travelled to. One said into London, one to Plymouth, one detoured back to Dover and one en route to Scotland. Either Caroline paid the witnesses to lie for her or there were very many coaches on that day and she tried hard to not draw attention to herself."

"And your inquiry into Miss Bingley's friends?"

"None of them had heard or seen her since she left with us for Hertfordshire."

Darcy thought for a few moments. "Do the stable man and maid have relations working with you too?"

Bingley jumped up from his seat. "I have questioned the staff here but I had forgotten that Harold, the stable man, is related to one of Aunt Pamela's maids. Good man, Darcy! I shall go there directly, to see if there is any news."

"I can come with you," Darcy offered.

"No, Bingley does not need an invalid to slow his progress," Colonel Fitzwilliam said. "Let me help him interview the servants."

"Yes," Bingley agreed. "You may return to your house and rest. I shall keep you informed once I have more news."

Darcy let them go reluctantly. He was a man of action and did not like to be left behind because of this minor injury. But he was aware that if he recovered sooner, he would be able to court his Elizabeth more ably, so he decided to return to Ashford Hall.

Halfway into the journey, he remembered the approaching engagement ball. Although the Darcy family had many pieces of jewellery, he wanted to present Elizabeth with something he had found himself. He knocked on the carriage roof and detoured to the establishment of Harveys, his family jeweller for many years, in Bond Street.

When Darcy entered the premises, he was led to its owner, Mr. Harvey.

"Good day, Mr. Darcy, what happened to you?" the elderly Harvey exclaimed.

"Just a riding accident," Darcy said. "But why are you returned to the business? Are you fully recovered?"

Mr. Harvey sighed. "I meant to visit you and apologise but I heard that you were out of town. I am afraid my nephew has let me down and abused your trust with our company."

Darcy bade him continue.

"As you know, I was struck down by a long illness late last year and had to remove myself from the business for a lengthy period. My nephew from France, Pierre, took over. And just a few weeks ago, I began to feel better and came into the workshop to fetch some tools so that I could work up some designs to occupy my time. There I discovered that Pierre was copying some of the exclusive designs that we had developed for clients."

"Did he intend to sell them?"

"That scheming nephew of mine intended more than that. He particularly concentrated his attentions on those with a delicate history, such as a diamond ring made by a certain Lord for his mistress, and he offered the design to the Lord's wife!"

"My goodness, you must have had a lot of explaining to do. What did he do with our family design … ?" Darcy asked – and a thought occurred to him all of a sudden.

"Pierre met with the daughter of a fashionable tradesman who said she knew you and had replicated the garnet cross your father made for your mother some twenty years ago. I did not know the significance of this piece of jewellery but he seemed to have sold it for a good price to this lady," Monsieur Harvey said. "I have notified all the clients who might be touched by Pierre's work and offered compensation. Do you want to interview my nephew to determine how and why the lady wanted that piece of jewellery? Of course, I am determined to pay for any compensation you deem necessary."

Darcy pitied the elderly jeweller. The Frenchman had been his father's friend for many years. Darcy was sad to hear that during the time of his illness, Harvey's business reputation had been blemished by one of his own family members.

"I would not want to cause you more stress by asking for any compensation. I am here today to seek out a special item for my betrothed. Perhaps after I have found the piece, I can talk with your nephew about the garnet cross," Darcy said.

Mr. Harvey was grateful for Mr. Darcy's generosity. Darcy decided on an exquisite ruby bracelet that matched the garnet cross. He asked for an inscription to be done post haste and the jeweller promised to have it completed within two days.

Then he was invited to Mr. Harvey's house in Stoke Newington where he was to meet Pierre Roux.

***

The Manor of Stoke Newington was situated on the north eastern outskirts of London. Many expensive and large houses had been constructed to accommodate London's expanding population of newly-enriched merchants.

Mr. Harvey, whose family had been in the jewellery business for many years, had done well to be able to house his family and certain of his relatives in this area.

As Darcy's carriage trotted at a steady pace along the High Street, he regarded the shops absent-mindedly. However, the carriage was pulled to a sudden halt that nearly sent him to the floor. He held on to the window and the top of the carriage to steady himself and glanced outside in time to see a buggy hastening past them.

Darcy did not see the man behind the horse but to judge from his own driver's curses, the reckless driver seemed to be a young dandy with fair hair. Darcy shook his head at the foolish behaviour of the other driver and felt lucky that his injured body was not further harmed.

Darcy met the young jeweller in a neat sitting room.

"Good afternoon, Mr. Darcy, my uncle has sent word ahead." Pierre did not rise from his chair but smoothed the shawl covering his legs. "I apologise for selling an imitation of your father's garnet cross. It was very generous of you not to send the magistrate after me. I shall answer all your questions truthfully."

Darcy nodded and began. "Mr. Harvey said that you sold the imitation to a lady. Can you describe the woman?"

"Yes, the tradesman's daughter called herself Jeanne. She was a light-haired woman with fair skin, tall, probably nearly as tall as you, and of sophisticated manner. She favoured feather and silk. If not for the slip of her tongue that showed her knowledge of commerce, I would have taken her for a woman from high society. We met in the Charing Cross Inn around late March. She was accompanied by a young man and brought a drawing of the garnet cross."

Darcy frowned. The description matched Miss Bingley. He had not foreseen that she might have an accomplice. Who was he? "What is the name of the man?" he asked. "What is he like?"

"He introduced himself as Nicolas. He had a figure very similar to your own, Sir. Very handsome and charming. Fair hair with a moustache. His gentleman's clothes were neat and of good quality."

"How did they know about you?"

"Nicolas seemed to know about my uncle's jewellery shop. They sent me a note at the shop, saying that they had heard about my work and requesting a meeting at Charing Cross."

"Why did they want you to work on the imitation if they already had the sketch? They could get anyone to accomplish the forgery. I imagine you did not offer your service cheaply."

"With so many years of apprenticeship with my uncle, I charged a high fee for my imitation. They wanted me to work on it because they wanted it to appear as genuine as possible and they did not have the design of the back of the garnet cross."

"They thought you could examine your uncle's records to make a more perfect imitation? But you nevertheless made them one that was inaccurate ..."

"Was it?" Pierre seemed unconcerned. "What was missing?"

"The inscription on the back."

"Ah, I see. Uncle likes to keep the inscription wordings in a separate location with the calligraphy book. I must have missed the footnote at the back of the design sketch and did not refer to the inscription file. At the time I was occupied with a great deal of work immediately before Easter."

Darcy breathed a sigh of relief. Thanks to Providence, he was saved from tying himself to the scheming Miss Bingley. He then continued with a few more questions about the initial meeting and the delivery of the product.

Finally, he was satisfied with all the details. Before he left, he asked, "What happened to your legs?"

"The nature of my work brought its own revenge. An imitation of mine created a scandal and a Lord – whom I will not name – sent someone to exact a measure of regret from me."

Darcy felt a pang of sympathy for the man, becoming an invalid so early in life. Greed and dishonesty had cost this promising young man dearly. Was there something lacking in his upbringing? From Pierre, Darcy's thoughts turned to Miss Bingley. He had no idea who the young man who had accompanied her might be, but he dearly hoped she would not face a similar fate as the Frenchman, for Charles would then grieve mightily for his sister.

***

The following day, Darcy's carriage drove across town again. When it had stopped in front of a neat townhouse, his valet helped him out and knocked on the door. A polite servant led Darcy into the parlour, where he found his betrothed quite alone.

"Fitzwilliam, what are you doing here?" Elizabeth abandoned the book she was reading, jumped up and went to assist him to sit. "Did the doctor not say you should be resting? Why are you visiting here?"

"I knew you would have arrived in town by now," he said. "I came to pay my respects to your aunt and uncle."

"My uncle is at the warehouse and Jane and Aunt Gardiner went out with the children. We planned to visit you tomorrow."

"You are here all alone?" he asked. Glancing around, and seeing that Winston and the servants had left, he lowered his head and whispered to her, "I miss you."

She drew in a short breath and replied archly, "I did not miss you."

"Indeed?" He blew air into her ear. She shivered.

Then she turned her head. He was not sure whether she wanted to avoid his ministrations or to welcome him, because with this movement her lips were very close to his.

"I have been busy, thinking about ..." Her sentence was cut off midway when he captured her soft lips. He nipped at the smooth skin, pressed his tongue gently into her mouth and drew hers out. When she sighed with a satisfied moan, he started sucking her tongue with vigour. Her arms came up to wrap around his neck, toying with his cravat. Her petite fingers traced a path around his neck. He forgot that they were in the parlour of her relatives. He pulled her close to his body by seizing her around the waist.

"Did you miss me, my dear?" he asked again.

"Yessss," she said with a low voice, and added after a pause, "That was why I slept with…"

"You slept with…?" – his mind was racing as he considered her thoughts – "…my pillow?"

Her face turned bright red, before she buried her face in his neck. "It is my pillow."

"Your pillow?" He turned to suckle her earlobe. "Ah…the pillow with my scent."

"You ruined it horribly."

"It was all your fault." He breathed in her sweet lavender scent. "You were naughty in my dream."

Her fingers moved lower to caress the lapels of his coat. "How?"

"You teased me to chase after you, all around Pemberley." His tongue licked the skin on her neck.

"You are becoming arrogant again, in the dream. That was why I was running away from you." She played with the button on his waistcoat.

"I caught you in the laundry room." He sank his teeth on her neck and bit her soft skin tenderly there.

She trembled and twisted the button a bit too hard, pulling it from his waistcoat. "Oh dear!"

"Now, you have ruined my best waistcoat," he said. His tongue went lower as he continued. "I expect repayment from you."

She fluttered her eyes and grazed her cheek against his. "I only have a little pin money."

"I prefer something more sentimental." He was touching her neckline now.

"My…copy of Shakespeare's poems?" Her hands lowered to his waist.

"I might consider your stocking ..." He found the mole on her bosom and started licking it.

Elizabeth moaned and squirmed. "Now?"

"Yes."

"The children will be back anytime," she panted. "They will be…scandalised, seeing me removing my stocking in the parlour."

"You must bring it to me when you visit me tomorrow, then."

She blushed but did not reply.

"In the meantime, I need another recompense."

"That is most unfair!" she protested. "I only drew out one button."

"But the entire waistcoat is ruined."

"I can repair it for you."

"Did I not hear your father say your sewing skills are lamentable? I am sure it shall not be fit for wearing again."

"Insufferable man!"

He held out his bandaged hand and said. "I shall be satisfied with your handkerchief for the moment."

She pouted, took it out and gave it to him reluctantly. Before he could pocket the cloth, she pulled it away and jumped from his embrace. "Not so easy!"

Darcy frowned. "Wait until my leg and hands have recovered!"

She sat on another chair far away from him and asked innocently. "Now we can start again. I hope you are well, Sir."

"I was quite well just a few moments ago. Now, I cannot say." He flexed his leg as he spoke.

"Is your leg hurting?" Elizabeth moved back to sit by his side and massaged his knee.

He felt abashed for playing on her caring nature. "Sorry, my dear. I am well. I just miss being with you and talking to you every day. Why did I agree to marry in February? It is still months away. How did you become so important to me in such a short time?" He rested his head on her shoulder.

"Do you resent it? The fact that I am dear to you?"

"Of course not." He gave her a kiss on the cheek. "I am ashamed of what I thought and felt when I first proposed to you. Now I can see beyond the obligation set by my late father, especially after you voiced your low opinion of me. Your pleasing form and passionate nature also appealed to me then. And I can see that you are caring, witty, intelligent and honest. I am delighted that you have agreed to be my wife. I am looking forward to sharing Pemberley and my life with you. Of course my body is aflame with desire to create some little Darcys with you."

"Men! Are they always ruled by their lust?"

"I am proud to say that my gentleman's education and upbringing have helped me rein in my carnal desire. I have never trifled with a maiden nor did I ever have a mistress before. And I never will."

"It is reassuring to hear this. I was afraid that you only lust after me, which I do not fully understand anyway. I am sure I am no more pretty, humorous, attentive or fair than some of the accomplished ladies you know in London. All my virtues are invented by you, for I think you love only my impertinence, which is so different from the women of the town like Miss Bingley. But people in love are usually blinded by each other's virtues."

"You walked three miles to take care of Jane. That is devotion indeed, and I can imagine you taking care of my sister when she is in need."

"Jane is such a sweet sister. How can I not care for her? I am sure Miss Darcy will be equally angelic. I would have no concerns about looking after her. But if I remember correctly, you did not approve of my roaming the countryside alone."

"I am simply worried that something evil may befall you, with no one protecting or assisting you. Promise me, if I am not around to accompany you, you will bring a servant when you ramble in the woods of Derbyshire."

"We will see. Perhaps I will become so enamoured with Pemberley's luxurious mansion that I will seldom venture into the woods."

Darcy shook his head at her teasing expression. "Pemberley's riches will not hold you, but I wager my agreeable love-making will detain you indoors."

"You? Agreeable?" she scowled and continued. "I shall be more enraptured if you stare less and converse more with me."

"Why would you want a young man that prattles away? That will leave you with no room for your own witty display."

"You accuse me of showing off?"

"Your liveliness is one of the qualities I love about you. But what of you? What do you find most endearing about me?"

"Your muddy appearance!" she said and laughed out loud.

"Be serious! Or I shall kiss you again."

She suppressed the laugh into a smile before continuing. "After rejecting your first charming proposal, I have already had second thoughts."

"Indeed?" Darcy sat up straight on hearing this.

"Did you not remember I wore the garnet cross at dinner at Netherfield the day you met my father and visited Longbourn?"

"Yes, I remember clearly how lovely you looked. You regretted rejecting my offer?"

"No. You were arrogant and condescending. I would never accept a man with such a disdainful attitude. But I thought about what part Providence had played in bringing our lives together, not just once, but twice. I believe in fate and was willing to give you another chance."

"I have to thank Providence once again, then."

"When we were at the Jones, I could see that you were an excellent master and brother, despite taking on the huge tasks of caring for your estate and a sister ten years younger than you. You seemed so altered, so perfectly well-behaved, polite, and unassuming with the tenants."

"I feel much more at ease with strangers when you are by my side." He patted her hands.

"There is also gratitude at play here."

"Whatever for?"

"I am thankful for the changes you have brought to my family. Much as I respect and love my father, I despaired of his liberal attitude towards the management of the estate and my younger sisters. I feared for their future, too, if my father should meet his destiny sooner. I would do what I could to help with the estate and educate my sisters. But I feel my effort alone would be like a tiny drop of water in the ocean. I am thankful for your appearance and your help. I respect, esteem, and am grateful to you. I feel a true interest in your welfare. It may not be a love at first sight, as for Mr. Bingley and Jane. But I am sure my journey to love is no less admirable than theirs. Fitzwilliam, you have become very important to me." She placed her arms around his waist and rested her head on his chest.

Darcy felt humbled, treasured and honoured. *Yes, their first impression of each other may not have been the most favourable.* But fate and their persistence in taking a positive regard towards their situation ensured that they had found and now loved each other. He hugged her in return and smiled happily.

That was how Miss Bennet, Mrs. Gardiner and her children found them in the parlour – a couple deeply in love and enjoying the simple warmth of an embrace.

## Chapter Twelve

Darcy released his betrothed with a flush in his cheeks. Introductions were made. Once he had learned that the mistress of the house hailed from Derbyshire and had a sensible disposition, he was more relaxed in his conversation.

"I would like to invite you and the Miss Bennets to meet my sister Georgiana tomorrow afternoon. She will arrive from Pemberley then and I am sure she will be eager to meet her future family," he said.

"Lady Susan has arranged for my nieces to go shopping tomorrow morning. We can arrive at your home perhaps at around two o'clock. Is that convenient?" Mrs. Gardiner asked.

Darcy agreed.

"But I have to apologise for Lydia. She will not be able to visit tomorrow," she added.

Darcy looked at Elizabeth. She drew in a deep breath and explained, "Lydia issued an invitation to Captain Denny and his friends to visit her when he has any leave from the militia, at Nevan House. It was apparently done without the hostess's permission. Lady Susan believed it fitting that Lydia should not be allowed to participate in any activity tomorrow, for her lack of understanding of true society."

"Oh." Darcy uttered the word. "I hope Miss Lydia is still in the best of spirits."

"Once she had seen Lady Susan's home and the room she was to stay in," Mrs. Gardiner added, "she quite forgot Captain Denny and her punishment. Anyway, enough of Lydia. Mr. Darcy, how did your business in town go?"

"It was not as successful as I would have hoped," he said honestly.

Mrs. Gardiner persisted. "I heard you came to assist Mr. Bingley with some family matters. I hope our visit to your home tomorrow will not interfere with your important affairs."

Darcy was momentarily lost for words. Looking at three pairs of curious eyes, he did not wish to disappoint. But he had promised his friend. "Not at all. You are most welcome to come tomorrow afternoon. Owing to my injury, I could only assist Mr. Bingley by way of making a few suggestions." He saw the eager expression on Jane's face and added, "Mr. Bingley told me he would come to call on you and apologise, Miss Bennet, once he has settled the family business."

"He should not trouble himself about me when he is busy with his affairs," Jane said quietly.

"Charles believes he did not behave politely when he last visited Longbourn. He wishes to apologise."

"Apology is not necessary. I do not wish for him to apologise. I only wish he will be able to share his burden with me," Jane blurted out with agitation. "I am sorry, Mr. Darcy. I should not be so presumptuous."

Elizabeth spoke up to help her sister. "Could you not explain more of the situation? Perhaps we could offer aid in some way."

He fidgeted in his chair before answering. "Mr. Bingley was able to acquire some intelligence about the matter from the servants working in his aunt's house. My cousin Colonel Fitzwilliam has accompanied him to Dover today to investigate further."

"Oh, I hope they do not need to cross the Channel!" Miss Bennet exclaimed. "It is not safe to go in such times as these."

"My cousin cannot be away for very long. He cannot leave the country without applying to his commander. I think they will simply try to confirm the information as far as Dover. Please do not be alarmed, Miss Bennet. Mr. Bingley will take the utmost care."

"Why are we both burdened with the most difficult relations? He with Miss Bingley and I with Lydia!" Jane raised her voice and then suddenly remembered that there was a guest in the parlour. She burst into tears, rose from the chair and curtseyed to Mr. Darcy. "Please forgive me!" Then she ran out of the room in haste.

Elizabeth jumped up to follow but her aunt prevented her. "Let me see to her. Mr. Darcy, I apologise for Jane's outburst. She has not been sleeping well lately. Lizzy, you can see Mr. Darcy out."

"Think nothing of it, Mrs. Gardiner," he said. Although he was happy to be left alone with his betrothed once again, he did not like the scowl on her face. "Elizabeth, I am sorry."

"Jane is genuinely worried about Mr. Bingley. She wishes she could do something for him. I think she has fallen deeply in love with him, despite their short acquaintance."

"We have known each other only a short time, too, and yet we are also in love. I can understand your sister's concern." Darcy said. "I think Charles has very deep feelings for your sister as well. If not for his family business, he would have spent all his time courting Miss Bennet."

"I think Jane is affected by how quickly we seem to have reached an understanding."

"Does she believe that I have had an easy ride to earn your agreement to marry me? Perhaps we should enlighten her concerning how furiously you had rejected me."

"Did I not reject you rightly in the first place?" She arched her eyebrows. "And you had the good fortune of previously meeting Papa and scheming with him to overcome my objections. But Jane has not seen Mr. Bingley for some days now. Her last remembrance of him was his agitated expression, the morning after the dinner at Netherfield. He was so different from his normal amiable and cheerful self. She was worried he would become ill with anxiety. What if he were to do something rash and hurt himself or put himself in harm's way? Pray tell, what actually happened the night of the dinner?"

"Please do not ask me, Elizabeth. I have promised Charles. I can only say that something unpleasant happened and Charles is trying to prevent a scandal about his family."

Elizabeth sighed. "Jane is normally the most patient soul. I think the clash between Lydia and Lady Susan this morning was the reason for her outburst. When we stopped to change horses at an inn, Lydia's unauthorised invitation was made known. When Lady Susan made her decision to not include Lydia in tomorrow's shopping, Lydia was so upset that she seized hold of something nearby, which happened to be Jane's fan, and twisted it in two. I saw Jane turn pale, then blush furiously while trying to remain silent, even after Lydia was forced to apologise. It was only after much persuasion did she tell me what was troubling her. She said that Mr. Bingley had commented to her how much he liked that fan. I think she felt sorry that every good memory she had of Mr. Bingley was destined to be ruined. And now you say he could be sailing to France. What if he does not return?"

"I am so sorry. Perhaps I should talk to Susan about her treatment of Miss Lydia. My cousin can be too vigorous sometimes."

"No, Papa and I are grateful for Lady Susan's efforts. I think Lydia is too set in her ways to be persuaded by her family to change. I hope a persuasive figure like Lady Susan will be able to do some good for her. I simply have to protect Jane from Lydia during this delicate time."

"We shall work together on this," he said, "to help Charles, Miss Lydia and Miss Bennet with their trials. After all, we shall be partners in life soon."

Elizabeth embraced him and rested her head on his shoulder again. "I hope we can get married sooner as well."

"I have met with my solicitor this morning concerning the settlement papers and I went to obtain the special license. We will be able to marry in the next few days." Wishing to lighten the mood, he added, "If it's true that you are tired of waiting for me ... ? After all, you have been waiting for your betrothal for twenty years."

She raised her head and looked at him with a scowl. "You have been very busy. Did you follow the doctor's instruction to rest? Have you been eating well?"

"I am well. Another two days and the bandages can be taken off. I accepted Winston's assistance during meals. Why is it that I have the feeling that you will turn into a nagging wife?"

She struck his arm and said, "Then you should treasure the months ahead, when you will be still single. In fact, I should reconsider postponing the wedding. With Jane so distressed and Lydia still rather silly, it may be another year or two before I can leave Longbourn without worrying about my family."

He touched his bandaged hand to her lips to prevent her from saying more. "St. Valentine's Day is the longest I can bear. Otherwise, I may resort to taking more liberties with you to advance the date of the wedding."

She kissed his wrist, sending shivers down his spine. "Am I really a bother?"

"No… but perhaps…" He swore under his breath and looked at her with wide eyes as she opened her mouth to lick his wrist. As the sensation coursed through his body, he closed his eyes to savour the feeling.

He trembled and waited for more. But there was none. She had left his side. When he opened his eyes, now blurred, he could see that she was walking with a suggestive gait to the door. "I shall endeavour not to exasperate you for the rest of my life," she added archly as she reached the door. "And I believe that is best done by our not spending too much time alone with each other." She waited for him to leave.

He knew he was in difficulty now. With the injury, how could he rise and leave with dignity? Winston was not here and he had to rely on Elizabeth. He tried to school his expression into one that resembled a lost puppy and said, "My dear future Mrs. Darcy, you will be far from a nagging wife. You shall be the most caring one, especially gracious enough to help your husband in time of need." He then raised his hands for her to take them.

"Since you asked so sweetly," she smiled, and then walked back to assist him from the chair. He of course took the opportunity to wrap his arms around her body tightly again and returned the favour by kissing her earlobe.

It was after many moments of kisses and fondling that the betrothed couple separated. He then left to return to Ashford Hall.

***

When Darcy arrived home, Mr. Fleming, an ex-bow street runner whom he had hired to search for Mr. Bennet and his daughter when he first learned of the garnet cross, was waiting for him.

"We have not met in several years, Mr. Darcy," he said as he shook Darcy's hand. The tall lanky man paced for a second before taking the seat in front of Darcy.

Darcy nodded. "What brings you here?"

"I came to beg for your forgiveness." Fleming said.

Darcy frowned but let the man continued.

"The occasions that I cannot solve the mysteries for my clients are few. Therefore, when you discontinued my service four years ago, I copied the sketch of the garnet cross and kept it with me at all times, in hope of revisiting the puzzle whenever I could."

A sense of foreboding loomed in Darcy's mind as Mr. Fleming continued. "Early this year, I happened upon a couple at an Inn in the North. They were whispering about Derbyshire and a garnet cross, thus piquing my interest."

"What was their appearance?"

"Both had fair hair and were tall. I struck up a conversation with them, pretending to be a jeweller who knew about rare jewellery. They introduced themselves as Jeanne and Nicolas."

The same couple who had hired Pierre Roux!

"We talked in depth about the history of garnet crosses. I deduced from bits and pieces said that Jeanne originated from France."

That could not be, Darcy thought; according to Pierre, Jeanne matched the description of Miss Bingley.

"Unfortunately, the couple got an upper hand over me. They must have surmised that I was no jeweller. In one unguarded moment, they must have put some kind of sleeping draught into my cup. When I next woke alone in the Inn, I found the sketch of the garnet cross gone. I spent some time trying to trace the couple, for I did not want to admit defeat and have to come to you to beg for your forgiveness. But they hid their whereabouts well. By the time I admitted to myself that I should bring the matter to your knowledge, you had already left for Ramsgate and then Hertfordshire."

Darcy's mind was in turmoil. So Jeanne and Nicolas knew about the garnet cross and its significance before they had possession of the sketch and asked Pierre to copy it. Jeanne might not be Miss Bingley, but someone who hailed from France. The couple could have known the Darcys well, for they knew about their family jeweller, Harveys. Who could they be?

"What else can you tell me about them?"

"They are not married but I saw that they were enamoured of each other. But the strange thing was that Nicolas seemed rather obedient to Jeanne. He looked to her for confirmation and approval many times during our conversation. I surmise that Jeanne is the clever one and the intelligence behind the whole affair."

"Affair…Jeanne… France…" Darcy murmured and exclaimed suddenly, "The Affair of the Diamond! They are using the swindler's name: Jeanne de Saint-Rémy de Valois who hoodwinked Marie Antoinette and the Cardinal of the diamond necklace and caused a scandal in the French royalty. Nicolas…but the only person with a similar name was the prostitute involved in the fraud. She was called Nicole, not Nicolas, and she was a woman ..."

Fleming nodded vigorously. "Why did I not think of it earlier? I had the distinct impression that despite the moustache, Nicolas looked rather too womanly. That was why it was odd that the man allowed Jeanne to dominate him. Could Nicolas be merely disguised as a woman?"

That meant that Nicolas could be Miss Bingley and she was associated with another woman who had conceived the whole affair. Who could that be? Darcy did not like the growing mystery.

***

Although Darcy seemed to have solved the puzzle of how Miss Bingley might have obtained a sketch of the garnet cross, he could not rid himself of the ominous feeling regarding her accomplice. He sent an express to Charles about the matter, hoping that he could perhaps talk to his sister's best friends once more.

Next morning, Darcy was happy to welcome his sister back to London.

"Oh my dear! What happened to you?" Georgiana exclaimed, forgetting the proper greeting when seeing her brother in bandages in the parlour.

He looked at his sister, gauging whether he should tell her about Wickham. She looked pale and had dark shadows under her eyes. Perhaps she had not overcome her disappointment yet. His aunt had told him not to treat her as a delicate flower and trust her to learn and mature after this ordeal. But he had no heart to burden her at the moment. After all, she was merely sixteen years of age. So he said, "I was robbed in Hertfordshire. But all is well. The bandages will be taken off tomorrow."

"How can people be so vicious? Was it not enough that they robbed you of your possessions? Why did they have to hurt you?" Tears pooled at her eyes.

He pulled her near and embraced her. "I am well, truly. Unfortunately, there are always people in the world who choose a wrong path through life."

"Like Mrs. Younge and Mr. Wickham," she whispered.

He raised her head and said with concern, "You should not think about the two blackguards. You look tired. Did you not sleep well?"

She lowered her head and said, "I have nightmares, from time to time."

"What are they about?"

"They are really quite silly ... You should not worry about me. I shall be well again soon."

"Georgiana, look at me."

She raised her head reluctantly and fixed her gaze on anywhere but her brother's eyes.

"Look at me, please," he urged softly.

She glanced at him tentatively.

"Tell me about the dreams. It may help you relieve the anxiety if you talk about them."

She sighed and commenced slowly. "It always begins in the same manner, with a woman giving me a present. Sometimes it is a book. Sometimes it is a dress. At other times, it is a plateful of delicious fruit. Then when I read the book or wear the dress, I feel a sense of elation for a few minutes, as though I want to play and sing for the whole world. I laugh and dance ... But then, not long afterwards, I feel a tightening in my chest. I collapse on the floor. My whole body feels insensate and then cold. When I struggle to speak or move, a heavy weight comes upon me and I can do nothing. I scream for you but you are never there. I call out to Papa and he is not there either. It always ends with…George…Mr. Wickham…looking at me, with a smile, before blackness encloses me. Fitzwilliam, the dreams frighten me. Sometimes I think that one day I will not wake from the dream. But then when I do wake and realize it is only a nightmare, I feel ridiculous. I feel so childish still."

"Sshh. It is just a dream." He embraced his tearful sister again and let her cry. "It will go away soon. We will concentrate our powers on driving it away, together. Tell me, who is the woman in the dream?"

"I cannot see her face."

"How does she dress?"

"I am not sure."

"And where are you?"

Georgiana turned her head and thought for a long while. "I do not concentrate on where I am in the dream. But it does look rather … foreign to me."

"As in the exotic Orient?"

"No, I think…perhaps…Greek….Yes, I think I am inside a temple…a Greek temple."

Darcy frowned. Why would Georgiana dream about being…poisoned…by Wickham…in a Greek temple?

"Have you been reading Greek mythologies lately?"

She shook her head. "No, I have been reading Shakespeare most of the time."

Seeing that she was trying hard to consider the Greek connection, he said, "You are tired from the journey. Take a rest now. Miss Elizabeth and her family will be arriving in the afternoon."

"Oh yes, would you tell me about your engagement?"

"I shall do that after you have taken your rest," he said.

"Do you think Miss Bennet will like me?" she asked timidly. "I have made so many mistakes in the past year. I am sure no one would want to be a friend of such a silly girl."

"You are not silly, my dear," he argued. "You are just too innocent about the world. Elizabeth will like you. She is the most compassionate and caring sister."

"I truly hope she will like me. Please do not send me away after you marry, if she does not like me. I shall try my best to behave and keep out of her way."

"Where do you get such an idea? Pemberley is your home as well as mine. You will always be welcome there."

Georgiana lowered her head again. "I overheard Miss Bingley once. She said she did not want me around when she married you. That was why I accepted Geor..." Then she halted in mid-sentence.

Darcy held back his irritation. The horrid Miss Bingley again! "You know now she was talking nonsense. I am not marrying her, after all, and Miss Elizabeth Bennet will be my wife. But tell me, Georgie, what were you saying ... the reason for accepting what?"

"You must think me extremely foolish."

"No, my dear. Tell me what was bothering you."

"Miss Bingley spoke as if the...marriage would take place soon, and I was afraid that you would send me away not long afterwards. That was...one of the reasons why I thought it would be good for me to marry George."

"That deceitful Miss Bingley!"

"I was relieved, when I received your letter, to learn that you are not marrying her."

"Elizabeth is nothing like Miss Bingley. She treats the servants and her father's tenants fondly. She will like you and you are always welcome at Pemberley."

"I am much relieved."

"You will discover for yourself soon. Now go and rest well before their arrival."

With that, Georgiana retired to her bed chambers while Darcy contemplated her strange dream.

## Chapter Thirteen

When the Bennet sisters arrived with Mrs. Gardiner and Lady Susan, Darcy was happy to see that Elizabeth greeted Georgiana warmly.

"I do wish that you would stop looking at your betrothed with those puppy eyes," Lady Susan's voice drew his attention away from his two favourite ladies. "Do you not wish to know how much of your money your betrothed has wasted this morning?"

"Good afternoon to you, Susan," he said formally. "I trust that means you all had a good shopping trip this morning?"

"I did not enjoy the shopping at all," she said with a frown.

"Why was that?" he pondered. "Ah, the Bennet sisters did not allow you to tell them what to do."

"Elizabeth has very decided opinions of her own, for someone that young. I am sorry for you, my dear cousin. Your married life will be doomed. You shall find yourself running around to fulfil her instructions. And what are your rewards? Her impertinence?" Lady Susan said with a wicked smile.

"That is very unkind of you, cousin, to predict that my future is doomed. Did they not even allow you or I to pay for a ribbon?" he asked.

"Obstinate girls! If your Elizabeth was not there, I was sure I could have spent an inordinate amount of your money on Miss Jane and Miss Mary. They are too nice to refuse the gifts. But the future Mrs. Darcy would not have it. She said you and I have helped her family in many ways. There was no need for us to pay for their bonnets, stockings or ribbons. And they already had the appropriate dress for the ball," Susan snorted. "As if I would believe any of that."

"Yes, Elizabeth is no fortune hunter. But I am sure you will soon fathom how to get your own way."

"Of course! I took notice of the most expensive fabric each of them had set their eyes on and talked to Madam Durand afterwards. Each of them will have the most exquisite evening gown in time for the ball. And I have placed them all on your account."

"I should talk to the Durands. They should not allow anyone but the Darcys to spend from our family account."

Lady Susan laughed. "Yes, tell Madam Durand I am the imposing poor relative."

"The money is one thing. But how do you expect me to persuade Elizabeth to wear this gown?"

"You have to beg on your knees then," she said. "Honestly, Fitzwilliam, I am very happy for you. Elizabeth is honest, clever, decisive and most importantly, caring. You cannot find a better woman who has the patience to take on your shy sister, your broody self and your whole herd of spoilt children. I should have saved my match-making effort these past five years. Uncle Darcy truly found a good wife for you."

"Yes, I know I am a lucky man. But I have already been forced to beg, too, before I persuaded her to have me."

"Indeed, why have I not heard about this before? Did the younger Miss Bennets and Mrs. Hurst fail to see your begging too?"

Darcy shook his head. "I will not feed you with more gossip. You just need to know you are hosting the engagement ball for us."

"Well, I have my way of digging up gossip, if I want to. I will leave you in peace for the present. Now, where have you sent my dear brother to? I heard young Charles and he were bound for Dover."

"Yes, I expect to hear from them tonight, if they have any news."

"That Caroline Bingley is a wretch. I hope Charles and Richard will arrive in time for the ball. Otherwise Miss Jane will be quite lost. You do know that your new mother-in-law will be coming back for the engagement ball?"

"Mr. Bennet said he would write to his wife, asking Miss Catherine and her to attend the ball and stay in London for a few days," he said.

"I have heard that Mrs. Bennet is something of a character. I shall enjoy seeing how you cope with her," Lady Susan said.

"I shall try my best, for Elizabeth's and her father's sake. Mrs. Bennet may seem silly but all her concerns are for the welfare of her daughters. She is a loving mother, at least more loving than Lady Catherine."

"Ah, how can we forget our great dame? But society will still laugh at your decision."

"I do not care for the opinion of society."

"You will have to prepare Elizabeth for the possible snubs. But I think she has considered it well before agreeing to marry you. See, she has even made Georgiana smile! That is the first time for several months."

"William, may I show the guests the music room?" Georgiana asked her brother eagerly.

"Of course, if I am invited to hear the rendition as well."

"I am going to persuade Georgiana to abandon her sad and lukewarm Médée for the great love story of Die Zauberflöte." Elizabeth said.

"I admit Médée is a sad story," Georgiana argued, "but I do not find it lukewarm at all. The atmosphere of the opera suits my mood, but I am eager to play Mozart's Magic Flute too."

"I have read that the opera was met with some indifference when it was first performed, and is hardly staged at all these days," Elizabeth continued. "And with Médée killing her two children, I shudder at the plot."

As Darcy listened to the conversation, he was astounded how Elizabeth could draw out the normally silent Georgiana. Suddenly something came into his mind and he asked his sister, "Georgiana, was Médée not based on Greek mythology?"

Georgiana looked at her brother blankly for a few seconds and then a smile broke out on her face. "You are right, brother! Miss Elizabeth, you are right, too. Perhaps I should not play Médée ever again. It is too sad and dark. I should have abandoned it after…the person who gave the music sheets to me left."

Darcy listened half-heartedly. In the opera, one of Médée's wedding presents poisoned her rival, Dircé. It fitted with Georgiana's dream. Who had given the sheets to her? Wickham? Why had he done so, an event that seemed to give her nightmares? What was the significance of the story? Perhaps Elizabeth could talk to Georgiana and get her to confide more about what had happened in Ramsgate.

***

Next day, the Darcy siblings and the eldest Bennet sisters were at Lady Susan's townhouse at about noon. It was agreed among the women on the day before that they would try out Lady Susan's pianoforte. Lady Susan would host a family dinner when the remaining three members of the Bennet family arrived from Kent and Hertfordshire. And the women would be called upon to entertain the guests, who would include Susan's parents, Lord and Lady Matlock.

Darcy would have liked to host the dinner at Ashford Hall but Susan persuaded him that the duty would be too strenuous for Georgiana. He agreed reluctantly.

Miss Lydia, who had been excluded from activities the previous day, joined the gathering. She pouted and sulked at the beginning, until the eldest Miss Bennet drew her out by asking to visit her bed chamber.

"Oh, the room was so spacious! It was larger than the parlour in Longbourn. Come, I shall show you the most elegant things I have seen in my life," Miss Lydia exclaimed.

"Lydia, did you forget something?" Miss Bennet reminded her and nodded in the direction of Lady Susan.

"Oh, yes. Lady Susan, may I invite Jane to visit my bed chambers?" Lydia asked. Darcy did not understand why she did not include Elizabeth.

"That is acceptable, Lydia. Georgiana will join you as well," Lady Susan said. "I am sure Elizabeth would like to visit the library instead. Darcy, would you like to take her on the tour?"

Elizabeth looked hesitant, not sure that she should abandon her sisters, or perhaps worried about leaving Georgiana with them. But Darcy had no qualms. He was thankful for Susan's manipulation, to have the time alone with his lovely Elizabeth. Springing up from the chair, as he had had his bandages removed, he bowed to the other ladies before taking Elizabeth away to the library.

"Charming!" Elizabeth exclaimed on seeing the marvellous library with volume after volume of books, both old and new.

"Charming indeed!" Darcy agreed, but his eyes feasted on her. "My love."

She arched her eyes at him for a moment but ignored his compliment. Walking into the room, she strolled towards the far end and started to inspect the books in the last shelves.

He followed her, his eyes devouring her form. "Why did you start browsing from here?"

Her face suddenly turned pink and she smiled in a slightly wicked sort of way which excited him. "There is no reason at all," she said.

"I do not believe you." He stepped closer to her. "I wager there must be some naughty reasons, for you look rather flustered."

Her breath shortened as she looked at his cravat rather than his face. She turned around to touch the spines of a few volumes. Ah, she was panting now! Her bosom was heaving up and down. What a pleasing sight!

He moved to stand behind her and traced his fingers along the books, just a few paces behind.

"What do you fancy?" He lowered his head, breathing in the sweet lavender scent from her earlobe, and whispered in her ear.

"Um," she stammered. "This one looks interesting," she continued and drew out a tiny old book from among the volumes.

"What an accomplished lady I am engaged to." The tip of his tongue caressed the lovely skin on her earlobe. She gasped out loud and he continued to whisper. "Is solving drainage problems high on your reading list?"

"I…want to help…the Jones's, now that they have to use the soil more," she muttered. "You know, with the glass house thing."

"Ah, the Jones's, perhaps I should see if Grandma Jones is telling the truth," he said. "You know, about you having wide hips." His hands moved to smooth over her waist and traced a hot path down her hips.

"Fitzwilliam!" she chastised breathlessly. "Do we not have more…important things to discuss? I am certain Lady Susan gave us some privacy for that reason."

"I am not so sure," he said. One of his hands was caressing her abdomen while the other grabbed hold of her pert behind. She squirmed and leaned her head back to his chest. He continued, "Perhaps she takes pity on me for not being able to properly court you in the past few days because of my injury."

The book slipped from her fingers and dropped loudly to the floor. She held the edge of the shelves tightly as her body moved against the stroking of his hands. "What about…Miss Bingley?"

His breathing became shallow as well. "I would rather not think about her." Her restless quivering heightened his arousal. "Do not move, Elizabeth."

"Why?"

"You will make me ruin my breeches. I shall not be fit to be seen by our family."

"Oh!" she whispered and tried to stop her movement. "But you have to stop…rubbing against me."

"I am trying."

"You need to try harder, for I may not be able to hold still."

Darcy stopped his wayward hands but still held onto her waist. His body embraced her tightly. Taking a few minutes to calm his ardour, he finally managed to suppress his arousal and moved away from her. He turned to grab the edge of the shelves behind, willing his own breath to become normal.

"We should not be alone in the future until we are married," she said.

"Or we should get married before Christmas."

She ignored his complaint and walked to sit on a chaise by the window. "Miss Bingley is still not to be found?"

Darcy shook his head and sat on the chair opposite her. "If Charles and Richard's mission were unsuccessful, they would return to London soon."

"What will Mr. Bingley do then?"

"We will think of something. But enough of her. Susan told me you refused any gift from her."

"Papa has given us some extra spending money."

"You know your refusal is futile to Lady Susan."

"What has her ladyship done?"

"All of you shall receive an exquisite gown in a few days."

"You should stop her! Instruct Madam Durand to stop the work. I do not want others to say that I married you for the money."

He took her hands and said, "I know that my wealth did not tempt you. And the most important people to us know that too. We cannot control what other people think. You should not get upset because of this."

She paused for a few moments, squeezed his hands and replied, in a calmer tone, "I am sorry. I usually do not have a care about what the world thinks, concerning our lack of wealth or connection. Perhaps Jane's worries have affected me. And I am anxious about how Mother and Lydia will behave in front of Lord and Lady Matlock."

"I am sorry to hear about Miss Jane. When Charles returns, I shall try to persuade him to see her. For my immediate relations, besides Lady Catherine, Lady Susan is – do not tell her I said so, though – the most difficult person to please. You will find that my uncle and aunt are like happy sheep compared to my cousin."

Elizabeth laughed at his analogy. "Well, then I need only worry about Mama clashing with Lady Susan."

"I do not think so. Susan always has a soft spot for we Darcys. And I have a soft spot for you and any one dear to you. So she will be good to your mother."

"Hopefully Papa will manage Mama's enthusiasm better."

"Do not underestimate Mrs. Watson. I think she may have already done a lot of good in instructing your mother in the past weeks."

She nodded her head. "But I really do not want expensive gifts from Lady Susan or you. I love you, Fitzwilliam, the man who is devoted to his sister, his tenants and his heritage. I am happy to be with you, even without any expensive things to adorn our lives."

He was touched, extremely moved by her words. This woman could burn his body one minute and melt his heart another. *How lucky am I!* He thought. He lowered his head and kissed her hands with an expression bordering on worship. Then he moved across and sat by her side.

"I am afraid you will have to get used to it. I will always spoil you terribly. Even at this moment, I have a gift for you. It is for our engagement."

She shifted her eyes to one side and shook her head in exasperation. He pulled a velvet box from his pocket and opened it for her to inspect.

"It is beautiful!" she exclaimed on seeing the uniquely designed bracelet constructed from several pieces of petite, deep red rubies. "It matches my garnet cross."

"Yes, I had it especially made by the same jeweller a few days ago."

"And there is an inscription," she murmured as she caressed the design on the front and back. "My…Only…One"

"Yes, Elizabeth, you are my only one. I am grateful to the Lord for allowing me to meet you, court you and love you. I vow to do my best for the rest of my life, to treasure and love you, to take care of you and our family. My only one!" He wrapped his arms around her and held her tight.

"What can I say?" Her eyes glistened with moisture and she ran her hands over his back. "Thank you, my love. Would you help me put it on?"

Darcy's mind was filled with love and his body shook with the need to join with her as one. With a deep breath and intense concentration, he tied the bracelet on her left wrist and then lowered his head to kiss her there, on every inch of the skin adorned with a piece of ruby.

Her hand trembled and she moved her fingers to caress his lips. Raising his head, he gazed at her for a long moment before kissing her. She drew in a loud breath and used the other hand to seize his hair. He could taste a faint hint of sugar, chocolate and fruit on her mouth. It was intoxicating. Nipping once, twice and three times, he devoured the varieties of zest on her lips.

She learned quickly, for she nibbled him in return. Now he was gasping for air as he felt her frantic biting. It was maddening, fast and hot. His heart was racing and his body was perspiring. Unable to stop himself, he pressed her down onto the chaise. As they continued to kiss each other with abandon, his hands moved to cup her breasts, his lower body imprinted on hers. The rubbing and friction were creating a heavenly sensation.

"Darcy and Elizabeth, are you done?" The loud voice of Lady Susan from far away in the corridor was like a pail of ice tipped over him. He tore his mouth from Elizabeth's bosom and sprang up from the chaise. Elizabeth raised and frantically tidied her clothes and hair as he dashed into the darkest end of the library.

"Susan has a frightful sense of timing!" he swore, panting heavily as his hands held onto the shelves tightly for the second time in a day.

Elizabeth hastened to his side and pushed something into his pocket. "I have something for you, too. Repayment for ruining your waistcoat the other day." She then skipped back towards the door.

"Lady Susan, you have a magnificent library," Elizabeth said.

"We are waiting for you to try the pianoforte. And where is that foolish cousin of mine?" Susan said.

"I am putting a book back up on the top shelf," Darcy cried out loud as he pulled the "something" from his pocket. It was her stocking! He groaned and could not stop himself from raising her intimate apparel to his nose. The scent was sexy, racy and spicy. He uttered the words under his breath. "Do not wait for me. I have found something…interesting to read. I shall join you ladies later."

"Do not ruin anything in my library, Darcy!" Susan's knowing voice was enough to cool his blood. When the door was finally closed, he leaned his body against the shelves and closed his eyes. That was a close escape. He had nearly ravished Elizabeth in broad daylight in his cousin's house. And

Elizabeth was not helping at all. She was too co-operative! *I shall conquer this. I must.*

## Chapter Fourteen

Darcy went to Gracechurch Street to pick up the guests the following evening.

"Oh, Mr. Darcy, let me welcome you to the family!" Mrs. Bennet's shrill voice was as charming as before. He bowed to everyone in the room with a forced smile and allowed her to embrace him. She did more than that and kissed him loudly on the cheek. There was no backing away for him this time. Fortunately she released him almost immediately and hastened back to the side of her husband.

Darcy saw Elizabeth trying to suppress a laugh while Mr. Bennet arched his eyebrows towards him with a smile.

"I was quite upset when Mrs. Philips wrote to me about Lizzy's engagement," Mrs. Bennet continued. "Mr. Bennet was so cruel, not letting me be in Meryton, to show Lizzy and you to Lady Lucas and others. But then I got over it almost immediately because once I told the people in the school, every one of them was so impressed. I had a wonderful time telling everyone about my little Lizzy and how her charm has captured one of the most eligible single gentlemen in the kingdom."

Darcy nodded absently. He could see that everyone allowed Mrs. Bennet to continue with her monologue. "I told them how your father met my little Lizzy and left her with the garnet cross. It was so romantic! Actually, why did he leave her with such an expensive piece of jewellery?"

Darcy opened his mouth, wanting to explain the story, when Mr. Bennet shook his head. But his wife did not seem to need an answer. "It did not matter. With the aid of Providence, you came to Meryton as a guest of your friend and *voilà*! You cannot keep away from my dear Lizzy. Oh, talking about *votre ami* – is that how 'your friend' is said in French, my dear Mr. Bennet? – where is Mr. Bingley?"

"He will join us at Lady Susan's," Darcy explained. He had tried to persuade Bingley to come with him to pick up the guests so that he could have some private moments with Miss Bennet; but he was not moved. Bingley was still worried and ashamed of his sister. He had not even wanted to attend tonight's dinner but he had not wished to disappoint Darcy. So he had reluctantly agreed.

"That is wonderful! I hope, Jane, you will sit next to him. Make sure you ask about his welfare. Men like that. But back to you, Mr. Darcy, why did you set the wedding date for St. Valentine's Day?"

"Um…" Darcy was lost for words. *Does she need more time to plan a bigger ceremony?* He looked towards Elizabeth who seemed not to know how the conversation would go either.

"It is too late!" Mrs. Bennet exclaimed. Surprised, he glanced at Elizabeth again. "I tell you, Lizzy, Mrs. Watson has given me many books to read about Derbyshire once she heard that my daughter would be marrying Mr. Darcy. One of the books said that it is very cold up in the North. As a landlord with so many tenants, he has hundreds of people depending on him. Of course, during the winter months and Christmas, it is only right that he stays in Pemberley. That means he is willing to share not just the bounty of the land but the…what should I call it, Mr. Bennet…seriousness?"

"Um…severity?" Mr. Bennet said.

"Yes, that shows Mr. Darcy shares the severity of the land with his tenants. Well, Lizzy, you will not see him for at least two to three months. Is that what you want? What if Miss Bingley comes back and tries to seduce him? Pardon me, I should not have said that. Miss Bingley is not a woman without virtue. I mean, would it not be better for you to get married before Christmas? Then you can help in the festivities. His tenants will respect you for sharing the winter with them, so soon after your marriage! Did I say that right, Mr. Bennet?"

Most of the people in the room had widened their eyes in shock. They did not expect such sensible words to come from Mrs. Bennet. Darcy had not thought it possible for Mrs.

Watson to completely transform Mrs. Bennet's behaviour in just a few short weeks. He looked suspiciously at the Master of Longbourn. He could see that Elizabeth did the same. But Mr. Bennet seemed as astonished as everyone else.

"Yes, I am sure I am right. Now I am certain you are going to marry with a special licence," Mrs. Bennet continued.

"Yes, I have obtained the licence already," Darcy said, before he saw Elizabeth's eyes staring at him.

"Marvellous, I shall arrange the wedding for the eighth day of December. I can help Lizzy choose the wedding clothes during these few days here in London. Magdalene, can you help with arranging the wedding reception when I am back at Kitty's school? You can order everything and have them sent to Hertfordshire. Mr. Darcy, you will not want us to spare any expense?" Darcy's head was whirling with all the information flowing from Mrs. Bennet's mouth. He nodded agreeably without thinking. Elizabeth opened her mouth, but could not edge a word in. "The school will break on the twenty-fifth of November. I shall have two weeks when I go back to Longbourn to complete the arrangements. That is excellent. All is settled. Are the carriages ready? Should we go?"

"But, Mama…" Elizabeth protested.

"Yes, my dear?" Mrs. Bennet replied absently as she stood up.

"December is too soon," Elizabeth said.

"Do you want to marry Mr. Darcy or not?"

"Yes, I do."

"Then there is no time too soon. Do I need to remind you how he was robbed, on Oakham Mount no less, and seriously injured? I learned this from your aunt's letter. What if he met with some highwaymen tonight?"

"Fanny, let Lizzy think about it. I am sure she understands your view," Mr. Bennet intervened.

"Yes, Mr. Bennet." She patted her husband's arm and then walked over to Darcy. "Mr. Darcy, can Jane, Kitty and I take the carriage with you?"

She then lowered her voice. "Let Lizzy take the carriage with her father and my brother and sister. Absence makes the heart grow fonder. She will miss you." With a wink, she took his arm and almost pulled him out of the sitting room.

"Perhaps we should wait for Mr. Bennet," Darcy said, hesitating at the landing.

Mr. Bennet came and took the other arm of his wife. "Let the young people ride together, my dear. I want to have a word with you."

"But I have so little time to talk to Mr. Darcy. He must tell me all about his family; otherwise I shall disgrace myself during the dinner. Oh, please excuse my manner. I am just so nervous about tonight. I could not stop myself from babbling. I promise I shall stay silent throughout the dinner." She let go of Mr. Darcy's arm. On seeing her daughters, she went to hug Elizabeth. "Sorry, my dear. I did not want to go on and go on just now. But I am very nervous. What if I say something silly and Lord and Lady Matlock persuade your betrothed to abandon you? I had asked Mrs. Watson to teach me how to talk to the lordship and his family. She reassured me they are nice people. Kitty spent the whole journey helping me to rehearse when we travelled back from Kent. I did not want to intervene with your wedding date. My dear Lizzy, please forgive me. But I am just so nervous. You should marry whenever you want."

"Oh, Mama!" Elizabeth hugged her in return. She felt guilty for the situation her mother was in. "Mr. Darcy told me Lord and Lady Matlock are very pleasant people. You know how Sir William Lucas is."

"Yes, Mrs. Bennet," Darcy added. "His lordship likes to say the word 'marvellous' all the time."

"Just like Sir William says 'capital' all the time." Elizabeth continued to run her hands over Mrs. Bennet's back. "You are a wonderful mother. We all love you, including Mr. Darcy. And you are right about the wedding date. I do not want any highwaymen to kidnap my betrothed away before I can preside over his magnificent Pemberley."

"Ooh! My dear!" Mrs. Bennet expressed her happiness volubly and then kissed Elizabeth soundly twice on the cheeks. "I knew there was a reason you were so clever. I really want you to settle down as soon as possible. You know, conceiving an heir takes time. If you are like me, it may take you years and many daughters before you have a son, you may as well start making babies sooner."

The eloquent looks she sent between Elizabeth and Darcy made the two of them blush bright red. "I am content and calm now. Mr. Bennet, yes, you are right. I shall ride with you." And after taking her husband's arm for a second, she turned back and embraced Elizabeth and Darcy separately one more time. "I promise I shall not go on and on tonight. I promise I shall not say one word too many." She walked to her husband. "That is what Mrs. Watson taught me. Repeat an important saying a few times every day and I shall be guided by it."

When Darcy finally settled in the carriage with the three Bennet sisters, he breathed out a sigh of relief.

"I do not think Mrs. Watson is a good influence on Mama," Elizabeth said.

"But Mrs. Watson is really good to Mama," Kitty argued.

"They spend a lot of time together?" Jane asked.

"Yes, Mother told me that each day when I am in classes, Mrs. Watson would talk to her about all the important people in society whom she may one day meet. They would read together about the different places she may travel to, such as Derbyshire, Kent and even Italy. She said that all the great mothers in the world take an interest in their children, married or single. Since Lydia and I like the officers," Kitty stopped and darted an embarrassing glance at Darcy, "Lydia may live overseas and Mother may visit her one day. It is good to learn more now. She also taught Mother how to balance the household accounts, and encouraged her to save money for our future use."

"It seems Mother has been doing a lot," Elizabeth murmured and looked at Darcy with a questioning frown. "I thought she was supposed merely to accompany you."

"Most of the day I am in a classroom with other girls. It is good that Mrs. Watson keeps Mother's company. She told her how she had risen from a poor vicar's daughter, to a companion of the great duchess to having her own school. Mrs. Watson told her she could achieve all the good things that she wants if she puts her mind to it. Mama told me she is less worried about us being thrown out into the hedgerows now.

And you will marry well soon. She is sure you will help us. And she thinks she can help Papa with saving money now. Mother said she wanted all the good things for her daughters. Not just being wealthy, but to be loved by their husbands and to have plenty of happy children, daughters or sons. Now that I spend more time with Mama alone, I know that she does not favour Lydia over me. I believe she loves all of us."

Elizabeth touched her sister's hands and gave her a squeeze. "You have grown up a lot. I am sorry I had doubts about Mama's changes."

"And did you enjoy school?" Mr. Darcy asked. He was happy that Mrs. Watson had started to influence Mrs. Bennet. The Mistress of Longbourn might not stop her babbling, but she was learning the correct way to take care of her daughters.

"It was difficult at first. There are so many rules to follow and so many things to do. I feel tired and scared that I would not do well. Some of the girls are very..."

"You do not get on well with some of them?" Jane asked softly.

"Everyone seems to be friendly with someone and does not need a new friend. But I get on better with a few now. And I like the teachers. They praise my drawings. I am doing one of Papa." She threw her hands to her mouth. "It is a surprise. You will not tell?"

"Our lips are sealed," Elizabeth said.

The ladies spent the rest of the journey from Cheapside to Mayfair in comfortable conversation. Darcy was content to listen to Elizabeth's caring and teasing banter with her sisters.

His gaze was uncontrollable, constantly devouring her sparkling fine eyes, her tempting full lips, alluring bosom and supple wide hips. Her evening gown was simple and elegant but he would have liked it better had she not been wearing it. He had a sudden vision of Elizabeth, sitting alone with him in the carriage, stark naked. What a magnificent sight! When his mind went dangerously awry, thinking of what he would do with her on such an occasion, he forced his eyes to look down to the carriage floor.

Ah! Even her shoes looked lovely. When he caught a glimpse of her stockings, his mouth curled up. *I still have to reprimand her about her naughty gift!*

It was lucky that they had finally arrived at Mayfair. He handed down the ladies and found a moment to detain Elizabeth inside. "It was remiss of me. I forgot to thank you for your delightful…stockings," he whispered.

Her eyes widened for a second before a twinkle appeared. "Did I say that they were my stockings?"

He was taken aback by this revelation. After a moment of inaction, he seized hold of her waist and demanded, "Whose are they, then?"

With a teasing smile, she said, "Perhaps they are Mama's …"

He should have known that she would fool him when she had a chance. How he wanted to sweep her up in his arms and get her alone to exact his revenge.

"Did the Darcy carriage manage to lose two passengers?" Lady Susan's interruption was unwelcome. He released his betrothed and bowed to his cousin politely.

Susan gave him a "tsk" "tsk" before walking away with Elizabeth arm-in-arm. All the guests except his uncle and aunt were present.

"Mary, Lydia, you look marvellous!" Mrs. Bennet exclaimed and hugged her daughters. "I miss you both."

"I miss you too, Mama!" Lydia returned the embrace. "Do you think I could rival Jane's beauty now?"

"Well, my dear," Mrs. Bennet said, "Each of you is special and handsome in a different way. I shall not be comparing you anymore, or Mrs. Watson will think me unfair to my daughters. Look at Mary here, she looks positively elegant."

"Thank you, Mama," Mary replied with tearful eyes. "I am glad you like this gown. I was unsure of the neckline. And I miss you too."

"No, the gown suits you. But you look happier…what is the word…more certain of yourself. I must thank you too, Lady Susan, for inviting my daughters to stay with you. We are so blessed."

"You are welcome, Mrs. Bennet." Susan replied. "If my brother and cousin had listened to my advice as your daughters do, I could have married them off years ago."

"Oh, but Mr. Darcy is destined for my Lizzy. I am glad he did not listen to you."

Darcy wished to hug Mrs. Bennet. Finally here was someone sensible enough to defend him from Susan's matchmaking. Elizabeth's face had a lovely shade of pink. He could see that she was proud of her mother and siblings. She said thank you to him silently and then moved to join her father, who surprisingly had sought out Mr. Bingley.

"Fitzwilliam, Bingley was telling me about the bustling town of Gillingham on the way to the south. Do you think it would be a good market for our winter crops?" Mr. Bennet asked.

Darcy was thankful he had not mentioned Dover in front of Bingley. He murmured a reply. Miss Bennet also came to join them at this moment. The normally quiet lady greeted Bingley first.

"Mr. Bingley, it is good to see you again. I can see that all that travelling has tired you out a bit," she commented tenderly.

"Um, yes, Miss Bennet," Bingley stammered. "I do not sleep well in strange beds."

"I always find it calming to have a sachet of dry flowers under my pillow," she nodded. "Then no matter where you sleep, you are reminded of home and the people you love."

"Oh, that is a… a wonderful idea," his stuttering continued.

"I like the smell of pansy flowers," Jane persisted. "What is your favourite flower?"

"Um, pansy is great. Yes, I like pansies too." Bingley's tongue-tied conversation was a torture to behold.

"If you do not think me too interfering," Miss Bennet continued with a blush, "I could talk to Mrs. Fossett, your housekeeper in Netherfield, and ask her to prepare some pansy sachets for you."

"No…I mean, you are not interfering. This is very kind of you. Yes, I would love to have some of your…I mean…my favourite scent with me. Lord knows where I must travel to next."

With Miss Jane finally managing to draw Bingley out, Darcy sighed with contentment. Not long afterwards, Lord and Lady Matlock arrived and dinner was served. Susan took pity on him and let his beloved sit next to him.

"Marvellous, Fitzwilliam, Georgiana and you will have a great family in the future," Lord Matlock said.

"Papa, are we not a marvellous family to him now?" Lady Susan asked.

"My fault! My dear Susan," his lordship exclaimed, "The Darcys have a marvellous set of relations now and will have an additional excellent set when he marries."

"I do not think so, father," Colonel Fitzwilliam said. "Susan has caused rather a lot of pain to Darcy throughout his life."

"Nonsense," Lady Matlock refuted. "Susan looks out for Fitzwilliam and Georgiana, in her unique manner, since she is so much older."

"Mother!" Susan protested. "I am not that old. If Lord Barrymore did not possess such an old title and wealth, I think I would leave him this instant and charm young Charles to run away with me."

Darcy and Bingley both choked on their wine on hearing Lady Susan's outrageous claim. But the pleasant company of Miss Bennet had soothed Bingley's wary soul. He replied decidedly more like his old self. "Please take no offence, Lady Susan, but whatever your age, I still prefer fair to dark haired beauty." His eyes settled on Miss Bennet's mane of shimmering yellow hair.

"Marvellous!" Lord Matlock laughed out loud. "Well said, Bingley."

The joyful dinner was suddenly interrupted by loud voices. "Where is my brother? I demand to see Lord Matlock this instant!"

"What a marvellous surprise," Lord Matlock said to his sister.

"Who would have served beef with fish together? What wine can your guests settle on?" Lady Catherine commented on entering the room.

"Aunt Catherine," Lady Susan's lips tightened. "As father said, what a surprise. Should Father and you retreat to the study to discuss the urgent matter that brings you here?"

"You!" Lady Catherine's eyes flashed on seeing Elizabeth at the table. "What is this shameless hussy doing here?"

Several voices, including Mr. and Mrs. Bennet and Darcy's were raised in protest at such an outburst. But the loudest was Susan's. "If you cannot respect my guests, I demand you leave at once."

"Is that your attitude towards your older relation?" Lady Catherine replied. "Andrew, I told you before, you should have sent her to the seminary in Kent. They are stricter there. As for your so-called guest, she is not fit to be present in polite society. She assaulted my pastor! I have talked to my magistrate and will have her arrested soon!"

This piece of intelligence made a few people in the room gasp. "You meddling old..." Susan swore. "It was not Elizabeth who injured your *lackey*."

"Mind your language! Andrew, you have let your daughter run wild for too long. Rein her in. And Mr. Collins told me himself. My man called me back to Kent before I could visit you to tell you about this shameful business of George Darcy promising his son to some unknown woman. When I returned to Rosings, I found Mr. Collins seriously ill. He was injured during his visit to Longbourn. In his high fever, he was muttering about Darcy and this Elizabeth Bennet, how she tied him up, used the whip on him and did all sorts of foul things with his body for many hours."

## Chapter Fifteen

After such a detailed account of that horrid night, Mrs. Bennet swooned, Bingley broke his wine glass and the younger women gaped in disbelief. Elizabeth turned to Darcy and he held her hand with a squeeze.

"Desist, Catherine!" Lord Matlock's usual jolly countenance turned grey. "Not one more word here. We will discuss this in the study."

"There is not much to discuss with this harlot. I shall inform the chief magistrate in London to have her arrested." She took the seat vacated by Mrs. Bennet, who had been helped to rest in a guest chamber by the younger Bennet sisters. Mr. Bennet and Georgiana, who was always fearful of her aunt, had also retreated with them.

Darcy rose. With hands on the table, he told his aunt squarely, "The night the incident occurred, Mr. Collins did not stay in Longbourn. Miss Elizabeth could not have hurt him. There is a whole household of people who can assure you of that."

Lady Catherine sneered at him. "They would only be the words of the family of this brazen woman against Mr. Collins's. Of course they would protect this harlot. I have faith in my clergyman's integrity. Your mental capability is dulled by this woman's arts and allurements and your eyes are blinded by your desire."

"You are absolutely wrong, Lady Catherine!" Bingley also rose up tensely. "Mr. Collins was staying in my estate, Netherfield, when the incident happened. I will not allow you to tarnish Miss Elizabeth and her family."

"Who is this person?" Lady Catherine looked him up and down for a second. "You must be Bingley, my nephew's friend in trade. And what are you? A mere carriage maker's son who bought an estate and pretends to be a gentleman? You are deluding yourself if you think you will be accepted by the first circles of society. I have demanded that my nephew, Darcy, distance himself from you for years. And now see what has happened? You have invited my nephew to this far-flung country where savages live. Did you work with this Elizabeth Bennet to ensnare my nephew? Or did Fitzwilliam pay you to say this, in order to cover the hussy's transgression? There is no use twisting the truth of the matter. My magistrate will not listen to anyone but me. He has already agreed to contact the magistrate in Hertfordshire to arrest this ... this predator. Now that I know she is in London, it will hasten her detention when I speak to Bow Street tomorrow."

Elizabeth's face turned pale. Darcy sat down and held her hand tightly again. Bingley was struck silent by the sheer intolerance of the enraged elderly woman.

Lord Matlock rose up this time. "You will do no such thing. I am sure the incident was as Darcy has said. I shall not allow the name of this marvellous young lady to be associated with such an outrageous scandal ... She is to be Mrs. Darcy soon. Susan, ask your man to prepare my carriage. I shall take Catherine with me to my townhouse. Tomorrow, I shall go to Kent with her to interrogate this Mr. Collins and stop this ridiculous business with the magistrate."

Lady Catherine protested. "You may be the head of the family. But I am Sir Lewis de Bourgh's widow. I have my own influence in the crown as well. And I shall not be removed to your house. I prefer to stay close to this trollop, in case Darcy hides her away."

Elizabeth retorted. "I do not think I require a companion, your ladyship, especially one so full of contempt."

"See what you are getting yourself into, Darcy? She has no respect for your relatives, rank or authority. She has no remorse for what she has done to Mr. Collins. Perhaps she intended to injure my pastor in order to cut the entail which will reduce her sisters to poverty one day."

"I have had enough of your false accusations!" Darcy rose up once again and walked to Lady Catherine's side. "Lady Catherine, I shall escort you out myself. And I shall have my lawyer prepare legal action against you for slander tomorrow."

"I am not afraid of you and I am not to be moved!" the ladyship cried.

Darcy nodded to his cousin. Colonel Fitzwilliam nodded in return and sprang to Lady Catherine's other side. The two men gave the ladyship a deep bow before each taking her arms and raising her bodily from the chair.

"Put me down this instant!" she demanded. "I am not to be manhandled! Andrew, where did you bring up your son? He is acting like a savage! Did someone knock the senses out of all of you? Did this siren place a spell on all you men? I shall petition to the Prince Regent, for how could you…"

Lady Catherine's torrent of abuse continued to ring in Darcy's ears. Lord and Lady Matlock followed them out to the stable yard, which had been almost deserted save for his Lordship's men. Darcy had to congratulate Lady Susan on being clever enough to prevent any servants being about, in order to minimise gossip, for it took the three men several minutes before they could "settle" her ladyship into the carriage.

"Should I come with you, Sir?" Darcy asked.

Lord Matlock shook his head. "Richard and I can restrain her."

"Are you to be part of this scheme of battery, brother? They are hurting me. Richard, Fitzwilliam, you will be sorry for how you treated me today…"

The usually genteel Lady Matlock took out her handkerchief and stuffed it into Lady Catherine's mouth.

"You ... um ... oh ... um …" Lady Catherine continued to argue under the gag.

"Sorry, Andrew, your sister's shouting is giving me a headache," Lady Matlock said.

"Marvellously done, my dear," her husband replied. "Nephew, you take care of the Bennets. They have suffered too much abuse tonight. Do send my apology to them. I am sorry your engagement dinner is ruined. But let Miss Elizabeth know that Lady Matlock and I welcome her into the family. She is a marvellous woman. It is a blessing that your late father secured this union for you. I shall sort out Catherine before the engagement ball. Now, let me get my sister back to the townhouse. Darcy, you ask Susan to make sure Lady Catherine's servants are well behaved and send the doctor to Matlock House. My sister needs to be sedated."

Darcy bowed to his relatives as they left and said, "Thank you, Lady and Lord Matlock and Richard."

"And you would do well to keep Miss Elizabeth close to you, Darcy, in case Lady Catherine's fool of a magistrate tries to take matters into his own hands. I shall come back to your house after I have helped Father settle down her ladyship," Colonel Fitzwilliam added.

"You are right, Richard." Darcy replied. "I shall persuade her to stay with me or Susan for a few days until the matter is resolved."

After Darcy saw off the carriage, he returned to the house and requested the services of the family doctor for Matlock House. Then he returned to the dining room, to find that everyone had moved to the sitting room, where the joyful atmosphere seemed to have returned.

Bingley greeted him first. Although he still looked grave, his countenance had a touch of optimism and steel in it. "Darcy, I have told Miss Bennet and her family a brief version of what happened that night and apologised for the abuse they received because of my sister. I am sorry this regretful mess left behind by Caroline has caused the disagreement between Lord Matlock, yourself and Lady Catherine. But as we are to become a family soon, we shall have to bear what we can from our pitiful relations."

"Are we?" Darcy repeated and then saw the blush on Miss Bennet's face.

"Mr. Bingley and my sister are engaged," Elizabeth said with a smile.

"Congratulations!" Darcy shook Bingley's hands and raised Miss Bennet's hand to bestow a kiss. "But that is quick work, Charles."

"Yes, definitely the fastest declaration and acceptance I have witnessed," Mr. Gardiner added.

"I am sorry to have missed that interesting episode," Darcy said.

"I shall tell you all later on," Elizabeth said.

"Yes, we need some cheerful news tonight, after Lady Catherine's ghastly interruption," Lady Susan said.

"Should I go and ask Mr. Bennet's permission now?" Bingley asked Miss Bennet.

"Perhaps after Father comes back downstairs," she replied.

"Susan, did your men have a word with Lady Catherine's servants?" Darcy asked.

"All is taken care of. They would not dare to breathe a word."

"Mr. and Mrs. Gardiner, may I request a private meeting with Miss Elizabeth for a moment?" Darcy said. When his request had been granted, he asked Susan for permission to use her library and took his betrothed there.

Once inside the library, Darcy embraced her. She laid her head on his shoulder and drew in a deep breath.

"My dear, how are you feeling?" Darcy asked with concern.

"I am well."

He hugged her silently for a few more minutes before taking her to sit down on the settee. "And your mother? How is she?"

"Mary sent word down that Mother has woken up but is resting. Lady Susan is very kind. She has asked Papa and Mama to stay here for the night."

"That is excellent news. I do not want her over-excited after such shocking events. And can I beg Miss Bennet and you to do the same and stay here?"

"I am well. I do not want to impose on Lady Susan with our whole family."

"As Bingley said, we are to be family soon. Susan will not find it imposing. She loves to be busy and entertain. Since Lord Barrymore is away in Ireland for some months, I think she secretly loves having much to do." Wishing to lighten the discussion, he added, "Especially if that means I owe her a good turn for which she can exact repayment in future."

"I do not wish Aunt and Uncle Gardiner to feel that we are abandoning them, all because of a superior social connection."

"Nonsense, your aunt and uncle are the most sensible people. I think they would understand. And there is a reason I want you to stay here."

"Why is that?"

"I am afraid Lady Catherine's magistrate may stir things up, once he hears the news that you are in London. Nevan House is better guarded," he added gravely.

Elizabeth's lips trembled on hearing this. She had been very brave the whole time during Lady Catherine's abuse but suddenly Darcy's quiet warning about the magistrate seemed to finish her off. Tears welled in her eyes and she stuttered the words out, "Could he…could he…really take me away on the basis of such…erroneous accounts from Mr. Collins?"

He embraced her once again, letting her sob out her worries. "No, I would not let anyone take you away. I shall always protect you and take good care of you for the rest of our lives."

"Thank you, Fitzwilliam," she said into his chest. "I do not know what I would do without you."

"I love you, Elizabeth." He cradled her face in his hands and wiped away the tears with his fingers. Then, lowering his mouth, he kissed her shivering lips tenderly, trying to give her warmth and strength. A few moments later, when he released her, she looked calmer and content. "Will you stay here, my dear?

She nodded and rested her head on his shoulder again.

***

Later that night, Darcy was nursing a glass of port with Bingley and Colonel Fitzwilliam.

"I am sorry about causing trouble between your father and your aunt," Bingley said to Richard.

"Stop apologising! If she were not Father's sister, I would have told her to cease giving her stupid, interfering advice many years ago."

"I do not understand why Mr. Collins would confuse Miss Elizabeth with my sister," Bingley said with a frown. "His senses must dulled by the fever. I did blame myself for not leaving him with better care. After all, I punched him accidentally and then Caroline injured him further."

"We asked the doctor to see to him before we left. Either he refused the service later on and became feverish and talked nonsense or Lady Catherine is in alliance with him, trying to invent excuses to ensure Darcy does not marry his fair maiden."

"If the latter was the case, I shall make sure the Archbishop knows about Mr. Collins's character," Darcy said bitterly. "Collins will find himself preaching in the Orkney Isles soon and Longbourn would never be passed to him, if I could find a way. I am torn between staying here in London to protect Elizabeth or going with you to Kent to confront this onerous clergyman and the magistrate."

"You stay here," Richard suggested. "Stay close to Miss Elizabeth and help Bingley continue his search for the origin of the trouble. Father and I will send news as soon as possible."

"So this young servant Harold sent a false message to his relative who works for your Aunt Pamela?" Darcy asked. He had not yet discussed in detail with Bingley his futile journey to Dover.

"Apparently. Harold said he would visit another relative in Dover, as he had to drive his mistress there for a visit for a few days. But when we inquired at the inns around the area, and Harold's relatives, none of them had ever seen a party that fitted the description."

"It is a pity you did not receive my express before you left Dover," Darcy said.

"Did you have new intelligence?" Richard sat up straight.

Darcy told them of the meetings with Pierre and Fleming.

"I hope," Bingley said with a trembling voice, "this Fleming fellow is wrong. Surely Caroline cannot be…enamoured with a woman. I have not seen her behaving strangely with other women."

"I am more concerned about the connection to the French," Richard said. "What if this Jeanne is a French spy?"

Bingley took out his handkerchief and wiped the sweat from his forehead. "Caroline may be hanged for treason…"

"Do not think of the worst possible situation yet," Darcy reassured his friend. "Why would a French spy take so much time and effort to induce Miss Bingley to marry me? I may be quite wealthy in the North, but I am not the richest man in the whole of England and I have no connection to the workings of government, save for being Lord Matlock and Lady Catherine's nephew."

"I do not want to exaggerate things," Richard said to his cousin. "But in the matter of war and national intelligence, your wealth and position are already very useful."

"I am still not convinced." Darcy disagreed. "Miss Bingley acted without composure whenever I interrogated her about the inscription on the garnet cross and during her search of Elizabeth's belongings in Netherfield."

"I am not saying Miss Bingley was a spy. I am saying she was used by Jeanne, who seems to have been plotting the whole thing for nearly a year. She either did not prepare Miss Bingley well for the assignment or Miss Bingley was caught off guard with the appearance of the real garnet cross and acted without Jeanne's instruction."

"Please, Richard," Bingley shifted uneasily on his chair. "This spy and assignment talk will give me nightmares!"

"I did wonder how they came to discuss the garnet cross at the inn in the North, in front of Fleming, so many months ago," Darcy conceded.

Richard stopped his train of thought on seeing Bingley's pale complexion. "Yes, let us not jump to conclusions. Perhaps talking about some happier news will be better. How did you come to be engaged so quickly?"

"Yes, Elizabeth did not have time to tell me yet," Darcy added.

"I think I am doing the wrong thing. I should not have become engaged to Miss Bennet." Bingley cradled his head with his hands. "What if Caroline was really involved with a French spy? It may bring shame and trouble to her family and you, Darcy."

"No more of this self-sacrificing talk," Richard said.

"Yes, you have to carry on with your life, no matter what happens with your sister," Darcy added. "I seldom talked about this. But Elizabeth has been very good to me and convinced me to tell her. I was very resentful of Father when he died, for promising my future to someone I did not know and, more importantly, for dying. I was not ready to become master of so many responsibilities and guardian to Georgiana."

"Indeed, you had so much emotion contained within you?" Richard said. "No wonder you have been so grim and solemn for so many years. You did not look any better than Lady Catherine at times!"

Bingley finally smiled at Richard's teasing of Darcy. Darcy punched his cousin on the shoulder and continued, "Remember, you are the head of the Bingley family and landlord, at least for a year, to many tenants. Many people now depend on you."

Bingley drew in a deep breath and said, "Yes, you are right. And now Miss Bennet has entrusted her future in my hands. I cannot disappoint her."

"So tell us," Richard urged. "How did you get yourself shackled so quickly? I did not think it took Father, Darcy and I more than a minute to subdue Lady Catherine. Ah, and for Mother to gag her."

The three men laughed as they remembered Lady Catherine being gagged by Lady Matlock. "Well, I am not quite sure how it happened. One moment I was telling the party about that night when Caroline…The next moment, I was recriminating myself for not being a better brother and Jane came to me and then she embraced me. I was overcome with emotion and I told her I loved her. She said the same and then she said let us face the fire together. I nodded my head and kissed her lips, only lightly, it was so heavenly, and then everyone rushed to interrupt and congratulate us." Bingley scratched his head. "I do not remember if I actually asked her to marry me. Perhaps I can still wriggle out of this?"

"I do not really believe you want to," Darcy said.

"I agree. Darcy will challenge you to a duel, being the only fit male of the Bennet family, for trifling with Miss Bennet in front of her family."

"Well at least neither Jane's father nor younger sisters were witness to my transgression," Bingley smiled embarrassingly.

"Or I shall have to endure Miss Catherine and Miss Lydia's constant teasing for the rest of my life."

"Perhaps more than that," Darcy teased him. "Miss Catherine said she has been mastering her drawing at school. She could have easily captured your first kissing scene on paper and demanded a ransom."

"Darcy, it is not yet Sunday night! How can you be so awful, as if you had nothing to do but jest about my future?"

"Miss Elizabeth is definitely tormenting him with her wit and clever banter," Richard laughed.

"I have an idea." Darcy sat up straight suddenly.

"If it is another jest about my first kiss," Bingley covered his ears. "I do not need to hear it."

"Miss Catherine's drawing skill. What say you if I persuaded Fleming to come here and asked him to tell her what Jeanne and Nicolas look like?" Darcy continued.

"That is an excellent idea," Richard said. "If Miss Catherine can draw a likeness from his description that would be most helpful."

"We will go to visit them early tomorrow," Bingley agreed excitedly.

"If Miss Catherine can only draw cows, you will at least have a good excuse to visit your betrothed," Richard grinned.

"I shall send a servant to check for Fleming's availability first," Darcy said.

"If he is not available, you can always take the Miss Bennets to Pierre Roux at Stoke Newington. It has some nice shops," Richard added. "You can take your dearly beloved away from worry for a day."

"How do you know the area so well?" His cousin asked.

"We foot soldiers have to ramble around the country to work."

"Or you may have a fair maiden hidden away there," Bingley joked.

The three men laughed out loud and continued to chat light-heartedly for some time.

***

The next day, as Fleming was out of town on another assignment, Darcy requested the help of Pierre via his uncle. Miss Catherine was unsure about her drawing ability but her sisters agreed that if the main mission for the day did not work, they would at least enjoy a walk in the market, for the weather was agreeably sunny for a November day.

Miss Mary and Miss Lydia had a dancing lesson and did not want to go. Their mother wished to observe them while they studied. Mr. Bennet preferred to stay in the enormous library.

The party of six, consisting of the three Miss Bennets, the two gentlemen and Lady Susan was divided into two carriages. While Darcy took Miss Catherine and Miss Elizabeth to Pierre's residence, the remaining three went for a stroll around the stalls and enjoyed the light refreshments on offer there.

After hearing descriptions of Nicolas, Miss Catherine was convinced that *he* was Miss Bingley in disguise. So Pierre and she concentrated on sketching Jeanne instead. It took Miss Catherine almost half an hour to complete the drawing. When Darcy took one look at it, his lips tightened and he frowned darkly.

After they settled back in the carriage and were on their way to meet Bingley's party, Elizabeth took his hand and asked with concern, "Do you recognise this Jeanne?"

"She is Mrs. Younge!" Darcy uttered the words with vehemence.

"That horrible governess?"

Miss Catherine seemed to be intimidated by the heavy tension in the carriage. So she leaned closer to the window to watch the scenery instead. Suddenly the horses reared and the carriage shook from side to side. The steady pace of Darcy's carriage had been interrupted by one passing at high speed.

"People always seem to drive recklessly in Stoke Newington," Darcy murmured, remembering the last time his visit to the area had nearly ended with a collision of carriages.

Miss Catherine turned back to Darcy and Elizabeth and said in an agitated state, "The fair-haired man driving that buggy that passed us just now … *He* is Miss Bingley!"

## Chapter Sixteen

Darcy knocked on the roof of the carriage and called out, "Turn the coach around and follow that buggy!"

The carriage lunged from side to side a few more times, stopped and then finally turned in a road large enough to manoeuvre. By then, the buggy had disappeared around a corner.

Darcy's party gave chase to the end of the road but the corner was too narrow for the carriage to turn into. Darcy and one of his menservants jumped down from the carriage and ran after the buggy. There were several narrow lanes meandering towards different parts of the village. When the two men dashed to examine each one, they were surprised to have lost sight of the buggy.

With lips closed tight and an angry scowl, Darcy returned to his carriage. "We have lost sight of her."

Elizabeth looked at him with a sympathetic expression.

"I shall talk to Bingley and send some men to investigate," he murmured.

They met Bingley's party at the market soon afterwards. One of the menservants was sent back to town to bring more men to start a discreet search.

"How was it possible for Caroline to conspire with this Mrs. Younge?" Bingley said in an agitated tone. "I do not recall meeting Georgiana's governess before."

"Yes, I have been thinking about it as well," Darcy said. "Fleming met them in Doncaster early this year, before I even engaged Mrs. Younge's service."

"So they heard about my garnet cross, found the design and imitated it," Elizabeth murmured, all the while holding Darcy's hand to give him support. "Then Miss Bingley showed you the jewel accidentally when Mrs. Younge entered your household. What sort of reference did she have when she applied for the position?"

"It was from one of the distant relatives of Lord Barrymore in town," Lady Susan said angrily. "Mrs. Younge worked as a companion for two ladies slightly younger than Georgiana for two years. Then their mother remarried and they moved to Scotland. Mrs. Younge did not wish to go with them. There had been no incidence of inappropriate behaviour. That was why I was furious about what happened at Ramsgate. I felt responsible."

"What happened at Ramsgate?" Bingley asked.

"Mrs. Younge allowed George Wickham to visit Georgiana without my permission," Darcy glossed over the incident lightly.

Bingley did not ask further. His mind was occupied with the wellbeing of his sister. "I cannot imagine Caroline being happy to stay in one of the less salubrious townhouses in this area."

"But how did Mrs. Younge know about Miss Bingley?" Elizabeth asked. "If you had not met the governess before, Mr. Bingley?"

"We spent the first few months of this year in Scarborough, except..." Bingley thought hard and suddenly cried out loud, "Caroline stayed with the Barrymore sisters at Cusworth Hall for about three weeks. Cusworth is very near Doncaster."

"Are they Lord Barrymore's sisters?" Elizabeth asked.

"No, distant cousins," Darcy said.

"Yes, Mrs. Younge could have been at Cusworth Hall at that time because her former charges were from the same maternal great-great grand parents of the Barrymore sisters," Susan murmured. "Perhaps she accompanied them on the way to Scotland before she returned to town. I shall enquire after her movements at that time."

"But I thought Miss Bingley found the Barrymore sisters 'annoying'. How did she come to visit Cusworth Hall?" Darcy frowned.

"Well she would not forfeit any chance to befriend any of your relatives, no matter how distant," Bingley replied.

The party visited the shops with heavy hearts. Before they were ready to return to town, several men from Darcy's household arrived. The two gentlemen talked to them about their tasks. Equipped with an illustration of Mrs. Younge, disguised as Jeanne, they were dispatched to scout Stoke Newington discreetly.

After the gentlemen returned the ladies back to Lady Susan's townhouse, they went back to Ashford Hall. Darcy's servants reported back soon afterwards. They had located a modest townhouse rented by Jeanne and a man. But it had been deserted prior to the search party's arrival. As the owner was not available, Darcy's servants could not gain access to search inside the house.

A disappointed Bingley declined to have dinner at Darcy's townhouse and returned to Grosvenor Place soon afterwards. Darcy hoped his friend's enthusiasm for the ball in two days' time would not be dampened by this latest incident. After a quiet dinner with Georgiana, Darcy retired to his study. He was determined to think of Miss Bingley and Mrs. Younge no more and contemplated the pleasure of dancing with Elizabeth at the engagement ball.

The next day, Georgiana went to Nevan House to assist with the preparation of the ball. Darcy was forbidden from attending as the hostess foresaw that the ladies would be busy with lace and ribbons. He had instead entrusted a letter for Georgiana to take to Elizabeth.

Darcy blushed when he thought about the love letter he had composed the previous night. Like a lovesick youth, he had gazed with a distant expression for a long time into the fire in his study. His reverie on marital bliss had been interrupted by the arrival of Mr. Bennet.

"My boy, I need a refuge from this non-stop talk of dances, silk and feather," Mr. Bennet said.

"You have come to the right place, Sir," Darcy smiled. "Would you like me to show you the library?"

Mr. Bennet clapped Darcy's shoulder and said, "Definitely! No wonder my Lizzy forgave your arrogant ways so quickly. You are a master of the heart's desire of every Bennet!"

Darcy was not sure if he should be offended or pleased by the elderly gentleman's teasing. He shook his head and led the guest to the library.

Mr. Bennet gasped on seeing the vast and priceless collection. He ignored his future son totally for several minutes. Darcy decided to leave him alone.

"Fitzwilliam, before I forget, you have made my Lizzy quite silly as well. She flew upstairs like a butterfly once she received your letter and did not come downstairs again for nearly three quarters of an hour. She has been blushing, sighing and smiling for no reason at all since then."

"Oh!" Darcy said. His face turned bright red too.

"Now, here is Lizzy's reply." Mr. Bennet drew a letter from his pocket and handed it to Darcy with a wink. "And spare me your blushing and sighing. Off you go!"

Darcy took the letter with two hands and quit the library in haste. He dashed back into his study two steps at a time, astonishing the footman in the corridor. With trembling hands, he tore open the seal. The first page was blank, except for several red ruby lip shapes on it.

He gasped at Elizabeth's bold action. Heat surged in his body as he imagined her branding his body with the same scarlet colour everywhere. He had to close his eyes and draw in deep breaths for a few minutes before continuing. He then raised the paper to his lips while he perused her message on the second page.

*Be warned, Sir, that in future you should not pen such correspondence to any Bennet lady. For my mother is skilled at intercepting our messages and will read them aloud to the entire family.*

Darcy's eyes widened. He was distressed to know that his rather amorous letter might have had such a fate.

*But you have the good fortune of being engaged to a sensible lady like your correspondent. I locked myself in the room to read your letter immediately after I received it from Georgiana.*

He breathed out a sigh of relief and continued to peruse her teasing reply.

*However, I am seriously rethinking my future, for it seems that I am to wed a man of limited means, instead of a gentleman of ten thousand a year.*

*Are all the chairs in your library so broken that you suggest I sit on your lap to read Shakespeare's poems together? Is the cost of a candle so great that you prefer us to waltz in the balcony under moonlight? Am I to be deprived of a lady's maid as you engage in taking off my dresses?*

*That cannot be borne. I demand a lifetime of luxury.*

*I expect you to ruin the linen not just in my chamber, but half a dozen of the rooms as well. I wish for a chaise fit for the King and Queen in the conservatory so you can read the sensual tales of the Orient to me while I feast on the most exotic fruit. I expect you to tear my old gowns in haste so frequently that I will have an excuse for buying new ones more often.*

Darcy's mouth gaped open on reading such counter-offers of marital activity.

*Last but not least, I am not satisfied with just two little Darcys, for how can we test the sturdiness of the carriages if we do not have at least half a dozen children?*

He smiled at the image of their six children, all looking as mischievous and cheerful as their mother, jumping up and down inside the carriages.

*Although I cannot call you loveliest Fitzwilliam, as it is most unbecoming for a gentleman of your stature to be judged as lovely, I must agree that you have fast become my dearest as well.*

*In return for your gesture of gifting me a lock of your curly hair, I send you several imprints of my lips, with the taste of strawberry and chocolate. I am desperate to place them on your strong body to see how you respond.*

*Until tomorrow, my dearest! I shall commit every word of your letter to memory and strive to discuss it with you during our dance.*

*E.B.*

Fortunately Mr. Bennet did not ask him to read the letter in the library. Darcy felt his body burning after reading it. He wished to retire to his bed chamber, hug his pillow and imagine all the delicious little things he wished to do to his teasing Elizabeth. But of course that could not be done. He had a guest in the house and it was the middle of the day. He locked himself in the study, gulped down a glass of port to soothe his heated constitution, and began to read and re-read the letter until he knew each word by heart.

About an hour into his idle day, Darcy was interrupted by a knock on the door. He thought Mr. Bennet was ready for company but an express was brought to his attention instead. Seeing its seal, his mind broke out of its happy daydream.

*Darcy,*

*Mr. Collins is still feverish and talks nonsense. But he did not accuse your lady. All was Lady C's doing. Her little magistrate has been busy and written to his counterpart in Hertfordshire. Father has talked to late uncle's lawyer and found a way to threaten Lady C. Money will stop flowing if she does not desist. She seems to acquiesce for the moment, though reluctantly. An express was sent out by his lapdog to correct the matter in Hertfordshire. Father and I will return. Cannot wait to see your lovesick face at the ball.*

*Your handsome cousin*

Darcy was relieved and yet angry. What a jealous and manipulative old woman Lady Catherine was! At least she did not manage to blacken Elizabeth's good name to the magistrate in London. And he had talked to Magistrate Robinson of Hertfordshire before. Robinson seemed a sensible man who would not act rashly. Darcy suspected the magistrate knew enough about local gossip, judging from their meeting concerning the incident of Wickham's robbery, to know about Miss Bingley's involvement.

Soon afterwards, Mr. Bennet took his leave.

Darcy spent a quiet night with his sister who refused to reveal any of the details about Elizabeth's preparations for the ball. He spent a great deal of time envisioning his betrothed in evening gowns of different colours and styles. But none of these images could replace the gorgeous vision he had conjured up of Elizabeth naked in all her glory.

***

Finally the engagement ball arrived.

Georgiana went over to Lady Susan's townhouse early in the morning. She would not be attending the ball as she was not yet out in society. But her cousin invited her to stay over, to keep Lydia and Kitty's company. The youngest Bennet sisters were not allowed to attend, much to their despair, in accordance with custom. Their parents had promised them a trip to the seaside early the following year to placate them.

About an hour before the ball commenced, Darcy arrived at Nevan House alone.

The servants and the hostess were in a flurry of activity so he was left to his own devices. He was disappointed that he could not have a private moment with Elizabeth before the ball and retreated to the library. After nursing a glass of port and reading a few poems from Wordsworth, he ventured out to see if the ladies were ready.

When he walked near the grand ballroom, he came upon a vision. It was Elizabeth! They were within twenty yards of each other, and so abruptly did she appear before him that he thought a goddess had come down to grace the earth.

His breath caught and his heart stopped beating for a moment. She was wearing a simple yet elegant white silk gown. He blinked several times, not believing what he saw.

Did the dress look as though it was held together by shimmering ribbons adorning her shoulders and waist? Under the bright candles burning in the house, her body seemed to sparkle. He had never seen her wear white before. The colour brought out the pink blush on her skin and accentuated the deep red colour of the rubies on the garnet cross and the bracelet.

Her hair was piled on top of her head in an alluring fashion with some pink rose petals woven into it. Several unruly curls escaped the confines of the pins and framed her face and delicate neck. Darcy itched to roll those mischievous curls with his fingers and pull loose the ribbons to reveal her lush body.

But nothing could compare with her fine eyes which dazzled like diamonds. They widened on encountering his intense gaze.

"Fitzwilliam," she whispered.

"Elizabeth," he murmured hoarsely.

He walked towards her in a haze, slowly breathing in her fragrant scent and devouring the rosy colour of her body. He did not stop until he was inches from her. Her breathing quickened. Her bosom rose up and down in quick pace. With mouth open in a tempting curve, she raised her head to keep eye contact with him.

His muscles felt the closeness of her soft skin, as the air vibrated and transmitted the heat from her body to his.

"You look very handsome, sir," she sighed.

He was lost for words for a second. Instead, lowering his head, slowly, he repeated "Elizabeth," before touching his lips against hers.

She gasped.

He could feel her tremble. Her lips were moist and hot. Her quivering sent a wave of shocks through his body. He did not dare to deepen the kiss nor wrap his arms around her waist, for if he did, he would carry her out into the night and worship her beauty in the most intimate manner until eternity.

He simply continued to brush her lips, in this slow and light manner for some time. When he broke off to catch his breath, he felt he had already united with her, in spirit and mind, as one soul.

He looked at her with devotion. The blush on her face and body was heightened yet again. It almost rivalled the colour of the garnet cross. Unable to help himself, he raised his hand and traced his fingertips along the porcelain smooth skin outlined by the jewel. He swore he could feel the pulse of her blood and the beating of her heart through his skin.

His wits seemed to have deserted him. Once again whispering "My dearest Elizabeth," he lowered his head further to worship the garnet cross which sat upon her cleavage.

She squirmed and moaned in a husky voice.

When his tongue tasted the sweet scent of her body, he was in heaven. Not able to think coherently, he bent down to pick her up in his arms. He wanted to go somewhere and he did not know where. But he walked on and found the stairs leading to the balcony on the second level of the grand ballroom. She seemed so overcome with emotion that she did not protest but rested her head on his shoulder.

Not two steps up the stairs, Darcy encountered a musician carrying a violin who looked at them with wide eyes. That finally woke him from his sensual cloud. With a scowl at the violinist, he slowly walked back down the steps and put Elizabeth down. Once she seemed to have found the use of her legs, he took her hand, placed it on the crook of his arm and led her to the front parlour, where their family would be assembling to greet the guests.

Elizabeth was silent for a few seconds. But once they had turned a corner, she chuckled.

Her infectious laughter spread to him and he grinned.

"What are you smiling at?" She arched her brow and glanced at him.

"Nothing."

"There can be only two reasons for such a display of cheerfulness."

"And are you going to enlighten me, madam?"

"Either you are happy that it was not my father who interrupted your impulsive act or you believe you look handsomer when you smile."

He threw back his head and laughed out loud. "I think the word impulsive better describes your character than mine. But I thank you for admitting that I look handsome."

"Me? Impulsive?" A crease appeared on her forehead. "Never! And I admit to nothing."

He raised her hand and kissed it. They engaged in light-hearted banter all the way to the parlour.

## Chapter Seventeen

Darcy scowled at the Duke of Bedford. Bedford was leaning entirely too close to Elizabeth. The Duke's eyes drifted low all the time, gazing upon her bosom. Bedford might be considered handsome by women but he had mistresses enough to fill Longbourn's dining room.  And why were they laughing together so much?

Finally the music drew to a close. Damn the Duke! He took his time to bring Elizabeth back. Darcy had suffered such torment many times throughout the evening. After Lord Matlock had congratulated Darcy and Elizabeth on their engagement, men flocked to their sides and filled Elizabeth's dance card in no time.

Darcy could only manage to secure her opening, middle and last dances. He had danced with Susan and the other two Bennet sisters and had no humour for other ladies. Elizabeth did persuade him to dance with two sensible sisters of Lord Matlock's friends but he stayed clear of all the "merry" married women who had been governing his time. All evening he had busied himself protecting Elizabeth from the lecherous men with his fearsome stare.

She had danced with Richard and Bingley too. But after that, she seemed to be monopolised by all the notorious dukes and lords in the whole empire. In truth, not all of them were really scoundrels. Some of them were as respected and sensible as he himself. But still, they were not Fitzwilliam Darcy of Pemberley. He paced around angrily at the thought of them, until the Duke and Elizabeth halted before him.

"Darcy, your betrothed is refreshingly charming." The Duke winked.

"Yes," Darcy nodded and then grabbed Elizabeth's hand and put it on his arm.

"Please excuse us," he murmured quickly and then walked as fast as he could away from Bedford, despite the crush of people in the ballroom.

"Fitzwilliam, what is the rush?" Elizabeth murmured.

"Bedford is a notorious rake," he whispered.

"I know, he has many mistresses," she replied in a low voice. "Lady Susan told us the juicy background of every guest last night."

"Good. Then you will not fall for him."

"But he has more land than you."

He stopped immediately and looked at her. On seeing her teasing smile, his pent-up emotions finally disappeared. He led her out of the ballroom and up the stairs into the second level. Once he had found a secluded alcove, he sat down on the window ledge, wrapped his arms around her waist, pulling her down to his lap, and frowned at her again. "You laughed too much with him."

"Well, the Duke is more charming than a certain young man from Derbyshire," she retorted.

"I cannot dance with you the entire evening," he stated, resting his head against her neck. "Of course, I am displeased."

"Did we not talk about what gentlemanly manners should be?" She did not return his embrace.

He remembered her chastising him for being condescending and arrogant towards Mr. Collins some weeks ago. "But this is different." He nuzzled her neck as he uttered the words.

"How?" She seemed to sense his vulnerability and wrapped her arms around his shoulders.

"All the men who danced with you are charming."

"Perhaps more charming than you."

"That is why I am not happy. I do not know how to smile flirtingly or give out frivolous compliments. I do not know how to rattle away. What if you found them more gentlemanly than me? What if they were less proud? I am afraid you will leave me for one of them. Your father warned me that could happen."

She pushed him slightly away and looked at him steadily. "Fitzwilliam, I am not a fickle youth. I have been taught good principles. I take my commitments very seriously. I have promised to be by your side and I shall not withdraw from that promise."

He raised his hand and traced the curve of her jaw with his thumb. "I am fearful, Lizzy. What if I make you unhappy? I was never a cheerful sort of person and I grew up to be rather taciturn. I would hate to turn your amiable and cheerful smiles into misery."

"Society may give more consequence to a man's wealth, his way of dress and his manner of discourse. But I am taught to look for more." She brushed the lapels of his coat as she explained further. "Your manner might need some softening but your judgement, information, and knowledge of the world will benefit me greatly. I admire the prodigious care you have provided for Georgiana, the strong friendship you offered to Mr. Bingley. I am certain you will protect our children and me. I shall have such extraordinary sources of happiness, by being your wife," she declared and touched her lips to his mouth.

Elizabeth's gentle and positive feelings about their future helped eased Darcy's worries. He returned the kiss as solemnly as she had given it. The attachment they felt for each other was remarkable. They pledged their future together, to work and achieve a happy and successful union.

When the music of the last dance began, Darcy led Elizabeth down to the dance floor again. They had eyes for each other only. They moved down the room as one. They swirled around in unison. He felt an aura of admiration, devotion and completeness. He might not be holding her hands every minute of the dance but he felt connected to her with every breath he took.

Finally the music stopped. Guests once again came forward to congratulate the engaged couple. Darcy held her hand throughout the farewell. A small smile adorned his face and he stood proud and tall.

"Oh, Lizzy, you were such a huge success!" Mrs. Bennet exclaimed, when all the guests had left. "Several duchesses said they would invite us for tea after you return from the wedding trip. What a marvellous chance for Mary, Kitty and

Lydia. I am sure every duchess has some single relatives with large fortunes."

"Mrs. Bennet, let us not get ahead of ourselves," her husband said. "I do not intend to let Kitty and Lydia out until they have mastered their studies."

"I know, I know," Mrs. Bennet waved her fan. "I shall talk to Mrs. Watson to increase Kitty's lessons. Then she can learn every thing she needs to learn in no time. I am sure Lady Susan will help prepare my Lydia very well too."

At this moment, Kitty flew down the stairs like a mad woman and cried out, "Papa, Mama, Lydia…"

"What is it?" Mr. Bennet said.

By the time she reached the bottom of the stairs, she was out of breath and panting heavily. "Lydia..."

"Something is wrong," Elizabeth added. "Let me go upstairs to investigate."

Barely two steps up the staircase, another person dashed down. "Brother, Lydia is poisoned!" Georgiana said, rushing towards Darcy.

"Susan, please call the doctor immediately!" Darcy said. He gave Georgiana a hug and led her and Elizabeth up the stairs. Colonel Fitzwilliam followed them while Lady Susan gave instructions to the servant. Mr. Bennet told Jane to take care of her mother before racing up the stairs too.

When everyone arrived at Lydia's chamber, Darcy could smell the rank odour of vomit. He saw that she was lying on her bed, pale and motionless. A maid was putting a compress on her forehead. Elizabeth and Mr. Bennet dashed to her side and took her hands.

"Lydia," Elizabeth called out. "Her hand is very cold!" she said to all.

"What happened?" Darcy asked his sister. "Why did you say she is poisoned?"

Georgiana had started crying when they arrived upstairs. In between sobs, she said, "We were…playing… Piquet for a while. And Lydia said she was bored. She wanted to see the…the ball."

"I was afraid of being caught," Kitty added. She was in tears too. "I did not want to incur Papa's wrath. I tried to stop her. But Lydia was adamant."

"I told them about the secret passage," Georgiana confessed. "I remember Richard showing me once. I took them to the study so that we could peer into the grand ballroom."

"We watched the dancing and laughing," Kitty said. "And we danced for near an hour. It was a lovely ball. I could have been satisfied to watch it the whole night. But soon Lydia was bored again."

"She saw the gifts for Elizabeth and you. They were piled high in the room."

"Lydia started going through them," Kitty raised her voice. "We told her to stop. But she wouldn't listen to me. I should have tried harder. I am her elder sister. Georgiana begged her as well. But Lydia still would not listen."

Georgiana continued, "And one of the boxes fell open. Inside there were some lovely macaroons dipped in orange syrup."

"Lydia popped two into her mouth!" Kitty explained. "I told her we should not touch the presents. They belong to you, Mr. Darcy and Lizzy. But she said the box was opened, Lizzy did not like orange anyway and she was hungry. Then she continued to explore the other boxes for some time. There were a few that were not securely tied. But they were a silver set, a clock or some other decorative items."

"When we were walking along the secret passage back to our chambers, she complained of pain. Not long after we reached her room, she started vomiting. I should have called the doctor earlier."

Georgiana was weeping so hard that Darcy could hardly understand her words. He embraced his sister and let her cry. He turned to ask Kitty. "How long has Miss Lydia continued in this manner?"

"For almost half and hour, on and off," Kitty said.

"Then what happened?" Richard probed.

"She was resting one minute. And then the next minute, she dropped back to the bed, hardly responding to our calls."

"We pushed and...cried for her to wake up," Georgiana said. "But it appeared that she had gone."

"I heard the clock strike midnight. I thought the ball should have finished," Kitty added. "So I rushed down to get Papa."

"When you left," Georgiana continued, "Lydia... opened her eyes suddenly and exclaimed that she was poisoned, exactly as in a novel she had read recently."

At this time, the doctor arrived to examine the patient and asked everyone to leave the room.

"Was there a card that came with the present?" Darcy asked his sister.

Georgiana looked at Kitty and said, "I do not... remember."

Kitty thought for a moment and replied. "I think there perhaps was a note."

"Can you help me retrieve it?" Colonel Fitzwilliam asked. On Kitty's agreement, the two of them went downstairs to the study.

"Who would dare to do such a thing?" Susan paced around angrily. "And in my house no less!"

"I am sorry, Cousin Susan," Georgiana said. "I should not have taken them downstairs."

"Stop blaming yourself, Miss Darcy," Mr. Bennet said for the first time. "If anyone should be blamed, it is I who is at fault. I let Lydia run wild for too long. She does not listen to anyone. We should only think to the future now. But the poison, it must have been intended for your brother and Elizabeth!"

Georgiana's eyes widened and she dissolved in tears anew. "How could anyone be so...wicked or want to harm you, brother?"

Darcy tightened his fists. He would not allow his family to be harmed. He hoped Miss Lydia would recover from this ordeal, or he would not be responsible for his actions when he caught the culprit.

Colonel Fitzwilliam came back upstairs again. He was holding a letter. "It was addressed to you, Darcy."

Darcy's lips had become thin. He tried to take the letter from his cousin but Richard stopped him. "Do not touch it. We do not know if poison has been smeared on it." Darcy's hands dropped back to his sides. He saw that Richard was wearing gloves.

"What does it say?" Mr. Bennet demanded.

*Congratulations, Sir, on reaching an important stage in your life. I wish your betrothed and you all the best you deserve. The flame of life is short. Enjoy it while the heat is still hot.*

*Your equitable friend*

"The letter reveals nothing," Lady Susan said, in frustration.

"Indeed, the culprits would not reveal their intentions," Richard stated. "They wanted Darcy and Elizabeth to partake of the sweets and swallow the poison. But I sense bitterness there."

"We are not sure Lydia is poisoned yet," Mr. Bennet reminded everyone.

"I am afraid Miss Lydia is in fact poisoned," The doctor came out of the sick room and announced.

"Are you certain?" Lady Susan asked.

"I have seen patients with similar symptoms," Doctor Warwick nodded. "And I have examined what she has ... disgorged."

"Will she be in danger?" Darcy queried.

"If the poison does not consist of many different kinds of drug," the doctor said, "the herb combination I gave her has a good chance of helping her through the danger. But I cannot say for sure. It will also depend on her constitution."

"I can never fault Lydia for her hearty constitution," Mr. Bennet declared. Elizabeth went immediately into the chamber to assist Lydia.

"Can you see my wife too? She has taken the news very hard." Mr. Bennet asked.

"Yes, of course."

When the doctor, Mr. Bennet and Kitty had moved away, Darcy turned to his sister, "You have had a difficult night. Do you want a sleeping draft to help you sleep?"

Georgiana shook her head. "I do not want to sleep yet. I want to stay with Lydia, to wait for her to wake up."

"Come, my dear," Lady Susan took her hand. "Lydia has taken some medicine. She may not wake until the morning. And Elizabeth is with her. You can sleep now and guard her then."

"Yes, we will wake you if there is any important news," Darcy added, as Susan led Georgiana away.

"Do you think it can be the work of Mrs. Younge and Miss Bingley?" Colonel Fitzwilliam whispered.

"It is one thing to want money from me, by getting Wickham to elope with Georgiana, or trapping me to marry Miss Bingley," Darcy frowned. "But to poison Elizabeth and me? What purpose does it serve? Why would they have so much hatred against us?" He shook his head, left his cousin at the door and walked inside the sick room.

"Elizabeth," he greeted his betrothed.

"I want to stay with her." It was a statement that bore no argument.

"Perhaps you should change into something more comfortable," he urged her tenderly. "I shall ask a servant to set up a bed here for you."

Elizabeth stood up. Her eyes were like those of a ghost, devoid of any sparkle. Darcy felt his heart tighten. He put his hands around her waist and let her lean her head on his shoulder. They walked out to the corridor, slowly and in silence. Half way through, she stumbled. Darcy picked her up and pressed her close to him. She did not utter a word of protest, just wrapped her hands around his neck.

When he reached her bedchamber, a maid was waiting for them. But Elizabeth would not let go of him. She muttered, "Please do not go."

Darcy signalled the maid to leave. Then he sat down on a chair by the window, still holding Elizabeth tightly and caressing her back. "All will be well. The doctor said the herb combination will help Lydia through." He murmured words of reassurance to her for some moments.

At last she relaxed her grip on his neck. When he beheld her eyes, he was glad to see her spirit returned. The glow of her fine eyes was as bright as the moonlight that shone through the windows.

"Yes, we shall not let the villains be triumphant, no matter who they are." She scrambled from his lap and collected the nightgown the maid had laid out on the bed. "I can change without assistance. Thank you, Fitzwilliam. You may go."

But he was still worried about her strength, as she avoided looking at him. He was apprehensive that she might have merely rallied enough of her spirit to send him out of the bedchamber and then would fall back into her doldrums.

"I have sent the maid away," he said. "Let me help you change and take you back to Miss Lydia's chamber."

"There is no need," she shook her head, still avoiding his gaze. "I am all right by myself." She turned her hands around, trying to release the hook on the garnet cross but could not reach it.

Darcy stepped near to her. His hands touched hers. As he examined the intricate contraption of the garnet cross in order to release it, Elizabeth started to pull at the jewellery.

"Take it off me!" she cried out. "I wish I had not known your family and you. Lydia would not have been poisoned."

His heart tensed. He knew she was shocked by the events of the night. But her wild actions could cause her harm. He wrapped himself around her to restrain her hands and hold her close.

She burst out crying and murmured involuntarily, "I did not mean it. I love you, Fitzwilliam. Please, please do not leave me."

He turned her around and let her sob her heart out on his chest. "I know, my dear." He repeated the reassuring words. His hands continued to caress her back. "I shall love and protect you forever."

Finally her tears stopped. He raised her chin and studied her eyes again. This time she returned his gaze. He was satisfied that she looked normal, almost. "Let me take off the garnet cross for you."

She nodded and allowed him to remove the jewel. When he had completed the task, he gasped, "Your neck was grazed by the cross." He could not hide the tone of disapproval in his voice.

She shook her head and whispered, "I am sorry. But it does not hurt."

He traced his knuckles along the red mark on the alabaster skin and sighed. "You have to take good care of yourself, Elizabeth. You are mine now, as much as I am yours."

She nodded and put her finger on his lips. "I shall be strong. I promise."

He kissed her fingers tenderly, admiring the flame lighting her eyes again.

"Help me take off the gown," she requested.

He released the row of tiny buttons at the back. "I shall wait for you outside," he said, after finishing the task with trembling fingers.

"No, stay with me," she replied, removing the pins from her hair. As the rose petals dropped from her head slowly, his eyes devoured her. Elizabeth was like a Greek warrior. Behind the mask of refreshing beauty, she exuded determination.

As she unwound the ribbons which seemed to hold the white gown together, Darcy took in deep breaths. He knew that she did not need his amorous attentions at this moment. He steeled his nerve as his eyes followed the fall of the gown, the petticoat, the corset and the shift. He kept his eyes on the floor, over the pool of lovely white garments which spread across the pink petals and framed her adorable ankles.

Finally the sound of the sliding garments ceased. When he lifted his eyes, he could see that she had put on a night gown and a robe. She stepped near to him and held his hands. "Thank you, Fitzwilliam." They walked out of her bedchamber, hand in hand.

# Chapter Eighteen

Darcy stayed with Elizabeth in Miss Lydia's chamber for nearly half an hour. He looked on as his betrothed sang a sweet lullaby to her sick sister while putting a cold compress over her face and neck.

He was filled with admiration and love for Elizabeth. Her devotion to the ones she loved, regardless of their faults and failings, was truly amazing. He thanked the Lord for giving him an opportunity to know her, to be given a second chance to win her affection. He was certain their future children would be blessed and cherished with an abundant supply of love.

After reminding her to take some rest if she was tired, he left in search of his cousins. He found them interviewing the servants.

Once the investigation was completed, they shared the intelligence with him.

"Did the servants notice anything?" Darcy said.

"There is no servant missing and they did not discern anyone entering the house without permission," Susan replied, in an agitated tone.

"Who sent the present?" Darcy asked.

"A manservant claiming to be from Mr. Bingley's household delivered the package," Colonel Fitzwilliam added.

Darcy gasped. "So it is the work of Miss Bingley!"

"Perhaps," Richard said. "That is why I intend to go to Grosvenor Square to talk to Bingley now, no matter the hour. He left shortly after you went upstairs with Miss Elizabeth."

"I shall come with you," Darcy said. "Susan, I shall rely on you to make sure Elizabeth and her family have enough rest."

Susan nodded and promised to do her best.

***

Mr. Hurst's butler did not seem to be surprised at receiving two visitors so early in the morning. In fact the townhouse was illuminated, with people bustling around.

Not long after Darcy and Colonel Fitzwilliam had settled in the morning parlour, Bingley burst into the room and exclaimed, "I was about to send a note to ask you to come here!"

"Good God, what is the matter?" Darcy said with emotion. On seeing his friend's dishevelled appearance, he poured Bingley a glass of port.

Bingley gulped down the contents and explained, "Caroline! She is here."

"How? When did she return?"

"She arrived shortly after we returned from the ball. She was unconscious, with blood on her head. Her maid and driver brought her back. The doctor is seeing her at this very moment."

"We have come with alarming news too," Colonel Fitzwilliam said.

"About what?" The younger gentleman wiped the sweat from his forehead. He clearly had had enough troubles for one evening.

"The gift which might have contained the poisonous macaroons was believed to have been brought by a manservant from here." Richard delivered the bad news.

Bingley sat down heavily on a chair. He cradled his head in his hands and groaned out loud. "What am I to do?"

At that moment, the doctor came in and told them that Miss Bingley had regained consciousness.

"I am going to kill her!" Bingley sprang from the chair and darted towards the door.

Darcy pulled him back. "Charles, be calm! We are not sure what happened."

Darcy dismissed the doctor with much gratitude, before returning to the others to continue with their investigation.

"Perhaps someone posed as a servant from here and sent the poisonous gift," Richard said. "Is Mrs. Hurst with your sister?

Perhaps I should go and interrogate Miss Bingley alone. If Doctor Warwick's medicine does not work for Miss Lydia, we will have to rely on your sister to find the right antidote, if she is truly involved. You are too distraught at the moment to get to the bottom of things."

"Richard is right. Bingley, come, take another drink with me while we wait."

"Perhaps, you are right. It may not be Caroline's doing." Drawing in a few deep breaths, Bingley declared. "I shall restrain myself. She is my sister. I do not want her to wake up from a traumatic experience to be immediately subject to questioning by someone she does not know well." He paced around for a few more moments and continued, "Come, we shall all go. And let me do the asking, please."

Darcy and Richard agreed.

When the three men arrived at Miss Bingley's chamber, Darcy and Richard stayed at the open door. Darcy could see that her head was heavily bandaged. Her skin looked pale and coarse. Besides the injury on her head, she had some bruises on the neck and arms.

"I am sorry!" Miss Bingley burst into tears on seeing her brother.

Mrs. Hurst was sitting on the edge of the bed, holding her right hand. Mr. Hurst was standing near the window with a glass of wine in his hand. Bingley sank onto the bed, taking Miss Bingley's left hand.

"Who are you apologising to?" Bingley asked, almost tenderly.

"I am sorry, Charles, for running away." Her lips trembled. "But I cannot marry that toad-like clergyman."

"How did you hurt yourself?"

"And I am sorry, Mr. Darcy," she continued. Her voice was raw. "I should not have made a copy of the garnet cross. I never imagined that the true owner would ever appear."

"How did you hurt yourself?" Bingley repeated, firmer and more impatient this time.

"I had an accident with the buggy."

"Where have you been staying?"

"In Stoke Newington. I have been waiting for a passage to America."

Both Mrs. Hurst and Bingley gasped on hearing this piece of information. "You are willing to leave London society?" Charles said, disbelieving what he had heard.

"I cannot marry that Mr. Collins. I heard that New York is becoming very fashionable. I know the Spaulding family from Summer Hill. I was going to write to you later and ask for my dowry once I arrived there."

"Who are you staying with in Stoke Newington?"

"Alone, with only my maid and driver."

"Do not lie to me." Charles shook his head. "We know about Mrs. Younge staying there."

"I am sorry. My head hurts!" Miss Bingley moaned out loud, before swooning.

Mrs. Hurst and Bingley became frantic. The doctor was called to return.

Darcy and Colonel Fitzwilliam waited impatiently outside. After several minutes, Bingley came out.

"The doctor has given her a sleeping draught, to help her pain," he said. "Why must she insist on withholding the truth? Jane will blame me for the rest of my life if Miss Lydia does not recover."

"Should we not interview Miss Bingley's maid and servant?" Darcy suggested.

"Yes!" Bingley agreed.

"I think interviewing them separately would be better," Richard added.

They called Harold, the carriage driver, to come in first.

"Tell me what happened," Bingley said. "From the day Miss Bingley left Kent until today."

"Not much really," young Harold murmured. "The Mistress went to Stoke Newington. We've been there ever since."

"But why did you tell your relative at my Aunt Pamela's that you would be going to Dover?"

"Oh, that. The Mistress did it. She said London was getting cold. She wrote the note to my relative – you know I can't write – to help her get some things. But we didn't go to Dover."

"And who was with her at Stoke Newington?"

"Mrs. Younge."

"How do you know Mrs. Younge?"

"The Mistress met her a few times."

"Where? And how many times?"

"Hmm, I think in Cusworth Hall, at the Friars Inn at Doncaster and at the Charing Cross Inn."

"Just those three times?"

Harold scratched his head. "As far as I can remember."

"Were there any other people with them, during their meetings?"

"Well, at Cusworth Hall Miss Bingley was visiting the Barrymore sisters. There were many other people there too. I'm not sure."

"And at Doncaster and Charing Cross? Was the Mistress acting strangely?"

"Hmm, I'm not allowed to say."

"Tell me at once!" Bingley said angrily. "This Mrs. Younge could be a danger to my family. I need to know."

"The Mistress dressed as a gentleman, then."

Bingley's lip tightened. "And did they meet up with anyone?"

"Yes, at the Friars Inn. There was a man."

"Who?"

"I don't know."

"What did he look like?"

"Hmm, ginger hair, tall, strong, he walked quickly."

Darcy mouthed the word Fleming to Bingley. The latter continued the interrogation.

"And at Charing Cross?"

"I think he was a Frenchman."

Bingley's face lost colour. "Who was he?"

"I heard the Mistress called him Pierre."

He sighed with relief. "How did Miss Bingley get injured?"

"I don't know. We moved to a new townhouse a few days ago. I was sleeping. I heard some screams and then I followed Marie into the Mistress's room. The Mistress was unconscious, with blood on her head. We didn't know any doctor in Stoke Newington so we brought her back here, as fast as we could."

"And did you do any errands for Miss Bingley or Mrs. Younge yesterday?" Darcy asked, taking over the interrogation as Bingley seemed to have run out of questions. Darcy needed to establish if Harold was the one who had delivered the macaroons.

"Errands? Hmm, I took them to the river."

"Did they say why they wished to go there?"

"They wouldn't say anything to me. I'm just a servant. The Mistress dressed as a ... as a gentleman, as usual, when she went out."

"But did you overhear their conversation?"

"I was not close enough to hear anything, but they did seem to be arguing …"

"About what?"

"… about you, Sir."

"Tell me exactly what you did hear."

"I didn't hear clearly. Just something like Mrs. Younge had not been helpful enough for the Mistress … um … to become your wife. And Mrs. Younge was blaming the Mistress for losing her temper by getting drunk. She blamed her for ruining her own scheme."

"I am not sure I understand your meaning. Who blamed whom?"

"Mrs. Younge blamed the Mistress."

"Did Mrs. Younge say what the scheme was?"

"Hmm …" Harold thought for a moment. "I don't remember. But she said something in another language."

"What language?"

"I don't know no other language."

"French? Italian?"

"Could be anything. Ah, but Mrs. Younge greeted the Frenchman at Charing Cross in his language. She must have spoken French."

Darcy and the other two men gasped. The French spy possibility was looming again.

"Did you remember the French words Mrs. Younge said?"

Harold scratched his head. "I don't know, ruler ... erm … fur … I can't say it correctly."

"Nothing more?"

Harold thought for a moment and then shook his head.

"Did they meet anyone else, from the time Miss Bingley left Kent?"

Again Harold said that they had not.

"No other woman or man?"

"No."

"What did they do after visiting the river?"

"The Mistress turned pale on hearing that Mrs. Younge was talking in French. She asked me to drive her back immediately. Mrs. Younge didn't come back with us."

"And did Miss Bingley leave the house after that?"

"No, she was in there the rest of the day."

"And Mrs. Younge?"

"She had not returned."

"Was this not strange to you, that she did not go back?"

"Not at all ... Mrs. Younge comes and goes as she wishes."

"Do you know where she stayed all the other times then?"

"I have no idea," Harold added.

"She never mentioned the name of a lodging the whole time she was with Miss Bingley?"

"I only drove them around. I never stayed in the house to listen to them. Maybe Marie would know more."

Darcy looked at Bingley and Colonel Fitzwilliam to see if they had more questions. They shook their heads. Bingley dismissed Harold but asked him to stay close by.

"Could Mrs. Younge be French?" Colonel Fitzwilliam murmured.

"When I interviewed her, she said she spoke French, German and Italian fluently," Darcy said. "I asked her when she learned them. She said she had married young and her husband had taught her."

"Her husband was of a high rank," Bingley said. "Why would he want his wife to speak so many languages?"

Darcy shook his head. "Mr. Younge was an elderly theology professor in Oxford, according to what she said. I believe he seldom came to London. And when he died, he did not leave enough means for her. That was why she had to become a governess."

"How did she come to marry an old man, at such a young age?" Bingley said.

"She said her family had all passed away. Mr. Younge was a distant relative," Darcy added. "Hmm, now that you have asked about it, I did not check on her original family. She came with a good reference …"

"What did she say her maiden name was, in the application letter?" Richard asked.

"I think it was … Vency."

"Are you familiar with it?" Bingley asked his friend. "Did she have a past history with your family?"

Darcy thought for a minute and shook his head. They pondered the mystery for a little longer, before calling Miss Bingley's lady's maid in to interview her.

"Tell me what happened, Marie," Bingley said, in the same fashion that he had started the interrogation of Harold. "Please start from the day Miss Bingley left Kent until today."

"The Mistress said she was going to visit a friend in Stoke Newington. When we arrived there, her friend had not yet arrived."

"Who was that friend?"

"Madame Younge."

"How did they know each other?"

"Through Monsieur Wickham."

All three men exchanged a look of concern. Colonel Fitzwilliam signalled to Bingley and took over the questioning of the maid.

"Do you remember when they first met?" Richard asked.

"I think early this year, when the Mistress stayed at Cusworth Hall."

"What can you tell me about this meeting?"

"*Je ne sais pas*," Marie said. "Only one night, the Mistress…" She stopped mid-sentence, looking at Bingley.

"Your mistress is injured," Colonel Fitzwilliam said in his commanding voice. "The culprit is still at large. You must tell us everything you know, or you may be considered an accomplice to the assailant."

"I understand, sir. Well, one night, the Mistress stayed in another part of Cusworth Hall till the early hours of the morning. When she returned, she asked for a bath. I noticed ... she had some red marks on her bosom. I asked if I needed to help her put some salve on it. She asked me to prepare a high-necked morning dress for the day. When I was tidying up in the dressing room, she murmured to herself in front of the mirror that Monsieur Wickham was not very satisfactory."

"Wickham was staying at Cusworth Hall at the same time?"

"I had not seen him. But one of the maids said he usually came around at night, to visit Madame Younge."

Darcy's face turned grave.

"Was that the first time your Mistress had been with a man?" Richard asked. Bingley's face was the same colour as the gowns Miss Bingley usually wore.

Marie darted a look at Darcy and shook her head. "I think she has been with a few other men, three or four."

Bingley sat down heavily. His hand clutching his head.

Colonel Fitzwilliam nodded and continued, "How did you know Wickham introduced Mrs. Younge to Miss Bingley, instead of the other way round?"

Marie thought for a moment. "I am not certain. But one of the maids told me she saw them in the woods one day. Since then, Mrs. Younge has visited the Mistress late at night from time to time. Miss Bingley said I was not to say a word about it or she would send me to service the Redcoats," Marie said with a trembling voice.

"What other things did you notice about her meeting with Mrs. Younge?"

"I think ..." She stopped mid-sentence.

"Go on!"

"They had carnal knowledge of each other."

Bingley's smacked his fist onto the arm of the chair. Darcy patted him on the back.

Marie continued. "Immediately before we left Cusworth Hall, she had some bruises on her ... bottom."

"She was forced!" Bingley exclaimed. "I cannot believe Caroline has this kind of inclination."

Marie stopped what she had intended to say.

Richard urged her on. "Why did Miss Bingley have the bruises?"

"*Je ne sais pas*. But she murmured to herself that she loved it, when I was tending her wound." Marie looked at Darcy again. "She said Madame Younge was very exciting, much more so than the men she had bedded. She speculated … that having Monsieur Darcy in her bed would be quite a chore."

Bingley jumped up, walked to the farthest end of the parlour and beat his head on the wall this time.

Darcy pulled him back and whispered to him, "Maybe you should retire now. Richard and I can continue the interrogation."

Bingley shook his head and said in a low voice, "How could she have gone so wild?"

Darcy suddenly thought about his childhood friend George Wickham. *What had set him off, down the path of self-destruction?* He shook his head and could not offer Bingley any opinion.

Charles continued to murmur, "I have to deal with her. I must stay calm. Father would have wanted me to." His eyes were bloodshot and his face turned red and white alternatively. "And I have to be strong. For Jane's sake. But what am I to do? How could she have lost all her virtues? All the servants seem to have known about it for some time. I have been deluding myself to fulfil Father's dream of becoming part of higher society. Everyone must be laughing at the Bingleys. You should not have befriended me. I should not have asked Jane to marry me. Our children would be the greatest laughing stock in society for having such a trollop in the family."

Darcy held his shoulders and spoke to him slowly. "People from higher circles are not always perfect. You have been a good son, brother and friend."

"But I have failed miserably as a brother! Caroline only talked to me when she needed more allowance."

"Do you honestly believe she would confide in you about her … um, unseemly behaviour? Perhaps she sees you as too young to understand her."

"Then what am I to do?" Bingley murmured again. "What am I to do?"

"Take some deep breaths and we will continue the questioning. We need to see if we can find some intelligence to help cure Miss Lydia."

Bingley did as he was told and they went back to join Marie and Colonel Fitzwilliam.

Richard continued the questioning. "Did Miss Bingley ever talk about or meet Wickham after that?"

Marie shook her head.

"And were you aware of other meetings your Mistress had with Mrs. Younge before Kent?"

"I did not know myself. But I have heard Harold talk about it. The Mistress …" She stopped and looked at the men for a moment before continuing. "She dressed as a gentleman when she met up with Madame Younge. She did not need me to accompany her."

"What about the red garnet cross? Were you aware of the origin of this piece of jewellery?"

"The Mistress only gave it to me to put away with her jewellery one day."

"She did not talk about it?"

"Not to me. But I did overhear her talk to herself then. She said it would be the …" Marie thought for a moment, " ... the perfect piece for her grand scheme. But I remember a few nights before we went to Hertfordshire, she threw it on the floor."

"Why?"

"I did not ask." Marie shrugged her shoulders. "The Mistress liked to throw things from time to time. It is best to get away from her at such times rather than ask. But I remember her swearing about the inscription."

Darcy pondered the events. *Miss Bingley met Mrs. Younge and Wickham in Cusworth Hall early this year. Did Wickham introduce Mrs. Younge to her? Darcy was not certain. They had an imitation made of the garnet cross around Easter time. Miss Bingley thought she would be able to get me to marry her. But after I questioned her about the inscription the first time she wore it in London, she knew the imitation was incomplete and got angry about it. At the same time, Mrs. Younge applied to work as Georgiana's governess and allowed Wickham to spend time with her in the summer.*

Trying to uncover the whole wicked scheme, Darcy jumped in to ask, "Did Miss Bingley have any contact with Wickham or Mrs. Younge during the time she was in Hertfordshire?"

"When the Mistress returned from the Assembly, she sent out an express," Marie replied.

"Did you know the direction? Was it to London? Was it to Wickham or Mrs. Younge?"

"I didn't know."

"Bingley, I want you to send an express later on to ask the housekeeper in Netherfield about it," Darcy said.

Bingley nodded.

"What about today?" Colonel Fitzwilliam said. "What did your Mistress do? Tell us in detail until the time Harold and you brought her back here."

"She did not do much until late in the afternoon. She changed into her gentleman's clothes and asked Harold to drive her to the river."

"Did you not go with them?"

"No, she wore gentleman's clothes. She did not need a maid to accompany her."

"What happened when she returned from the outing?"

"She closeted herself in her room at first. Harold told me she had an argument with Madame Younge. Then she asked me to pack up her belongings. She said we would have to leave tomorrow."

"Did she say why?"

"No. She just murmured fou and Français when she left the room while I packed."

"Mad Frenchwoman? Could she be talking about Mrs. Younge?" Richard said. "Is she French?"

"Madame Younge?" Marie shook her head. "I heard her sing Médée once. She sounded very fluent. But there are still some awkward English accents here and there. It is more like someone who has learned French. I don't think she was born of our people."

On hearing the mentioning of the opera Médée, Darcy paced around agitatedly. *Could Mrs. Younge be the one who gave the music sheet to Georgiana?*

"Did Miss Bingley say where she would be going, after Stoke Newington?"

"She said she wanted to visit a friend in Ireland."

"Not America?" Bingley asked.

"I don't think the Mistress would want to go to America, too savage. She often said that about the Spauldings."

"And how did you find the Mistress injured?" Colonel Fitzwilliam continued.

"I don't know. I was sleeping. I heard her screams so I dashed into her bedchamber. She was there, as if dead. So horrible, so much blood. Harold came in. He helped me bring her back here. I was so worried she would die in the carriage. The Mistress may be mean-spirited and harsh. But I do not want her dead."

The three men nodded. Her story matched Harold's. Neither Harold nor she fitted the description of the servant who delivered the gift to Nevan House. After a few more moments of frustrating discussion, the gentlemen decided to retire, until they could talk to Miss Bingley again.

Colonel Fitzwilliam and Darcy went back to Susan's townhouse. Darcy preferred to be close to his betrothed, though he knew Elizabeth would still be busy tending to Lydia. He also wanted to talk to Georgiana about the sheet music. Then he would need to help Charles to get the truth out of Miss Bingley later in the day.

## Chapter Nineteen

When Darcy arrived at Nevan House, most of the occupants had retired. The doctor told him that Miss Lydia had responded to the herb he gave her. The vomiting had stopped and she had been sleeping. Darcy asked the servant about Elizabeth and was shown to Miss Lydia's room.

From the partially-open doorway, he could see that Elizabeth was sleeping on a makeshift bed beside her sister. And Mr. Bennet was sitting on the edge of the bed against the headboard, having also fallen asleep.

Darcy decided not to wake the guardians and retired to a guest chamber.

The next morning, bright sunlight woke him from a deep sleep. It was nine o'clock, much later than his normal waking hour.

Colonel Fitzwilliam had left early, apparently at his commander's summons. Darcy went in search of his betrothed and found that she was no longer in Miss Lydia's room. The other three Bennet sisters were there instead. After greeting them, he found Elizabeth taking breakfast alone in the morning parlour.

"Are you well, my dear?" he enquired with an intense gaze, examining her countenance for signs of fatigue.

She gave a radiant smile and nodded. "I am well, thank you. Lydia woke up for a few minutes this morning, feeling much better. The doctor said she is on the mend. She even protested weakly that she would not survive if the doctor only allows her broth and confines her to the bed for the next two weeks. Father went to sleep after that and Mother has not woken up yet. Jane, Mary and Kitty took their turn to watch over Lydia."

"It is good to hear that Miss Lydia is recovering. Did you get any rest?"

"I fell asleep on and off. I feel in excellent spirits. Did you find out who sent the poisonous gift?"

Darcy debated with himself whether he should tell her about the return of Miss Bingley. Aware that she would be angry with him for keeping secrets, he eventually told her about the interrogation of the servants and what had happened at the Hursts' townhouse.

"Miss Bingley, Mr. Wickham and Mrs. Younge …" she said in a trembling voice. "They seemed to be after your position and wealth at first, but now it has turned towards violence and murder. Why? Could it be as sinister as Colonel Fitzwilliam said, that it is somehow related to a French spy?

He took her hands and squeezed them. "I do not know. I shall talk to Georgiana first and then go to Grosvenor Square to see if Miss Bingley has woken up."

"Georgiana and Lady Susan came to check on Lydia around dawn," Elizabeth said in a worried voice. "Your sister mentioned that she had had a nightmare and could not sleep. The doctor persuaded her to take a sleeping draught. I think she may not wake up for a while."

They went to check on Georgiana and found Lady Susan sleeping on a chaise in her cousin's bed chamber.

"Lady Susan must be exhausted," Elizabeth said, as Darcy and she retreated from the room. "She organised the ball, questioned all the servants and then supervised the settling in of my whole family last night. Perhaps we should return to our Aunt and Uncle."

"Do not worry. Susan is the most energetic host I have ever known. I do not think that it will be good for Miss Lydia and your mother to be travelling across town or anywhere so soon."

As she nodded in agreement, the butler brought in a note for Darcy.

Darcy read it quickly, then said, "It is from Bingley. His sister has awakened. I shall go. It is a pity Richard is not here. He is very good at interrogation."

"I shall come with you," Elizabeth said.

"You are well rested?"

"I want to hear the truth from Miss Bingley. She must not be able ever to harm my family or you again!"

Seeing the determined glint in her eye, he nodded. "Should we ask your sister to come along? To give Charles support?"

After learning the circumstances from Elizabeth, Jane went to prepare for a visit to her betrothed. They were ready in half an hour.

Even though Grosvenor Square was within walking distance from Nevan House in Mayfair, Darcy asked for a carriage to convey them there. He thought the two eldest Bennet sisters would be too tired to walk, especially after taking care of Miss Lydia for some time. Anyway, a cold November chill had set in. It was a grey morning; most of the streets seeming rather deserted.

The carriage rattled along at a slow pace. Jane and Elizabeth were chatting about Miss Lydia, when suddenly the carriage took off at frightening speed.

"What is happening?" The ladies held onto the edge of their seat.

"I do not know!" Darcy leaned out of the window but the carriage was lunging from side to side at high speed. He nearly got thrown out when it turned a corner suddenly. Elizabeth held onto his coat and pulled him back.

"I cannot see Morgan," he said. He had a sense of foreboding. Lord Barrymore's driver and footman were always very careful. They would not take on such speed in crowded London, even though this morning the streets were quite empty. He glanced outside and saw that they had turned off Park Lane, that led to Grosvenor Square, and into Hyde Park. Opening a secret compartment in the seat, he reached down for the gun Lord Barrymore kept there.

On seeing him frown, Elizabeth said breathlessly, "The gun is gone?"

He nodded.

"Father keeps his gun in a similar place too," she said. Both ladies turned pale, holding onto each other.

Darcy moved to sit beside Elizabeth and held her other free hand. His mind was racing. How could he protect them? He could not wave to the passing horses in Hyde Park, as the carriage was travelling too quickly. After a moment, the carriage turned west towards Baynard's Watering at breakneck speed. After that, Knottynghull came into sight. Finally it came to a screeching stop on a deserted hill.

He jumped down as soon as it was safe and outside, with a gun in her hand, stood Mrs. Younge! With her head in a cap and dressed in driver's clothes, Darcy would not, from a distance, have realised that she was a woman. Her dark brown eyes showed a glittering fire that looked as menacing as the gun she held.

Darcy took a quick look at the driver's seat. He saw that Lord Barrymore's driver, Morgan, who was a rather short man, was sprawled over the seat. Mrs. Younge must have replaced the footman immediately after the passengers had boarded, since she was equally tall, and held the driver at gunpoint throughout the journey. Then she would have taken the opportunity to knock out poor Morgan.

"Don't move!" Mrs. Younge instructed. "You women! Out!"

"You are after me only, Mrs. Younge. I insist that you leave the ladies alone."

"You will feel the pain more," she smiled, "when I burn these good ladies alive!"

Darcy heard the Bennet sisters gasp.

"Come out at once! Or I shall shoot him!"

He wanted to turn and assist the ladies out of the carriage but Mrs. Younge waved the gun and stopped him.

Elizabeth came down first. Then she turned to help Jane out. The latter was shaking and shivering.

"Why do you want to harm Mr. Darcy?" Elizabeth said. Her voice held strength. "What did he do to deserve this?"

"Shut up! I do not need to answer any of your questions. Now, move towards the pits."

He looked ahead and saw that there were several gravel pits a short distance ahead.

"If I am going to … to die anyway, I shall not die without knowing the reason!" Elizabeth retorted. "Either you tell me now or you will have to shoot me. I will not give you the … pleasure of burning me alive."

Darcy felt himself breathing shallowly. While he was looking for ways to disarm Mrs. Younge, he did not want Elizabeth to be injured by provoking the apparently mad woman. But when he looked at his betrothed, she gave him a reassuring gaze. He trusted her judgement. There seemed to be a reason why Mrs. Younge wished to harm them in this way. Perhaps by getting the truth out of her, they could subdue her in the process.

Mrs. Younge's eyes widened and her pupils turned a more intense shade. Her hand tightened on the gun and the other hand balled into a fist. Darcy was prepared to shield Elizabeth if the woman fired. But after a moment that felt more like an hour, Mrs. Younge stepped forward and shouted at Elizabeth.

"You wish to know why I want to harm him? What about your father choosing to save him, instead of my father!"

"Your father ..." Darcy murmured, putting the puzzle together.

" ... was at Bromley Inn twenty years ago?" Elizabeth completed the sentence.

"I was there too," Mrs. Younge said. "I begged your father."

"Father would not have refused to help," Jane said.

"He said my father was gone," Mrs. Younge told them. "He pushed me to run away and ran to rescue Mr. Darcy instead." She waved the gun at Darcy before continuing. "I knew that Father was not yet dead. I knew that. I could feel his gaze when I left the Inn. I knew that! It was all your fault, Fitzwilliam Darcy!"

"Why now?" Elizabeth called Mrs. Younge's attention away from Darcy. "Why did you wait for twenty years?"

"I did not know your father had rescued someone else." Mrs. Younge had tears in her eyes now. "Until George Wickham got drunk and blurted the story of the garnet cross to me at Cusworth Hall in January. It was then that I knew what I had to do. I did not know who had taken the help intended for my father back then. But I vowed to have revenge to hurt you, Mr. Darcy, as much as your existence has hurt me!"

"So Mr. Wickham, Miss Bingley and you plotted this together?" Elizabeth urged on.

Mrs. Younge laughed, wiping away a single tear that had dropped from her eye. "They were just useless pawns! I had drugged Georgiana and handed her to Wickham on a platter last summer. But he wanted to marry her instead, to get more money out of it. He was afraid she would kill herself if he had taken her without her consent."

Darcy gasped. His fists tightened. He had not been in time to protect his sister at Ramsgate. He realised ironically that, thanks to Wickham's twisted logic, Georgiana's virtue and life had been spared.

"But you love Miss Bingley!" Elizabeth continued.

"Love? What is that?" Mrs. Younge retorted. "Father and I left France to find love here. But instead where did it take us? He was dead just a few days after we arrived."

"You left behind much in France?" Elizabeth said.

"I was a D'Arcy too, with a grand estate in Paris. I will never understand why my father had survived the persecution there only to be killed in a stupid fire in the middle of nowhere, leaving me all alone in the world! And you, just another Darcy! You have lived a life of luxury and comfort ..."

Darcy drew in a deep breath. He had not known of their distant family ties.

Mrs. Younge continued, " ...while I was taken to work as a servant all my life, until I married Younge. I thought my fortune would turn for the good. How wrong I was! The great old ugly theology professor, loved by all his students in Oxford," her laugh turned evil, "for being kind and gentle. He loved no one but himself. He loved his whips," Mrs. Younge said. "It was a pity he left me no money, after I got rid of him with poison."

Darcy, Elizabeth and Jane gasped. Mrs. Younge had killed her husband with poison! It was fortunate that Lydia had survived.

"You taught Miss Bingley how to use the whips." Elizabeth kept the assailant talking.

"Stupid woman! She lost her composure when you appeared. If Caroline had waited for my instruction, I would have found a way to get rid of your father and you, and left

Darcy to her. He would have suffered a lifetime of misery, married to Caroline."

"You sent the engagement gift?"

"An inspiration from Médée. I pretended to be a manservant from Caroline's household, delivered the exquisite macaroons and was waiting to hear about the loss of the great Fitzwilliam Darcy. But what did I hear from the servants? That the youngest Miss Bennet had fallen ill! Nothing goes according to plan. When I expressed my anger to Caroline, she said she did not want Darcy dead, she would tell her brother. Dim-witted girl! Even Wickham! I sent him to Hertfordshire to help Caroline and he just turned back with his tail between his legs. And your youngest sister too. All so stupid! Why did your sister have to take my precious poison instead?"

"So you planned this?"

"It is all too simple," Mrs. Younge laughed out loud. "Lady Susan's footman was so easily tempted. It was not difficult to drug him and find the gun. Then it was a matter of waiting for the great Mr. Darcy to climb aboard and then subdue the driver. What a bounty that you are here too, Miss Elizabeth! He will suffer all the more on seeing you die in front of his eyes. Now, no more questions! Move to the pits at once. I've already prepared straw and hay there," she lowered her voice. "For the fire..."

Mrs. Younge's eyes had taken on a strange steady glint. Darcy's mind was racing. It was now or never. If she had prepared the pits the day before, managed to steal the gun away from the carriage and overcome the footman, she would not leave anything to chance. He had to take action now or both Elizabeth and Jane would be hurt.

He looked at Elizabeth. She raised her hand to brush her eyelashes and blinked a few times. Then she touched Jane's hand. The latter bit her lips and squeezed her eyes tightly for a moment before looking down at the ground.

Darcy had never seen Elizabeth stroke her eyes like this before. After a moment's thought he understood her message.

The ladies walked up the hills for a few moments. Darcy followed slowly. Mrs. Younge was walking to their right, a few steps away, the gun steady in her hand.

Suddenly Jane swooned and dropped to the ground. Elizabeth cried out, "Jane!" and crouched down beside her sister.

Mrs. Younge's face turned angry, annoyed with the delay. She stepped closer to them and demanded, "Help her up, now!"

That was the moment Elizabeth seized a fistful of gravel and threw it in Mrs. Younge's eyes.

Mrs. Younge yelped in pain and raised her hands to cover her face. "Stay clear, Elizabeth!" Darcy barked out the command, then sprang forward and knocked the gun from Mrs. Younge's grasp.

"You will die!" she screamed as she lunged for the gun, but her eyes were still blinded by the gravel.

He grasped her hand and twisted it backward, preventing her from reaching the weapon.

"I shall kill you!" she continued her tirade as she raised her hand and tried to scratch his face.

He turned away his head to avoid the claws, momentarily losing his grip on her hand.

Diving for the gun once again, she finally took hold of it. Before she could turn her body to fire at him, he gripped her arm while she was still face down. At that instant, the gun went off ...

"Urgh!" Mrs. Younge moaned out loud and rolled on the ground, twisting with pain.

Darcy knocked the gun further away before inspecting her. The right side of her face had been caught when the gun was fired. Blood obscured a large part of her cheek and her right eye was closed. She raised her hands to touch her face but the pain was so severe that she cried out even louder. "I shall kill you! For my father's sake!"

He took out his handkerchief and pressed it to the wound.

She screamed, "You will die!"

"Are you hurt?" Elizabeth said breathlessly, finally coming to kneel near them.

"No, thank you."

"I shall check the carriage for some wine to help ease her pain," Elizabeth said.

"Let me go," Jane said. She had only pretended to swoon and had risen as well.

"Pray check on the driver too," he said to her. Jane nodded.

Elizabeth stayed to hold Mrs. Younge's hands still, to prevent her from further injuring herself.

"Let go of me! I need to kill Fitzwilliam Darcy!" the injured woman cried. "And I need to kill Thomas Bennet!"

When Jane returned, she was followed by Morgan, who was rubbing his head and had a bottle in his hand.

"I am sorry, sir. She knocked me out," the servant apologised.

Darcy nodded and helped Mrs. Younge drink the brandy. She gulped down the contents in no time, until she no longer moaned in pain.

"Le fer!" She mumbled: 'fire' in French. "Please do not hurt me. Je brûle…I burn…It hurts…"

"We have to take her back and send for the doctor," Darcy said as he pocketed the gun.

With the help of the servant, Darcy settled the half-conscious, half-delusional Mrs. Younge in the carriage. Elizabeth sat by her side to calm her.

When the carriage arrived at Lady Susan's townhouse, most of the occupants were up. The doctor was called for to tend to the injured woman.

"Will she live?" Lady Susan asked.

"I believe so, if there is no infection set in," the doctor said, "but her face will be scarred and she will have no use of her right eye."

The extent of her injury shocked the people gathered.

Once the doctor had left, Lady Susan asked her cousin, "What are we to do now?"

"She admitted poisoning her husband. I think we have to call the magistrate for this. We do not have to tell the magistrate about the imitation of the garnet cross and her attempted murder with the macaroons," Darcy said.

"Her father was dead before I came upon him at the Inn," Mr. Bennet murmured. "I was so sure about it."

"Father, I think Mrs. Younge was only wishing her father not dead," Elizabeth squeezed her father's hand. "I am sure your judgement was correct."

"I encountered a little girl of around ten years of age, crouching near the body of a man, after I asked the late Mr. Darcy to take Lizzy out of the Inn," the older gentleman sighed. "I checked on the man's pulse and he was gone. So I hurried the girl out of the Inn and came back to get you, Darcy, and your mother. It seemed the body of Mrs. Younge's father was the one I mentioned to you. We stepped past him on our way out to safety."

"Mr. Bennet, you did the right thing," Lady Susan said. "Mrs. Younge was a child. She could not be sure about what had happened then. And you saved Aunt Anne, Fitzwilliam and even Mrs.Younge's lives."

"Mrs. Younge hurt Miss Bingley too, did she not?" Elizabeth said.

"We better go to Charles soon," Jane said. "He will be frantic waiting for our arrival."

Darcy sent a note to inform Bingley they would be joining him later in the day. Another note was sent to summon the magistrate.

When the magistrate had arrived, accompanied by two officers, Darcy informed him of what happened at Knottynghull, without going into detail about Mrs. Younge's other schemes.

The magistrate took custody of the injured woman. Soon afterwards, Jane, Elizabeth and Darcy were on their way to Grosvenor Square once again.

## Chapter Twenty

When the party arrived later that afternoon, Bingley greeted them anxiously. Jane however asked her sister to stay in the library, instead of joining the questioning of Miss Bingley.

"I'm sorry to cause you any trouble, Mr. Bingley," Elizabeth addressed her future brother-in-law instead. "But I have a right to know about your sister's actions. She may be involved in trying to harm Fitzwilliam."

Jane jumped in before Mr. Bingley could reply. "But Miss Bingley has been through a lot as well. In a moment of drunkenness, she has sealed her future. Then she had to run away and almost died. Could we not allow her some comfort first? She has been jealous of you, of your good fortune in securing Mr. Darcy. I am worried your presence would give her a good deal of anxiety. Lizzy, would you do it for me? Please, stay here."

"Jane, you have the greatest heart." Bingley held Jane's hand and then turned to her sister. "Miss Elizabeth, I would truly appreciate it if you could do as Jane asked. Even with the doctor's sleeping draught, Louisa told me, Caroline has been quite restless the last few hours. I talked to Caroline after she woke up. She had a countenance of true despair. She could not utter more than a few words and the tears simply kept flowing."

Elizabeth bit her lip and pondered for a few moments. Then she pulled Jane aside and talked with her in a low voice for almost a quarter of an hour. Darcy could see the older sister nodding her head all the while.

"Well," Elizabeth said when they had finished. "I shall learn to be as patient and forgiving as my sister."

"Thank you," Bingley said.

"Do not worry, my love." Darcy took Elizabeth's hand and gave it a kiss. "I shall relate all the detail to you afterwards."

She nodded. Darcy followed the other two out of the library.

Miss Jane entered Miss Bingley's chamber and took the chair by the bed. Bingley stood behind her. Mrs. Hurst was sitting on the edge of the bed. Darcy remained at the door.

"Are you well, Miss Bingley?" Jane asked in a soft voice.

Miss Bingley opened her eyes and replied, "Yes, my head … does not hurt too much."

"We have had an eventful morning," Jane continued, rather than engaging in questioning the injured woman. "Mrs. Younge tried to harm us when we were on our way to see you."

Caroline gasped. "She … You are well?"

Jane nodded. "Yes, we are not harmed."

"And she?"

"She has been taken away, by the magistrate." Jane did not mention Mrs. Younge's injury. *Perhaps she does not want to worry Miss Bingley*, Darcy thought.

"She won't be free any more?" Her eyes darted to her brother and then towards the door.

"She confessed to poisoning her husband." Jane took Miss Bingley's hand. "I do not believe she will ever be free again. She will not harm you."

Miss Bingley burst out crying and said at the same time, "I did not know she had … had done evil things before."

"You love her." Bingley's and Mrs. Hurst's mouths dropped on hearing Jane's statement.

Miss Bingley stopped sobbing and looked at Jane, with wide eyes. "You do not think me … strange?"

"It may not be accepted in the eyes of the church," Jane mused for a moment. "But I cannot fault a person for it, if he or she has not done harm to anyone."

"Jehanne is very … determined." Miss Bingley had a faraway look. "She is so … strong. At first it was like an adventure. She taught me to dress as a man. There was so much freedom. We could go places I could not have gone before, as a woman. She made me laugh, day and night."

"Her name is Jehanne? Not Jeanne?"

*So Mrs. Younge's maiden name is Jehanne D'Arcy*. Darcy tried to remember whether the family book had mentioned this distant relative before.

"Yes. She said we would be Jeanne and Nicole, who outsmarted the French Queen and the Cardinal ... to gain possession of the diamond necklace. They upset the French royalty and earned a place in history."

Darcy shook his head. Miss Bingley was quite naïve. Did she not know that the real Nicole was a prostitute? Mrs. Younge's mind was very twisted.

"And then?" Jane probed.

"Jehanne became … a little crazed. She was insistent on carrying out her scheme."

"Crazed?"

"When she learned from Mr. Wickham about old Mr. Darcy offering the garnet cross to an unknown baby at the Inn of Bromley," Miss Bingley continued. "We were in the woods. I was visiting the Barrymore sisters at Cusworth Hall. Jehanne was so angry. She grabbed Mr. Wickham's whips and hit an old bush without cease for a long while. We, Mr. Wickham and I, were quite afraid."

"How did Mr. Wickham learn about the cross?" Jane continued. Darcy wanted to know too.

"He had known about it for quite a long time. He overheard the solicitor talking to his clerk, shortly after the late Mr. Darcy had died. But he had not thought of a way of using the information to his benefit. And he did not have the sketch of the jewel either."

"Why did he mention it only then?"

"He came upon someone at Doncaster, a Mr. Lamington. They were playing cards and got a bit drunk. Mr. Lamington lost some money to Mr. Wickham. When he took the wallet out, a piece of old paper dropped out. Mr. Wickham caught a glimpse of the sketch of a garnet cross."

*Ah, Fleming disguised as Mr. Lamington*, Darcy thought.

"He knew this was the sketch of the late Mr. Darcy's garnet cross?"

"Mr. Darcy was looking over the sketch at their family jeweller in London. Mr. Wickham was with him, though he was quite young then. But he remembered it, as it had quite a special design. He said his godfather told him at that time that it was made for Lady Anne."

*When could that be, Darcy thought. Father and Wickham in London...Ah...We were all in London at that time. Mother and I were visiting Lady Matlock. I remember now. Father said he had business to attend to and Wickham wormed his way into going with him. And when he returned, he boasted about seeing the King's crown. I was quite jealous about it.*

"And Mrs. Younge came up with the scheme?"

"She said she would help me become the Mistress of Pemberley," Miss Bingley continued. "So we disguised ourselves as a couple and obtained the sketch from Mr. Lamington."

"And then?"

"She told me to come up with the money to make a copy of it. I did not know that Miss Eliza … your sister ... had the real jewel."

Jane patted her hand. "Did you hear from Mr. Wickham afterwards?"

"I did not see him after I left Cusworth Hall."

Darcy breathed out a sigh of relief on hearing Miss Bingley's words. If she had been involved with hurting Georgiana in Ramsgate, he did not think he could forgive her.

"Why did Mrs. Younge become Miss Darcy's governess?" Miss Jane asked.

"Jehanne said she would like to stay close to me when I became Mrs. Darcy. She said if I had a grand estate of my own, I could have even more freedom. We could be together, forever."

Darcy's mouth tightened. *What would have been my fate, had I married Miss Bingley?*

Jane nodded. "Did she tell you about her family in France?"

"She told me about it, once," Miss Bingley said. "How horrible the French were, seizing her father's estate. Their situation … had turned bad for some years. Her father decided to come to England, to start a new life, with a distant relative."

"What happened to her father?"

"Jehanne never told me that. She became rather angry when she told me about the time they left France."

"How did you get injured?"

"Jehanne hurt me," Miss Bingley said in an agitated manner. "She was mad when she came into my room last night. She said nothing had gone as she planned. Mr. Wickham was impulsive. And I had no discipline. She would do the work herself. In fact, she had done it already. Mr. Darcy and your sister would die. I swear I did not know that beforehand. I argued with her, wanting her to tell me what she had done. So I could come back, to tell Charles. I only wanted the status and wealth of being Mrs. Darcy. I do not want to harm anyone. I do not want to be hanged. She became so mad. She grabbed something and hit me … hit me … hit me. It hurt, so painful. I thought I would die too. Please, Miss Bennet, you have to believe me. I did not want to harm anyone. I just wanted to be part of society. No one from school would look down on me again just because my father was a carriage maker. I am so sorry. I am so sorry. Please, Charles, do not send me to jail. Please, I cannot marry Mr. Collins. I shall die."

Bingley went to embrace his sister and let her sob her heart out. "Calm down, sister," he murmured. "I shall see what I can do." He called in the doctor, who gave Miss Bingley something to drink and helped her to sleep again.

While Miss Bennet and Bingley engaged themselves in seeing to his sister, Darcy had gone in search of Elizabeth, who had settled in Hurst's library. After he related the detail of Miss Bingley's revelations to his betrothed, he commented, "I'm surprised by Jane's way of questioning. She handled it very well."

Elizabeth's eyes brightened for a moment.

"Ah," Darcy said, "you instructed her how to interrogate Miss Bingley."

She did not reply directly but her lip curled smugly.

Pulling her hand to his lap, he said, "The future Mrs. Darcy is quite the brightest jewel in Hertfordshire."

"Only in Hertfordshire?" she exclaimed.

"And Derbyshire."

She pouted.

"And in the heart of the Master of Pemberley."

"That is a much better declaration," she laughed. "Though you sound quite like Sir William Lucas."

"Capital!" He tried to suppress a grin and imitated Sir William's favourite word. "I shall spend my life devoted to presiding over assemblies in Lambton."

"And I shall spend my life gossiping about the wealth of the men who come to attend the assemblies. Perhaps they would take pity on one of our six daughters." Once the words left Elizabeth's mouth, her face turned crimson.

He raised his hand and traced his knuckles along her jaw. Her skin was smooth and warm.

"I shall feel blessed for the children we will have, no matter whether they are boys or girls."

"Thank you, Fitzwilliam," she whispered, gazing at him.

He admired her beautiful complexion in silence. She drew in a deep breath and then wetted her lips. Naturally, he lowered his head and touched his mouth to hers. She tasted of wine, a full and mellow kind that was addictive. Her sensual lips felt quite different from when he had last tasted them.

Was it just last night that they had kissed, at their engagement ball? How eventful the last few hours had been! He shivered as his mind raced through what had happened and what could have gone wrong. As if to erase the memory of their brush with death, he embarked on celebrating life by deepening the kiss. As his mouth fused with hers, he felt his body and soul connected to hers. They became one person. She gave him warmth, strength and the energy to face the world.

When he reluctantly released her mouth, she laid her head on his shoulder. He embraced her silently and considered their lives. It was a blessing to him that their paths had crossed at two defining moments: the Inn at Bromley and the Meryton Assembly. Perhaps the Lord had mapped out their paths. It was fate. But then, why did the Lord deal some people a poor hand?

"Why is life so cruel for some people?" he said. "Like Mrs. Younge. Perhaps she only turned violent because she had a hard life, from her childhood onwards."

"I do not know, Fitzwilliam," Elizabeth raised her head, took his hand and pressed it to her face. "Why am I a gentlewoman and others are maids? I do not quite understand why we need to have this order in society. And the entail on Longbourn does make me wonder from time to time, had Father died early, life could be very different for all my sisters and for me. We might have had to cross the social divide, never to return."

He nodded, considering the possibility. Elizabeth could have become a governess or worked in a shop. Their paths might never have crossed. That could have been disastrous for him. He could not foresee a future without her by his side, now that he had known her.

"Does it make you … unhappy about your father?" Darcy commented. "For not preparing more for his family, financially?"

She tilted her head and thought for a moment. "He has been very good to me, teaching me his love of books, and learning about life and the world from them. Some may say that he should have hired a governess and be stricter with Kitty and Lydia. But I can see some merit in his liberal attitude. We are not forced to endure lessons we don't like. We can spend more time on what interests us most. I think it is finding a balance that is most important, to allow children the freedom to grow and yet give them enough structure. But should children really expect their parents to provide for them? Perhaps we put too much burden on parents."

"I am worried," he said.

"About what?"

"What if I am not a good father? Life requires so many decisions. What if I teach my children badly and they take the wrong course?" he continued. "The day I learned about Miss Bingley using the whip on Mr. Collins, and that she had used cutting spurs harshly on her horses, I did wonder why she turned out like that while Bingley was such a good-natured man. They have the same parents."

"From what she said, I think it was the censure of her school friends that set her off in her youth." Elizabeth squeezed his hand. "When people are faced with being belittled on a daily basis, they may learn to use similar cruel methods on those from lower circumstances – even animals."

He nodded. "Perhaps that is why she was so determined to become my wife."

"We cannot fault the late Mr. and Mrs. Bingley for providing her with the right education," she continued. "It was unfortunate that Miss Bingley met some cruel girls at school. But some people rise against adversity. She did not. Perhaps she did not study as hard as she could, to learn from the events and ideas of the past. The wisdom of past scholars could have given her fortitude to withstand the force of spitefulness."

"You are right, my love," Darcy said. "We shall read with our children and help them become strong."

She nodded and squeezed his hand.

Their musing was interrupted by the arrival of Jane and Bingley.

"What will you do about Miss Bingley?" Darcy asked Bingley.

"Caroline may have put up the money to copy the garnet cross, but she is not involved in harming Miss Lydia or you," Bingley said. "I hope Mr. Bennet and you would not object that when she recovers, I shall let her go abroad. I do not want to force her to marry Mr. Collins. Caroline has suffered greatly. I hope she has learned a lesson."

Darcy heard Elizabeth give out a sigh. Did she think Miss Bingley was let off lightly? Or did she breathe a sigh of relief for Bingley's sister? He did not know.

Miss Jane added, "Miss Bingley tried to come back to tell Charles about Mrs. Younge's scheme and got injured in the process. I think she is not so very bad. Please Mr. Darcy, Elizabeth, pray give her a chance. Surely there can be no occasion for exposing and punishing her dreadfully."

Elizabeth walked to take her sister's hands and replied, "Jane, you are truly very good." Darcy looked at his betrothed. Elizabeth seemed to have accepted Bingley's decision for Miss Jane's sake, whatever her feelings about Miss Bingley were; or perhaps she believed Bingley's sister had been telling the truth. Darcy's admiration for Elizabeth rose yet again.

Not long afterwards, Miss Jane, Elizabeth and Darcy took their leave. Before dinner, Darcy and Elizabeth talked to Georgiana about Mrs. Younge.

"She is one of our distant relatives?" Georgiana could not believe it.

"Very, very distant, I believe. I shall check the family book about it. Did she give you the Médée sheet music?"

"Yes, we were having tea when she gave me the music." Georgiana thought back to the day. "She was telling me about the sad story behind the opera. I felt quite hot. Perhaps it was the weather. All this talk about rivalry and poison made me feel a bit dizzy. I thought I might have stood up. Or did I dance around? I was not sure. Then I felt the world floating around me. A heavy weight, like a stone, weighing heavily on my chest. I struggled and cried out. But when I woke up, I was in my bedchamber and ..."

"And?" Elizabeth took over the questioning.

"... Mr. Wickham was there."

Darcy clenched his fist. Elizabeth squeezed Georgiana's hand and urged her to continue.

"He was sitting on a chair, by my bedside. He said I had fainted in the drawing room. He had carried me up to the bedchamber and Mrs. Younge had gone to fetch the doctor."

"And did she come back soon?"

"I was scared. It had been some time since I had last seen him. And he was suddenly there, looking at me with this strange expression. He ..."

"What did he do?"

"He touched my face, with his hand. I trembled, called out for Papa and shut my eyes. Then I felt unwell again."

"What happened afterwards?"

"I woke up the next day. My head hurt."

"And your body? Did you hurt yourself, with the fainting?"

"No, I felt well."

"You did not have any pain or ... bruising?"

"No. I did not believe I hurt myself when I fell. But the nightmares started soon afterwards. And Mr. Wickham came to call on me, from that day on. He was polite, charming. He did not have that strange look again. I began to warm to him and thought I was in love with him."

Darcy tightened his lips. He was thankful that Georgiana did not remember what Wickham had tried to do. Wickham might not have taken Georgiana's virtue but he had tried. If she had not fainted again, or if she had not called out for Father, Wickham would have forced himself on her.

***

The next morning, Colonel Fitzwilliam and Darcy went to the gaol to visit Mrs. Younge. They wanted to ask if she knew where Wickham was. Mr. Bennet asked to go with them.

"Are you sure about this, sir?" Darcy asked.

"Yes, Fitzwilliam," Mr. Bennet nodded. "Perhaps my appearance will lay her mind at peace, finally."

Darcy had asked the magistrate to take good care of Mrs. Younge, when the latter had taken her away the day before. The party found her in isolation, in a relatively clean cell.

She lay on the floor, looking at the visitors curiously, without motion.

*What can you say to someone who hates you so much?* Darcy pondered.

Mr. Bennet approached her first. "Does your eye hurt? Could we get a doctor for you again?"

Mrs. Younge gazed at the elderly gentleman, still listlessly. But there was fire in her eye. After a long moment, she said, "You are … him?"

Mr. Bennet nodded. "I am sorry about your father."

Her face turned grave and she uttered the words slowly in a trembling voice. "He was not dead when you rushed me out of the inn."

He shook his head. "I am sorry. His skin had turned blue and I had checked his breathing."

"No!" She cried out and turned her body toward the wall, away from the gentlemen. "How could that be?"

"He smelled of alcohol. He had been drinking," Mr. Bennet said firmly. "He died from drinking too much alcohol."

Mrs. Younge stiffened. After another long silence, she spoke, still facing away from the visitors. Her voice cracked with a strange sharpness, sounding like a little girl. She murmured, "He loved to drink, when he had had a hard day. He hated to work. He had been drinking a lot on the ship to England too."

"And that night?"

"I was woken by the noise. Father was gone from the room. I saw him lying on the floor round the corner, near the stairs. Someone must have pushed past him, trampled on him," she said. "I could not reach him at first, because of the people. I cried for him to wake up, from a distance. He did not move or hear me. When I reached him, he just lay there, at an awkward angle. His body was cold. I pushed him, begged him to wake up. I tried to drag him. He did not respond."

"He was dead, by then," Colonel Fitzwilliam commented. "You should not blame yourself, or anyone."

"I had hidden his bottle earlier. He must have gone down to drink at the tavern." She turned around. Her eye focussed on Mr. Bennet. Then she continued, sounding more like Mrs. Younge and not the little girl who had seemed lost. "What did you want from me?"

"Where is Wickham?" Colonel Fitzwilliam replied.

She gave up the information without being difficult. "He is staying at my friend's house, at the other end of Edward Street."

When the three men were about to leave, she started coughing violently. "Urgh!" She yelled in pain and started twisting her body. The gentlemen looked at each other and Richard dashed to her immediately.

"Guard! Fetch the doctor at once!" he said.

Darcy crouched down near them as well. Mr. Bennet followed.

"She is poisoned." Darcy could see that she was trembling and shivering. White foam started to drip out from her mouth.

"I … swallowed … the poison … myself … just now," she murmured, her eye staring at Mr. Bennet. "You … should not … have…saved my life. It … was … an unbearable life."

Her hand, which had been holding her abdomen, moved to her dress. She pulled out a piece of paper, holding it out to the gentlemen. Suddenly, with another violent twist of the body, her hand dropped and she lay totally still.

Richard touched her pulse and shook his head. He took the paper, inspected it quickly and handed it to Darcy. It had Darcy's name written on it.

The doctor finally arrived and pronounced Mrs. Younge dead.

Darcy had a heavy heart. Mrs. Younge was a tortured soul with a difficult life. He pitied her circumstances and wished she could have risen above her life's tribulations instead of taking a path of destruction. He could not do anything to help her when she was alive, since they had not met until early that year. But he wanted to bury her properly now that she was dead. That was the only thing he could do now. He asked and the guard agreed, after the proper procedures had been completed in the following days.

When the three men stood outside the building, Colonel Fitzwilliam asked Mr. Bennet, "You remembered? Her father died of drinking too much alcohol?"

"I could not sleep last night," Mr. Bennet sighed. "Thinking over the event, over and over again. It was some twenty years ago. Memory failed me. I was afraid I really let the poor man down and let him die in the fire. When I finally closed my eyes and drifted off to sleep, I remembered his skin seeming blue when I inspected him. His body was ice cold. He did not seem to be overcome by the smoke. Then I remembered the smell of cheap port on his body."

"Mrs. Younge must have known about that too when she was younger," Colonel Fitzwilliam said. "She only placed the blame on you two when she knew about the garnet cross from Wickham early this year. She tried to block out what her memory was telling her. What did she write in the note?"

Darcy opened the letter.

*Life is a burning hell. No more scrubbing the floor. No more being slapped in the face. No more being whipped on the body. No more carrying a cross on the back.*

*So I leave this world, for a better one. I was born to a weak man and you weren't. Life is not fair so I didn't play fairly. It is time to go to a nicer world. - Jehanne D'Arcy*

"She was still very bitter when she wrote this note," Darcy commented.

"She was not brought up wisely," Mr. Bennet said. "We all carry a cross on our back. We just need to find a way to prevent it from weighing us down."

With these last words, the gentlemen parted. The younger ones left for Edward Street, while the elderly one returned to Nevan House to monitor his youngest daughter.

When Colonel Fitzwilliam and Darcy arrived at the boarding house, the owner told them that a man of Wickham's description had stayed there before. But he had left the day before. They found another letter awaiting them. It was in Wickham's handwriting, addressed to Mrs. Younge.

*Chère amie,*

*I have to say goodbye now. I did not tell you that I have been waiting for a passage to...*

*Well, I better not tell you the destination. In case any of my debtors or benefactors tries to get the information from you about my whereabouts.*

*With the money I "earned" and the proceeds from selling the magnificent horse I accidentally found in Hertfordshire, I have a good sum tucked under my belt.*

*England is quite a disappointment to me. After I left Derbyshire, my luck has not been good. I am sick of it, of sleeping in hard beds, sipping cheap wine and fornicating with silly wenches.*

*It is time I started a brand new life on brand new soil. I vow to start the journey as a gentleman and live the rest of my life as one. I have even chosen an excellent name for it.*

*What a joke it will be when you hear of my good fortune from afar.*

*I shall sign with my new name from this day on.*

*Au revoir*

*Richard Darcy*

"Bloody man!" Colonel Fitzwilliam swore. "He intends to blacken our names abroad. I shall inspect the passengers on all the ships that leave in the next two days."

Darcy shook his head. He had never understood Wickham since they had grown apart. Why did he have to continue to pursue this path? To bring shame to the Darcy name.

# Epilogue

Darcy gazed at Elizabeth, remembering the last time he had seen her wearing white. It was the night of another engagement ball, their own. Thinking about that night brought back dark memories of Mrs. Younge, Wickham and Miss Bingley.

"Can you help me my dear?" Elizabeth's request woke him from his musings.

He went to stand behind her, unhooking the garnet cross from her creamy white neck and releasing the buttons of her dress. Lowering his mouth, he kissed the skin at the juncture of her neck and shoulder and breathed in her scent of lavender mixed with her womanly fragrance. Closing his eyes, he savoured the feel of being alive.

"What is the matter, Fitzwilliam?"

"I was thinking about the last time you wore white," he whispered.

Elizabeth turned to look at him. "Pray do not remember the past that was unhappy. See, Mama has been behaving like a duchess the whole night and Mary and Kitty are very much admired. Georgiana is much loved. And Lydia is engaged to Lord Richmond, no less. Even Lady Catherine has ceased her silent treatment of me and sent Lydia an engagement present. Our dear cousin Collins followed suit. I could never have imagined that my wild youngest sister who spent all her time talking and dreaming about the Redcoats could be so elegant and gracious."

"Not as grand as you, Elizabeth," he declared, raising his head and looking at her intently. "You are right. Mrs. Younge's murderous attempt did have one good outcome. Miss Lydia has been confined to bed for nearly a month and has learned to reflect upon the importance of life. But the events of that day have still left me with an unhappy and troubled feeling, when I think about it. I could not find any reference of Jehanne D'Arcy in our family history. Mrs. Younge might have hated us without cause. And Wickham got away lightly. Richard could not find anyone bound to new worlds with either Wickham's real or fake names. "

"If he was settled in a new world, as an honest gentleman, as he said he would, perhaps that is the Lord's decision." She patted his hand.

Darcy picked up his wife. She gave out a mild curse and held onto the falling dress. He gently lowered her onto the bed. "You are always the wise one, my loveliest dearest Elizabeth."

Kissing her deeply, he tasted her sultry lips and soft tongue. When he stopped to breathe, he continued, "Perhaps you are right. The Lord has a way of mapping out our destiny. Miss Bingley would never have thought that she would live the rest of her life as a queen of savages."

"Yes, the Lord's wind blew away her plan to join society in New York and instead had her captured in the deep forest of the Amazon basin." She raised her lips to caress his neck. "Perhaps she is tremendously happy as the wife of the tribal chief."

Darcy did not reply. He still remembered the distress Charles had undergone on receiving news from his investigator. With the help of the missionary, the investigator had only managed to see Miss Bingley from afar, under the guard of the entire warriors from the tribe. The investigator described Miss Bingley as in good spirits, though her skin was coarse and her teeth were broken, probably due to the ship's accident at sea and her subsequent ordeal. The tribe was not ready to negotiate her release. Darcy still could not imagine Miss Bingley dressing in animal skins and leaves. At least Bingley knew that she was alive.

"Charles has had a difficult time these past years," he commented. "It is lucky that Jane has been by his side the entire time."

"Jane has the sweetest and most patient soul. She is truly a great match for Charles. Although their marriage was delayed and clouded with the disappearance of Miss Bingley, they seem to be much happier now."

"No one will be as happy as we are." Darcy pushed down the silk garment and bared her lush bosom for admiration. Her nipples were deep red, bigger than normal. "You gave me an heir last year and now perhaps a *Little Lizzy* this time." He palmed the bouncy creamy mounds and rubbed them the way she liked. He loved the way she moaned, the quickening of her breath and the tension in her face when she bit her lips with her teeth. He drifted lower to caress her slightly rounded abdomen as he lowered his lips to worship her breasts. They were ripe and full.

Pulling down the white gown further and pushing it out of his way, he devoured her valleys and mountains amid the candlelight. The sight of her alluring body was magnificent.

He still remembered the first time he had set his eyes on her nude body, on their wedding night. His need rose to an unbearable height and he had taken her rather roughly, their first time together. The tightness of her muscles, gripping his shaft for the first time, was a feeling he would always remember. It was beyond his erotic dreams and their passionate kisses before the wedding. He felt the earth move and his whole being exploded in his body when he came inside her.

Now, after almost two years of marriage, he still could not get enough of this feeling, of unifying with her in body and soul. Sometimes when his Mrs. Darcy sat in the library, reading a book and sharing a conversation with him about family and life, he would have this sudden urge to make love to her madly and acted on it immediately.

Other times, when she teased him, or when drifting off for a nap in the carriage, he would pull down all the curtains and take her fast and by surprise. The intense and explosive encounter often left them lost for words for the remainder of the journey.

He remembered the anxiety he had when she went into labour, having little Max. It took her nearly twelve hours to deliver the baby, who was just tiny. Max Darcy was an exact replica of himself, at least to Darcy's mind, quiet, shy and brooding. Elizabeth refused to agree that a baby could be brooding.

Darcy lowered his lips and kissed Elizabeth's abdomen again and wished for a little girl this time. Then his mouth trailed lower, to explore the bush at the apex of her thighs. Licking her secret lips as his hands continued to pluck her nipples. Her womanly scent and the texture of her skin bombarded his senses. Blood pounded in his veins as his arousal grew. Removing his clothes hastily, he devoured her body with his kisses.

Her moaning became louder and she squirmed under his ministrations. He enjoyed hearing the sound of lust escaping her mouth. It excited him no end and his arousal rose to new heights. His tongue lapped at her folds and thrust into her secret entry. Her taste was divine. Elizabeth arched her body violently a few times before screaming out at her peak.

Darcy loved to please her, to bring her to heaven, before joining her. Raising his body, he positioned himself on top of her, rubbing the sweat from her wide hips, from the valley of her lush breasts and her pink face.

Positioning his thick hard shaft at her entrance, he nibbled at her lower lips and brought her thoughts back to him. Elizabeth raised her legs, slowly wrapping around his waist. She had a seductive, satisfied and yet teasing smile on her face. Then she raised her body slightly, tempting him with a slow glissade. Her alluring movement pushed him over the edge. With one mighty thrust, he thrust into her strongly and buried himself deep inside her.

Darcy felt the trembling, the slickness and the scorching heat of her inner muscles, enveloping his manhood, bombarding and squeezing it. His breathing was shallow and his entire body was boiling.

His body engaged in the rhythm of mating on its own, thrusting in and out deeply, as his tongue imitated the same motion. Darcy poured all his love into making love with Elizabeth. On and on he went, until her hands dug into his spine and sent him over the cliff. His body exploded and his mind went blank. Stars burst in front of his eyes. Rainbows, clouds and an intense sun slid past his eyes as he reached heaven.

When he finally returned to earth, he hugged her tightly. "I am blessed since the day our paths crossed. Thank you, Mrs. Darcy!"

She ran her hand over his face and replied, "Thank you, Mr. Darcy, for loving me."

Made in the USA
Lexington, KY
25 April 2012